KU-486-648

DUNCAN KYLE

Green River High

FONTANA/Collins

First published in 1979 by William Collins Sons & Co Ltd
First issued in Fontana Books 1980

© 1979 by Duncan Kyle

Made and printed in Great Britain by
William Collins Sons & Co Ltd, Glasgow

For HMEB, CDAB, ALCB
to whom such code groups
are child's play . . .

Lines from 'Reveille' are quoted with the kind permission of the
Society of Authors as literary representative of the Estate of A. E.
Housman; and Jonathan Cape Ltd., publishers of A. E. Housman's
Collected Poems

CONDITIONS OF SALE
This book is sold subject to the condition that
it shall not, by way of trade or otherwise, be lent,
re-sold, hired out or otherwise circulated without
the publisher's prior consent in any form of
binding or cover other than that in which it is
published and without a similar condition
including this condition being imposed on the
subsequent purchaser

GREEN RIVER HIGH

DUNCAN KYLE was born in Bradford, Yorkshire, a few hundred yards from the house where J. B. Priestley grew up.

He started his career as a junior reporter on the *Bradford Telegraph and Argus*, later going on to the *Leicester Mercury* and the *Yorkshire Post*. In the mid-fifties he joined *John Bull* magazine – which later became *Today* – in London and from there he went on to become editorial director at Odhams where he wrote his first novel, *A Cage of Ice*.

It was the success of this book which persuaded him to become a full-time writer and to fulfil his long-held ambition to live deep in the country. He now lives in Suffolk with his wife and three children.

He has written seven novels, each more successful than the last: *Green River High* is the latest.

Available in Fontana by the same author

Black Camelot
A Cage of Ice
Flight into Fear
A Raft of Swords
Terror's Cradle
Whiteout!

CHAPTER ONE

It was Friday, and bound to be busy because Fridays always are; and it was going to be a bitch of a day because half the staff was off with 'flu, real or simulated. On awakening that morning I had contemplated discreet absenteeism : my bed was warm but the room itself, when the end of my nose tested the air temperature, was a place for penguins rather than people. I thought about it, and wanted to do it, and couldn't. But then I never could. They plant deep, those schoolmasters and sergeant-majors who ram currently official concepts into the fertile soil of youthful eagerness, and they've left me with more assorted handicaps than a Sunday-afternoon mixed foursome. Hold doors open for ladies, they said, and damn it I still do, while said ladies barge by with their parcels and their magpie eyes, treading on my toe as often as not. The good officer, they said, ensures that his men are fed and comfortable before any morsel of food or drop of water touches his own lips. So you do it, and when they're comfortably full and topping it off with a cigarette and the bar of chocolate they've all tucked away in their tunic pockets, you find they've scoffed the lot and are looking at you with eyes that plainly say : mug!

Duty – I'm part of the last generation that even recognizes the word, let alone understands its implications. But once its meaning and requirements have been hammered into one's head, duty awakens more effectively than any alarm clock, and compels attention to matters you've no wish to attend to. That, of course, being the whole idea.

So that Friday morning I clambered unwillingly from my bed, shaved (a clean soldier is an efficient soldier), cooked myself a solid breakfast (men collapse on parade from missing breakfast). I put on my shiny shoes and my almost equally shiny trousers, took a look out of the window and put on my mackintosh, then went out to catch the bus which, since the rain was heavy, was both late and full, and stood irritably among all the other irritable people, trying to sort out my problem.

If all the foregoing has given the impression that I'm a soldier, and I see that it may have done so, then I'm sorry. I'm a rather resentful *ex*-soldier, with the marks on me and in me, and I was on my way that cold, wet morning to the bank where I work – to make the final concession. Two days earlier I had been summoned to the manager's office and told that since the senior counter-clerk was retiring and I was next in seniority, the job and an extra hundred and fifty a year were to be mine. Birstall, the manager, said all this with the air of one conferring knighthood, and was taken aback when I asked for a couple of days to think about it. He was a dead-man's-shoes man himself, and promotions hadn't come so often in his life that he'd ever had to consider whether to accept. Head Counter Clerk, in Birstall's eyes, was a good couple of rungs up the heavenly ladder; I looked at it rather differently. Most of the rest of the counter staff were girls. They were husband-hunting, engaged, newly-married, or pregnant. A nice lot, certainly, but their commitment to banking as a career was loose-ish, and they took with relish and without hesitation their full quota of leave, sick leave and casual days off. 'The counter staff, of course, will be entirely your responsibility, Mr Tunnicliffe, you understand that . . .' – I understood only too well! – 'and I'm sure I can rely on you to look after their problems as well as their duties. It is, as you appreciate, a post of considerable responsibility. But then you have shown us over the past nine years . . .' He had nattered on while I began to contemplate those nine years. I'd been thinking about them and cursing them ever since and this was the day I'd promised my decision. I was going to accept, of course. It was just that I hated doing it. I knew that once I'd gone into the sanctum and said 'Yes, sir – and thank you, sir,' that was the end of George Tunnicliffe. Somehow or other, while all those years were sliding by, I had thought of the job as temporary, just keeping me fed and clothed until something better, something more excit-

ing, something more suitable came along. Now the bank's
stout door was going to slam behind me. Tied by one leg to
a bank counter and a lifetime of 'No, you can't have Thursday off, Judith', knowing all the time that blasted Judith
would take Thursday off and be damned, and I'd be short.
My job : Dealing with Important Matters, as Birstall would
say, With a Sense of Responsibility.

I remembered later what I was thinking.

Then the first thing happened. A little bloke beside me
on the bus passed out. There wasn't any warning; he simply
blacked out and fell down in the aisle among all the damp
feet. I yelled to the conductor to stop the bus, lifted the
man up and got him into a seat somebody vacated for the
purpose. He was pale and breathing a bit raggedly, but
after a minute or so he began to come round, a little dazed
but conscious, and I suggested to the conductor that he stop
the bus at the next phone box and call an ambulance.

'Hospital's only a mile,' he said. 'Be quicker if he stays on
the bus till we get there.'

So he did. When we reached the hospital, I picked the
old boy up and carried him inside. It wasn't very difficult:
he weighed about as much as a wet newspaper. They kept
me there, in the casualty department, for a little while, so
that I could explain to the doctor what happened, then
they hooked the old man up to a heart monitor and sent
me on my way.

The result was that I was a full half-hour late, which
irritated me because punctuality is another habit dinned
into me all those years ago and I can't shake free of it.
So as I hopped off the bus and began to cross the street
towards the bank's front door, by now already open, I
wasn't in the most cheerful of moods.

As I crossed, a blue van stopped in front of me, indicator
flashing for a right turn, waiting at the crown of the road
for a gap in the traffic, and as it did so, I got a passing
glimpse, through the rain-spattered glass, of an odd-looking
man in the front passenger seat. Odd because his face
seemed somehow formless, his features rudimentary and
indistinct like a sculptured head begun but not completed.

Then the van moved on and a couple of cars followed it into the turn and it was several seconds before my mind got to grips.

The van halted in the side-street beside the bank and even before the door opened, realization came: that odd formlessness was produced by a stocking mask. The bank was about to be raided! I slipped between the cars to the middle of the road and there, pretending to watch the oncoming traffic, kept the van in view out of the corner of my eye.

Four of them came out fast. Two shotguns, as far as I could see, and two pickaxe handles. A puffing exhaust, so the engine was running and number five would be still in the van. No running: they walked to the bank, quick and purposeful, and three vanished inside. Number four turned in the doorway, shotgun in hand and faced the street, the shotgun held low across his body, its butt against his right hip. A few cars went slowly by between us, then a lorry and a Green Line bus, blocking my view, and his too, and the bus halted just in front of me and a few people took the opportunity to step off. I moved round behind the bus to join them, keeping my eyes well away from him, and trying to look as though I intended to cross the side-street. The best thing would be to get to his right, where the gun butt would be in his way if he swung it quickly.

'Mum!' A child's voice, raised in sudden alarm.

I was seven or eight feet away, my back half turned to him, as I stopped at the pavement edge by the rear of the blue van. I heard him say, 'Shut up!' savagely. His attention was bound, however briefly, to be on the child and its mother. I put my hand on the side of the van to get leverage as I turned, then took two fast steps and dived at him, hands clawing for the shotgun, trying for barrel-up, butt-down, as per long-ago instructions. The damned thing was swinging at me horribly fast as I came at him, and almost as my fingers touched the metal, it went off with an infernal bang close to my ear. But by then he was too late: I was trained for this kind of thing and he wasn't and the gun was out of his hands and in mine and turning into a quarter-staff. I got his head with the barrel and his kidneys with the butt and then was up and away to the side where the wall offered shelter.

'Jack?' A questioning yell from inside, repeated twice with a sudden injection of fear. 'Jack? *Jack!*'

They knew, then. Perhaps they could see Jack on the pavement, dazed, moving sluggishly against the kidney pain. There was a moment of silence, then they came racing out. I'd no way of knowing whether there was a second cartridge in the breach, and no time to check, and firing shotguns level in crowded streets is pretty damn stupid anyway. I ducked down and tried to swing the shotgun like a flail, low at the approaching legs. Goodbye shinbone or kneecap if I connected.

It wasn't a bad try, but it wasn't wholly successful either. Bad tactics, forgetfulness, one or the other. I hadn't allowed for the van driver, or his arsenal. He must have fired his handgun as I swung.

I came to in the ambulance and I couldn't see. First blackness and nausea and an unbearable degree of pain in my head, then dull reddish and greenish flashes daubing my retinas and beside me a steady London voice saying, 'Hold hard, we'll be there in a minute.'

'I can't see!'

'There's a gauze dressing over your eyes. Now keep *still!*'

I kept still. Wounded eyes must stay still, I knew that well enough. I could hear the bell clanging and sense the speed of the ambulance. It swayed, then stopped, and I was carried out, laid on a table and the needle went into the back of my hand. Familiar enough. *Almost* reassuring because the pain would go. But that pain was all across my eyes and I went panicking into unconsciousness . . . Surfacing through all the anaesthetic confusion, trying to remember, remembering – and the panic was back.

'My eyes!'

A girl's voice then. 'Try to sleep again, Mr Tunnicliffe.' A tone intended to soothe, but when you're afraid you've been blinded, soothing tones are strongly counter-effective.

'What about my eyes?'

'Just a moment. I'll get the doctor.'

Rising panic. A lifelong terror of the one across the eyes. I've seen it, know about it. My raised hand touched bandages and pads.

Then footsteps and another voice, also a girl's. 'Leave the dressings alone, *please*!' Speaking sharply.

'What-about-my-bloody-eyes?'

Hesitation. Christ, she's trying to find the right words! Then: 'We think they're all right.'

'Think?'

'Believe,' she said. 'We believe they're all right. Not certain, but we believe.'

Not much, but I felt myself sag into a pallid kind of relief. Uncertainty was marginally better than certainty. 'How long before you know?'

'Fairly soon. Sleep will help.'

'What are the odds?'

'In your favour. Swallow this.' A tablet and a glass.

Later: the same woman doctor, speaking with fair precision. 'It's a question of possible damage to the nerve structures through bruising. There's heavy bruising to both eyes. The wounds themselves are almost superficial, but the eyes are very swollen. Shut tight, in fact—'

'Wounds plural?' I said.

'Two.'

'Both in the eyes?'

'I'm afraid so. But they're clean and stitched. Quite neatly if I may say so.'

'You the needlewoman?'

A smile in the voice: good medicine. 'My work and my hobby. There'll be scarring. A little. Interesting, rather than disfiguring, if you care for a female view.'

'How soon?'

'Will we know? Really it's just time, Mr Tunnicliffe. I know patience isn't easy.'

'No.'

'But I think, *really* think, it will be rewarded.'

'When?'

'A few days. A lot depends on the swellings. If it helps, you might like to know you're something of a hero.'

'It doesn't,' I said. 'Were they caught?'

'Three of them. One with a broken fibula, one with a badly bruised kidney. The other unhurt – I can't quite understand that. You're rather dangerous, aren't you?'

'It's instinctive, I'm afraid. The credit, if any, goes to an old Company Quartermaster Sergeant Instructor, name of Fox.'

'You were his star pupil?'

I thought about old Fox, killed by a booby-trap in Cyprus. 'No,' I said. 'He turned us out in hundreds. Tell me about the bruising.'

So she explained about the body's habit of cradling damage in fluid while the repair process had time to work and the general good sense of leaving it alone, if possible, to do its own efficient job. Then she asked if I could stand a visit.

'Police?'

'Yes.'

'Not much option.'

'I could hold them off for a while.'

'No, I'll see – ' I checked on the word. 'I'll talk to them.'

'You were right the first time. You'll see them. It'll be a little later, that's all.'

I made my statement. What I'd seen. What I could remember of the man with the shotgun and the bruised kidney. I described the van and blushed when they asked for its number, because I hadn't so much as glanced at the licence plate.

'Could you identify him, sir?' Flat foot right in it. 'Sorry, sir. What I meant – '

'If I can, I will.'

'When is that likely to be, sir?'

'Ask the doctor.'

When he'd gone, Birstall came. Everybody most, er, most, er, well . . . full of admiration for your, er, your . . . Mmm, yes and Head Office most appreciative and very concerned for your, well, you . . .'

I let him flounder on. Like most bank managers, he's good with the big stick and bad with the butter. He even reminded me in his fussy way of the Bank's Standing Instruction: employees should not take unwarrantable risks in defence of the bank's property. He didn't ask for my decision, though : not because he didn't want to, of course, but because he's properly cautious and the question of whether I'd be able to see to count the notes was as yet unresolved.

When he'd gone, I lay back and thought about that phrase. Unwarrantable risks. I'd had only two employers in my life and it struck me rather forcibly, lying there, that they had decidedly different attitudes in the matter of risks. I tried, by way of diversion, to visualize a discussion of the subject between Birstall and my mad old colonel, who took colossal chances as a matter of course, the way other people take two lumps of sugar. I once saw him rise cursing from behind the sandbags and fell with his walking-stick two screaming Chinese brandishing automatic rifles. It was a briefly enjoyable recollection, but the pleasure was ruined when I realized that confrontations between bank managers and colonels on retirement pay could have only one victor, more's the pity.

I won't go over the next two days. I was half-convinced my sight was gone, and sunk in gloom a lot of the time, wondering how blind men in hospital beds might contrive to blow their own brains out. I was counting the hours, hating them as they passed, dreading The Moment. When it came and my swollen lids were gently pressed apart, the light hurt and the woman doctor laughed.

And so, after a moment, did I.

The letter came two days later.

CHAPTER TWO

It was one among a very large number. After the raid, the London evening papers worked on me at length. WAR HERO FOILS BANK RAIDERS, said the *Evening Standard* deceptively. My war was Korea, now remembered only by those unlucky enough to have been present at the proceedings. The following morning there were variations in all the dailies (cuttings were kept for me by the ward nurses) and it was clear the newspapers had shown both enterprise and imagination. The hospital had not allowed reporters in, and the bank can have had no photograph of me, so the picture they'd all used was a notably pure example of very keen young lieutenant, more than a decade old, and supplied, presumably, by the public relations department of the War Office, which never sleeps. The stories published were fairly lucid, too. The *Daily Mirror* had me 'facing the armed bandits with the same cool deadliness he'd shown winning his Military Cross among the icy hills of Korea'. The *Daily Telegraph*, precise and accurate as ever, even knew how many toes I'd lost in those same icy hills, and the *Daily Mail* had dug up from somewhere a girl I'd once taken to a regimental dance. She remembered me, it seemed, as 'very much the strong, silent type'. It was amazing she remembered anything at all: she got very plastered indeed on a couple of glasses of champagne and was sent home, in his own car and well before midnight, by the scowling colonel. Next day, when I telephoned to ask after her hangover, her mother's voice was of a frostiness that would have made Korea's icy hills seem warm and friendly, so I took the hint and stayed away. I hadn't seen her since.

The mail, as a result of all this publicity, came if not in sack loads, certainly in bulky bundles. Very gung-ho, most of it. I can never quite understand why people sit down

and write emotional letters to total strangers, but I learned
then how many do. Some even reproached me for failing
to turn the shotgun round to blast its owner. But there were
pleasant ones too : a couple from old army friends I'd lost
touch with, and a telegram from my mad old colonel – he
was anything but really, though he enjoyed having the
reputation – which said simply, 'I know you – you enjoyed
it.' I grinned at it, at first. Then I thought about it. Then
I felt mildly ashamed.

The letter signed 'C. Franklin' contrasted sharply with
the rest. Not an exclamation mark in sight, for one thing,
and no heavy underlining either, and to be truthful I didn't
take much notice on first reading. But when, for the sake
of something to do, I began to answer the fan mail, I read
it again.

Dear Mr Tunnicliffe,

In reporting your exploits, *The Times* gave your full
name, and I wonder if it is possible you might be son to
the late Squadron Leader George Hawke Tunnicliffe,
RAF. If you are not, I hope you will forgive this enquiry.
If you are, perhaps you will allow me to visit you briefly.
I hope that the injuries to your eyes are, as the newspapers now report, unlikely to be permanent.

Yours sincerely,

C. Franklin

Bold, clear handwriting, a plain white bond paper, a
Birmingham address, no phone number, no indication of
why Franklin might wish to see me, or who Franklin might
be. I was a little curious, but no more. My father was
killed in a flying accident when I was fourteen, just after
the end of the war, and even at that time I hadn't seen
him for six years, so although I shed tears, his death wasn't
a matter of towering grief. From what I knew of him –
which means, I suppose, my mother's somewhat heated
descriptions, and *she* could hardly be called unbiased – he
was something of a rascal, and possibly a bit of a crook,
too. It therefore crossed my mind that gambling debts

incurred in some long-ago club or officers' mess might lie behind the letter. IOUs have a long life and are treasured and it's not unknown for them to be visited on later generations. The distance involved lent weight to that view : Birmingham is more than a hundred miles from my part of South London, and in my experience people don't travel a hundred miles for nothing.

But then I thought : what the hell – no harm could be done. So I scribbled a note giving hospital visiting hours, and sent it off. If Franklin wanted to see me badly enough to make the trip, decent courtesy seemed indicated. If the visit proved to be unpleasant in any way, I'd only to clap my hands to my twin black eyes and the nurses would say fast enough that time was up.

Perhaps you will have guessed Franklin's secret already. I honestly had no idea. What I expected, I suppose, was an elderly gent of ruddy countenance, probably with a considerable moustache and wearing an RAF tie. So when the door of my little room at the end of the hospital ward opened and a smallish woman entered, I merely thought she'd been sent to the wrong room.

'Mr Tunnicliffe?'

'Yes.' A little cautiously. The unworthy thought came that while gambling debts were now unlikely, it might turn out that I had an oblique kind of cousin somewhere.

'I'm Miss Franklin. I wrote to you.'

She pulled up the chair and was about to sit down, then stopped. 'You're staring, Mr Tunnicliffe.'

'I'm sorry.'

'Why were you staring?'

'Probably surprise. I suppose I was expecting a man.'

'I see.' She gave a brisk little smile and sat down. 'My signature, I imagine. It always seems so – well, *pusillanimous* – to put "Miss" in brackets afterwards.'

'You could always sign your full name.'

She began to peel off a pair of dark blue kid gloves. 'I have only one forename and have never cared for it.'

'What is it?'

She looked at me with level grey eyes. 'I answer, civilly

as a rule, when addressed as Miss Franklin.'

I said, 'All right, Miss Franklin,' and watched as the gloves were placed neatly beside the handbag on her lap.

'Now,' she said, 'you will be wondering why I wrote and why I wish to talk to you.'

Schoolmistress, I thought. Or hospital sister. Holy terror in either case. Probably retired. She was wearing a tailored blue suit, a crisply starched white blouse, a blue hat trimmed with white. All practical, all severe, all neat. 'Yes, I did wonder.'

'If you are the man I think you are, Mr Tunnicliffe, I have been looking for you, really quite hard, for nearly twenty years.' The bright grey eyes were intense, but there was something of amusement in them, as though to acknowledge that what she had said was just a little ridiculous. After a moment, she added, 'You're staring again.'

'Are you surprised?'

'Perhaps not. But I prefer that you shouldn't. When you stop we can continue.'

One of those dealers in reproof, I thought. 'Where do you suggest I look?'

'Mr Tunnicliffe, it is entirely preferable that people should look at one another as they talk. But you are not a snake and I am not a mongoose. You know very well what I mean.'

Cheerful conversation this was going to be! 'All right. *Why* have you been looking for me all these years?'

The question was ignored; she opened her handbag, took out an envelope and extracted the note I'd sent her. 'You say here that your father was George Hawke Tunnicliffe and that he was a squadron-leader in the Royal Air Force.'

I said, 'Yes. Were you one of his – ' and stopped sharply as her lips tightened. 'I mean, you knew him?'

That question was ignored too. The lady was going to do this in her own way, thank you very much.

She said, 'It is an unusual combination of names.'

'True.'

'Though none is of itself unusual.'

'Also true.'

She flicked a glance at me, one intended to quell; and it had a confident look about it, as though it had quelled many times before. She went on in a harder tone. 'There are, for example, a dozen Tunnicliffes in the London telephone directory.'

'Not including me. I'm not on the phone.'

'I'm aware that you are not. I have always checked all the directories as they have been issued.'

'From Birmingham?'

'Mr Tunnicliffe –' this with slight exasperation – 'you must know that it is the custom for public libraries to stock all directories issued by the Post Office. It is a relatively simple matter to check them.'

'Every year?'

'Certainly.'

'In a moment,' I said, 'I shall be staring again.'

She gave me a frown, and I said, 'Are you by any chance a schoolmistress?' It was unforgivable, I suppose, but that kind of woman has always brought out the worst in me, at least since I've been of an age to answer back.

The rebuke that visibly boiled inside her was suppressed. She sat and waited and I said, 'I'm sorry.'

She gave a little nod. 'Be patient. I really *must* be sure. Do you know how the combination of names came about?'

I said, 'Do you?'

'Simply tell me, if you can.'

'All right. My grandfather was a cricket enthusiast. No, he was more, he was a fanatic. He came from Yorkshire where there were and are thousands like him. Apparently there was a Tunnicliffe who played cricket for England, and my grandfather believed they were distantly related. When my father was born, he was given the names of two other celebrated players of the time : George after a man called George Hirst, and Hawke after Lord Hawke. My father handed the burden to me.'

Miss Franklin gave a tight little smile. Even teeth, all her own. 'Very well, I'm satisfied. Even a little relieved, too.' She opened the bag again, took out another envelope, and held it out towards me.

'What's this?'

'A letter,' she said. 'From your father.'

A momentary shudder went down my back as I took the envelope. I said, 'But he died in –'

'It was written as he was dying.'

'Was it?' I kept my eyes on the envelope, trying to decide how to handle this. The old question : how to get rid of a nut-case who's got you cornered. I said, 'But this writing isn't his, Miss Franklin. It's yours, isn't it?'

'He dictated it to me.'

I took a deep breath and looked hard at her. Plenty of the letters I'd received over the last few days had been from the mildly-mad, and this woman must be as mad as any of them.

'Look,' I said, 'my father's aircraft vanished into thousands of square miles of jungle. He was first posted missing, then missing-believed-killed, and finally he was presumed dead. How *could* he have written this?'

'He didn't write it, Mr Tunnicliffe. *I* wrote it, at his dictation. As I have explained.'

The idea was into my head and out through my mouth in an unconsidered flash. 'Are you a spiritualist? Some sort of medium. A message from beyond the grave, that kind of thing?'

'Are you *trying* to be offensive, Mr Tunnicliffe, or unable to help yourself?' Her eyes sparked with sudden anger.

'Well, it has to be something like that, doesn't it? Fingers touching and taps on the table!'

'I see!' She stood up instantly. 'You need a lesson in manners, Mr Tunnicliffe.'

'From you?' I said. But it was true enough, I supposed. I reached for a soothing cigarette and said, 'I'm sorry, please sit –'

'Certainly not.' The tidy grey head was determinedly shaken. 'You need the lesson and you shall have it. Furthermore, you shouldn't smoke.'

'Oh, for God's sake!'

'For your own!' At the door she turned and said coldly,

'I will say only this. Your father's aeroplane crashed and he survived for a while, though he was badly injured. It was then he dictated the letter. I have fulfilled his wish and my duty by delivering it to his son. If you wish to know more, as I expect you will, then *you* can come to see *me*, and if you then behave with propriety, perhaps I shall tell you.'

'Look, I'm sorry, I'm –' But it was already too late. By that time I was talking to the door.

I swore. At her, at the general unreasonableness of women and even, finally, at myself. Shouldn't have lost my temper, of course. But neither should she! And she shouldn't have nagged either. Bloody old schoolmarm, treating me like a five-year-old! My head was beginning to throb harder under the joint pressure of injury and anger, and I swore about that, too, because the headache had gradually been going away and was now all too clearly returning. I rang for the nurse and demanded codeine and she said, 'What's the matter then, had a fight with your girl-friend?' and gave a cheeky grin and dodged out of the door when I threatened her.

The headache got rapidly worse: migraine-style, with dazzling little lightning flashes and rising nausea. I don't get them often, but when I do they're fiendish, and I knew that if I didn't get off to sleep quickly, I was in for a rough twenty-four hours, so I put the letter away – by this time I wouldn't have been able to read it anyway – closed my eyes and tried to will myself into slumber. But Miss Franklin wasn't going to permit that kind of rapid escape. Her body might be on the way to Euston Station, but her sharp little personality had lodged itself inside my skull and was continuing to torment me. Suddenly there were lots of questions and no answers. My father had crashed shortly after the Far East war ended, in early October 1945. And I knew very well that Borneo had been occupied by the Japanese from 1941 onwards. So how and why had Miss Franklin come to be in Borneo? And if she'd seen him die, why hadn't she reported it? She certainly hadn't, because his death had never been confirmed, merely presumed.

Indeed, at one time in my youth I'd had a private fantasy of him as a new White Rajah, ruling lost tribes of head-hunters in mysterious mountains, had written to the Air Ministry to check, and had received by way of reply a fatherly letter inviting me to come one day as a guest to an RAF station, and assuring me with great regret that there was no chance he could have survived. The more I thought about it, the more puzzling it became. Had my father been flying alone? Were there other casualties; other survivors even? When he died, he must have been buried, so there was a grave. But where? Above all, why had Miss Franklin been looking for me for nearly twenty years? If she was one of my father's old flames, she certainly wasn't his usual style, at least if my mother was right; according to her he'd spent his life chasing barmaids. Duty? She'd used the word: 'I have done my duty in delivering his letter to his son.' That fitted in with her character; Miss Franklin was a duty-doer if ever I saw one. But in that case, why hadn't she reported his death? To do *that* had surely been her duty too.

It was infuriating. I had to read the letter, but the fierce-ness of the migraine flashes made that impossible for the moment and I knew it. I muttered, 'Blast you, Miss Franklin' and wriggled miserably for a while until some benign mechanism in my head finally cut off the supply of con-sciousness and let me through the sleep gate.

Next morning I read the letter. It was written in pencil on blue flimsy and none too clear, but there could be no doubt the sheet of paper was old : its corners were bent, and round the edge the blue had darkened and roughened with age. There was a small stain at the bottom left-hand corner and I thought of the steamy heat of Borneo and wondered about it. Sweat, perhaps.

Dear George,

I have been a rotten father. Blame the war for it, if you can, but a lot of the fault is mine and now there won't be a chance to make it up to you. Maybe I wouldn't anyway, much as I'd like to, but now neither of us will ever know. I'm thinking of you more than anything, just now, when I'm able to think and the shakes and horrors go away for a bit. You must be quite big, almost a man, and I think I can almost see how you must look. You were a lot like me as a child, so probably you still are. But better all round, I hope.

I've nothing to leave you except affection and this message. Not even a good name, though I did have that, at least out here, until quite recently. Now, no money, no valuables, nothing. But there are two things I'd like you to remember. The first is about your mother and me. We're neither of us up to much, and never were, and you must know that. It's a pity in a way that we ever met, because we'd both have been better off with somebody else who might have made something of us. As it was we made a mess of things and sort of dragged each other down and the only worthwhile thing we managed was you. But the thing about mothers is that you only get one in this world, so I beg you to be kind to her, and look after her. You mean more to her than you may think.

The second thing is a number and you'll have to work out its significance for yourself. Charity could have nothing to do with it. But if this letter ever reaches you, remember that it can be very important. The number is 156.5. Keep it carefully and don't forget it or lose it. What a terrible waste that would be.

I hope you will have a long, happy and successful life and be twice the man I've ever been. Goodbye from
your loving
Father

Oh yes, there was a tear in my eye at the end and I guessed that mark on the paper wasn't sweat. Difficult it might be to imagine Miss Franklin weeping, but she had been deeply moved by this; moved enough to keep the letter safe for the day she found me, even though it must have seemed she never would. I had seen people die, too; had written letters to parents and wives in the army's ritual attempt at comfort. But there were few I could even remember any more, and none I would think of seeking out.

I went back to the letter and read it again, thinking about him, and about her; he dying in some clammy jungle hut, fever high and probably incoherent most of the time; she taking careful notes of his ramblings and making of them a message a father might wish to send his son. The phrasing, certainly, had a touch of Miss Franklin about it, and I could imagine how she'd edit out the service phrases in the interests of supposedly innocent youth. He'd lain there demanding the letter be delivered; she'd listened, taken it down, and promised.

She must have thought, then, that it would be easy enough. The RAF would have an address and she would be able to send the letter, or perhaps, given her character, deliver it by hand. She'd have no way of knowing – indeed, I doubt whether my father knew – that we'd moved out of London two years earlier, out of England in fact, after my mother fell for the boozy charms of Mr Sean Emmett from the city of Cork and the pair of us followed him to Ireland. There were never any letters from my father, and though I wrote a few to him, no reply ever came. I doubt whether my mother wrote at all. She always refused to talk about it. 'We're parted,' she'd say, 'and that's that!' Occasionally, drink taken, she would treat me to stories of his cruelties, his inability to provide, his love of horse-racing and distaste for his family, his infidelities, his overall lack of character. But my mother always had a flexible attitude to truth and as I grew older I listened with the old magician's warning lively in my mind; believe nothing of what you hear – and only half of what you see!

Perhaps one day she'd have told me about him without all the embroideries, but then again perhaps she wouldn't. She was fairly good to me in most ways, but the sun didn't shine out of me the way it shone out of Sean Emmett, and she was so damned erratic that it's impossible to say she even had intentions, let alone try to define them. She had her practical moments, though. Having learned – I don't know how, but she did – of my father's disappearance, and later of the presumption of death, she hadn't allowed the Government to forget its obligations to widow and orphan.

She was killed two days before I was to go to Aldershot to join the army: too much Old Bushmills as usual and the car ran off the road and she and Emmett died together as it hit a tree. Nobody else was hurt, which is probably a fair summing-up': the pair of them damaged only themselves. And me, a little, but not really for very long. The army gave me compassionate leave even before I'd joined, and when, a bit late, I finally put on uniform, I quickly found a far better family life than any I'd previously encountered, and I stuck with it afterwards for as long as it would allow me to stick.

Looking at the letter and thinking about Miss Franklin, it struck me that bureaucracy has its odd ways. Miss Franklin must have been badgering the RAF in the hope of finding me, and the RAF hadn't been able to help. But just along the road, the army had found me smartly enough, Ireland or no Ireland, when my turn for conscription came. No escape when they want *you*; it's when you want *them* that the difficulties begin.

I decided that once I was out of hospital, I'd go up to Birmingham, eat the hefty slice of humble pie Miss Franklin was bound to cut for me, and get the questions answered. They weren't of vast importance, but I was intrigued and knew myself well enough to realize that my mind wouldn't leave the thing alone until it was cleared up.

Shortly afterwards, Birstall came to see me: briefcase, umbrella and bowler hat, and looking prim, which was as near as he could ever get to bonhomie. Most of the time he just looks bad-tempered but sometimes, with a great effort, he controls his facial muscles and succeeds in looking like a stern Victorian lady confronted with a favourite but recalcitrant nephew. As he sat in the chair, it struck me that he looked just a little like its last occupant, Miss Franklin, though with substantially less force of character.

'I – ah – understand your sight is in no danger, Mr, ah, Tunnicliffe.'

'So I'm told.'

'Good news indeed.' His lips pursed.

I thought: the damned old vampire wants his answer, and added carefully, 'Not quite sure yet, though.'

'Ah? But I understood —'

'Sometimes,' I said, 'there's delayed reaction. So they tell me.'

'How soon will you be certain?'

'A few days.' Better switch the subject. 'Was anything actually stolen, Mr Birstall?'

He frowned. 'No. We were – ah – very fortunate. The cash tills were actually in the process of being emptied. Those men were armed, you know!'

'Ah,' I said. 'So they were.'

'And there was a good deal of cash on the premises.'

'Yes, there would be. Well, so long as it's still there!' Your move, I thought. *Now* ask me how soon I'll be back.

He wanted to; that was why he was here. But even for Birstall there were limits. He fumbled in his briefcase and pulled out two hundred cigarettes and a bottle of Bell's whisky, and looked at them disapprovingly for a moment. 'The – ah – staff made a small collection to send you these.'

'Splendid. Thank them for me.'

'And there is some correspondence. Some – ah – people appear to have written to you.' He handed me a small bundle of letters with a rubber band round them, then closed the briefcase with a snap.

There was a pause, while he searched for the right words, and found them. 'We are all – ah – of course, anxious to – ah – welcome you back.'

'And I, of course, to come back.' I smiled at him, impervious.

But not as impervious as I thought. 'To your new position,' he said. The old bastard. I had to answer and he knew it and waited with miserable pleasure all over his face.

I hesitated, searching rather frantically for a reply. 'If I can see straight,' I said finally. 'There's a touch of double vision still. I won't be much use if I can't count accurately.'

'Very well.' He rose reluctantly. 'You must let us know if there's – ah – anything we can do.'

'Thank you. I will.'

He left then. People to harass, no doubt. I began to open the letters. There had been a kind of pattern to the correspondence I'd received. The London evening papers had said which hospital I was in, and most letters from the London area had been sent to me there. Others had been sent via newspapers or to the bank branch – its name having been much publicized. This batch seemed to have been forwarded from head office. I wasn't entirely surprised that two of them contained money: there had been pound notes and the odd fiver tucked inside several previous letters, usually with the instruction to 'have a good dinner with my compliments'. The senders probably believed bank clerks couldn't afford good dinners, and were largely right. The ones containing money seemed invariably to be anonymous, though, which was useful; no reply necessary and no way of not hanging on to the money.

But one of these new letters contained a hundred pounds! I nearly fell off the bed. It had felt a bit bulky as I picked it up and when I opened it I found ten ten-pound notes wrapped in a sheet of writing paper on which were four words : 'Well done. Good luck.'

In my astonishment I very nearly forgot about the rest of the letters. For several minutes I simply lay there enjoying the sensations : passing those new tenners from hand to hand in a shocking display of avarice. I tried to imagine myself shoving a hundred quid into an envelope and posting it off to a total stranger, and failed utterly. Not exactly the kind of thing I'd do. Or that anybody I knew would do. For a start, I doubted whether I knew anybody who had a hundred to spare, let alone the depth of generosity required. Eventually I tucked the notes away with the rest, but not before I'd counted it all with professional skill. One hundred and thirty-two pounds, by God! I counted it again, restraining myself from cackling like the miser in the cartoon, and reflecting that if Birstall were peering through the keyhole – not impossible, that – and had seen the display of dexterity, he'd have had me back on the counter the following morning.

There were three other letters. One lady wrote that when the thieves were convicted I sounded just the man to give them a damn good flogging. The lady regretted it wasn't possible. The final one bore a strange stamp. When I opened it, the letter resurrected the subject of my father.

> White Walls,
> Angels,
> St Mary's,
> Jamaica,
> West Indies.

Dear Mr Tunnicliffe,

I don't suppose you'll ever have heard my name, but I knew your father pretty well. (I'm assuming he was your father – you've got the same name.) Anyway, I see from the airmail edition of *The Times* that you put up a pretty good show the other day and caught a nasty one in the process. Well, I have a suggestion to make. That bank of yours owes you (1) a convalescent holiday, and (2) probably a reward. So why don't you come and spend all of (1) and part of (2) here in Jamaica? You can stay with me and it won't cost you anything much, and I promise you our climate's a sight better than yours, especially at this time of year.

Mind you, I'm aware (a) that banks can be mean and no reward may be forthcoming, and (b) that if it isn't, bank salaries don't run to Caribbean holidays. So: if the bank won't pay your fare, I will (though *not* BOAC first or any other class – fly charter!). And don't sit asking yourself silly questions, like 'How can I accept this from a stranger?' I may be a stranger to you, but you're not to me. Your photograph used to be shown to me quite regularly by your father. He was proud of you, and the pride now seems justified. Believe me, I'd be delighted to meet old George Tunnicliffe's boy.

Sorry if this is a bit out of the blue. I'd have written years ago if I'd have had any idea where you were.

If you fancy the trip, just let me know, and come.
                                Yours
                                      J. C. H. Ludlam

'Just how soon will you be back at the bank, Mr Tunnicliffe?'

'Not quite yet, I'm afraid, Mr Birstall. Apparently I'm scheduled for a little convalescence.'

'Oh.' Grudgingly. 'Well, I suppose if the doctors insist.'

'They're very insistent.'

'I see. And where can you be reached if, er – ?'

'I thought – Jamaica.'

'*Jamaica!*'

'No, she went of her own accord. Ha, ha! Sorry, Mr Birstall. I have an invitation, and it does seem a pity not to accept.'

Birstall in a cleft stick and knowing it. Can hardly hound the hero, and knowing that, too.

I lay back on my bed, going over this delightful and wholly imaginary conversation, and going over, also, the state of my finances. A hundred quid and an invitation to Jamaica in the same post – talk about Fate's intentions! I'd be mad to pass it up, now I could afford it. Even if I could only just afford it.

I pushed the bell for the nurse and she came and saw the grin on my face and said, 'You're quite well enough to run your own errands now, Mr Tunnicliffe.'

Reclining happily, hands behind my head, 'I only want some information, Sister.'

'I'm not a sister, as you know perfectly well. Stop buttering me up.'

'It's just a matter of time. Sister in a fortnight, matron in six months.'

She laughed. 'Some of us are busy. What *do* you want?'

'Haven't I seen a nurse who looks as though she might come from the West Indies?'

'Probably. There are several.'

'Then shoo one of them in here.'

'What do you think I am! Make your own approaches!'

'It's your job to lighten suffering. If she's from Jamaica, so much the better.'

'My – we are particular.'

'And in need,' I said.

The Jamaican nurse came in shortly afterwards, with a broad grin. 'What's it about, man?'

'Do you happen to know,' I asked her, 'if there's a nice cheap way to get to Jamaica?'

She knew the airline fare structures backwards: she herself was saving hard for a trip home to see her parents. Thirty pounds more and it was back to Kingston for her, she said. She knew the agents who ran charter flights and which of them to avoid; she knew how long the flight took, how long it was possible to stay on which of the available tickets. It was like talking to Thomas Cook.

When she'd gone, I exercised my privilege as an ambulant patient, went to the telephone and rang the travel agent she had recommended. Nice deep brown voice and businesslike manner. Single seat? No problem, sir. He might even, wait a moment, sir, yes he could: there was a flight on Tuesday of next week from Manchester and he had a coachload of passengers for it. Certainly I could go to Manchester on his coach. I'd have to join his affinity society, of course, and if I remember, it was a society of ornithologists. He'd backdate my membership six months, and it would all be nice and legal. If I'd either confirm in writing with my cheque, or call round with the cash?

I fairly skipped back to my room, confirmed in writing enclosing my cheque – bounce *that* one, Mr Birstall! – recalculated my financial state and, on impulse, slipped three of those ten-pound notes into an envelope and addressed it to the Jamaican nurse at the hospital. Two could play the anonymity game. I posted it later, though, from Manchester Airport.

On the way there, the coach by-passed Birmingham. Oh well, I thought, I'd visit Miss Franklin when I got back from Jamaica. In the meantime, perhaps I'd send a picture postcard. Of some palm trees.

CHAPTER THREE

Ludlam had cabled that he'd meet my flight at Kingston. As soon as I came out of Immigration I looked round for him. He'd be smartish and middle-aged, I imagined; probably early fifties and with the mark of the military.

But he wasn't like that at all. A bunch of drivers stood waiting, some from hotels, a few cabbies looking for custom. Ludlam stood among them, a piece of old cardboard in his hand with my name lettered on it in chalk. He was a small man, hair very dark, but sallow-faced, shrunken-cheeked, his thin body a little stooped.

'Mr Ludlam? I'm George Tunnicliffe.'

He grinned at me. His teeth were yellowish, his hand-shake limp. 'Tunnicliffe's boy,' he said. 'Well, well.' To put down the words is to make him sound hearty, but Ludlam spoke in an undertone. 'Crowded here. Let's get clear.' I followed him as he slipped between the noisy family reunions on the airport concourse. He wore shorts and sandals, the local uniform, and his bandy little brown legs moved him along in a curious, swift way as though he were half light infantryman, half ballroom dancer. I remember thinking he looked a bit rat-like and reproving myself for lack of charity. He had a toothless centenarian of an old Morris Minor tourer outside, and he pointed to my suitcase. 'Toss it in the back. Boot's full of junk.'

The passenger door stuck and he lifted his foot from the clutch and gave it a kick. 'It does that. Goes, though. Hop in.' The door hinge grated, the lock was broken, and the silencer no longer impeded the free flow of exhaust gases. The Morris had the roar of a Grand Prix car and roughly the acceleration of a bicycle. Ludlam nudged me, grinning. 'Nothing to worry about. She goes very well.' Somehow in my head, a phrase formed that I was immediately ashamed of. Ludlam looked like a rat bound for a carnival.

We roared slowly through and then out of Kingston. There was no conversation because the Morris's engine drowned anything but a shout and Ludlam's modest vocal equipment wasn't designed for shouting. So I just sat, looking around me, not thinking about anything much. It was warm and pleasant and the vegetation was luxuriant, and if my mind lingered on anything, it was on a mental picture of beaches and girls and palm trees.

That's not to say I was entirely blind. I saw some nasty-looking shacks, and then houses with nets hanging out in the sun, and I looked at those nets with weary familiarity. Ping and pong in the night; mosquito country.

But the road climbed, and so did we, and with luck the mosquitoes would follow the habit of their kind and cling to the low and the wet. We didn't climb far, though, before Ludlam halted the Morris beside a small house that had once been white, a house one could recognize as a blood relative of the car. It was battered and run down, and it was Ludlam's. There wasn't really much to be done except hide disappointment behind polite smiles. I was his guest, invitation given and accepted, and he was being generous to a total stranger.

'Leave you to unpack,' Ludlam muttered, having shown me to a dusty room. I opened and closed drawers and shutters and they all seemed to stick. I had just put down my suitcase when the Morris started up outside. When I opened the window, Ludlam gave a small shrug of apology, pointed at his watch, let in the clutch and vanished.

Well, no doubt he'd be back quite soon. Also he was of military background and would expect his guest to be thirsty and to show initiative. I went looking for the booze.

There wasn't any. A dusty-looking jar full of water stood by an evil-looking sink in the kitchen, and that was as far as the possibilities for refreshment went. I left it severely alone. Thirst may be uncomfortable but it takes two or three days to kill you. Water-borne bacteria, in warm climates, can do it faster and far more unpleasantly. I found a chair and sat on it. At a table. There was nothing to put on the table; not even a kerosene lamp to lighten my perceptions in the fast-deepening dark, and certainly no food. So I sat, and I waited. And finally, hungry, thirsty and, if not angry, at least irritable, I put my arms on the table and rested my head on them. Not as comfortable as a bed, but safer. Beds in warm countries can harbour more than one kind of trouble.

By morning I was still alone, thirstier, hungrier, and getting irritated. No house could be occupied and entirely bereft of sustenance. I had not looked hard enough. I would bloody well look harder now. And I did. In my time I was taught about searching on an army course by some fairly expert gentlemen from the Hong Kong police and I gave Chez Ludlam the Class III version – Thorough, But Don't Leave Tracks. But I'd been right the first time. There was nothing to eat and nothing to drink, and very little of anything else. Ludlam seemed to have no more than he stood up in. And still no Ludlam.

So I left. There were houses a mile or two away, and it was downhill. Okay, I'd walk.

Suitcase in hand I walked, and sweated, and thirsted, and cursed Ludlam. Finally a bus came, and I took it and found myself entering the town with the mosquito nets, Spanish Town, and one of the first things I saw there was a branch of the bank.

I went in, told them I was both customer and employee and would like to change travellers' cheques, and the counter clerk asked was I the George Tunnicliffe whose name was all over the staff newspaper? Next: the manager. Come in and have a drink.

Tea, please. I explained that I'd had no breakfast and so on and he asked why and I told him about my host. To that point, no name had been used. But the manager now said delicately, 'Somebody I might know?' And I said, 'Mr Ludlam.'

'Really!' He fairly sat up in his chair. 'Staying with Ludlam? Well, I'm damned,' and a fair amount more along the same lines. After a bit, he said, 'Tell me –' It was the most unbecoming behaviour in a bank manager, but curiosity had him gripped '—what's it like inside?'

'Well, there isn't much *there*. In fact, hardly anything.' And then I asked questions. 'Why,' I asked, 'are you so surprised I'm staying with Ludlam?'

The answer was that nobody stayed with Ludlam. Nobody had ever been *known* to stay with Ludlam. It was easier, the bank manager said, to insinuate a mastodon into the prime minister's private privy than to cross Ludlam's threshold. Which led us to Ludlam himself.

Ludlam was reputed to be rich. Alternatively, he was reputed to have been rich and lost it all. It was difficult to tell because he kept himself to himself, and had done so ever since he first came to Jamaica soon after the end of the war. It was during that war, apparently, that the riches, which might or might not still exist, had been acquired.

'How?' I asked.

'Well, I shouldn't be saying all this,' said the bank manager, who certainly shouldn't. 'But there's supposed to have been some fairly dirty work out in the Far East. I *did* hear there'd been a court-martial.' He remembered his position then, and changed the subject. Was I on holiday? I said I wanted to hire a car cheaply and needed an address where the rooms were cheap and the Caribbean was adjacent and to which I could retreat if necessary. He made telephone calls, and I got a discount on a small Ford. After that I got an invitation to go to his club any lunchtime.

When I left, Ludlam was sitting outside in his Morris, giving me a small, flat, unwinking smile.

'I've decided to hire a car,' I said. 'Mustn't put you to too much trouble.'

'No trouble,' he said. 'Hop in. You'll want some breakfast, I expect.'

'Thanks,' I said, 'but I've had some.'

'No, you haven't.'

'How do you know?'

'How do you imagine? I bloody well watched.'

'All right,' I said. 'You can buy me some breakfast. And explain!'

'Working out perfectly,' he said. 'Hop in.'

We went to a place that seemed to be built of plaster-board and held together by spit, and there I had a confection of assorted sea-food in some violent sauce, simultaneously exquisite and almost lethal. Afterwards coffee, and with the second cup, rum.

I pushed it away. 'Too early.'

'Never,' Ludlam said. 'Never too early. Sit and sip it while I talk.'

So I sipped and it was pleasant. I lit a cigarette and waited.

'What I wondered, you see,' Ludlam said, 'was whether you were anything like your old man. And you are. Uncannily.'

I have one old photograph of my father, and when I knew I was going to meet his old pal Ludlam, I'd put it in my pocket. Now I fished it out and said, 'Resemblance, maybe, but it isn't uncanny.'

He grinned. 'In the moral character, I mean. You've unusual skills for a man of probity. To name two, you can disarm men who carry loaded shotguns, and you can search a house so people wouldn't know.'

'If they wouldn't know, how – ?'

'I'm not people. I *can* tell. Manage to find out anything at the bank?'

'They cash cheques.'

'By Jove, but it doesn't take *you* long, does it? Give you an hour or two and you've searched your host's house from top to bottom and started furtive enquiries.'

'You shouldn't have left me all alone.'

'Oh, I'm not complaining. You might have gone off to bed and read a book and waited for me to come home. But you didn't. Not George Tunnicliffe's lad. Not likely. You're up and busy. What do you know about your father?'

'Not a hell of a lot. My mother told me a certain amount. I remember him vaguely.'

'Your mother said he was a wastrel, I'll bet. Spent his money on heavy-footed horseflesh and lively ladies.'

'Did he?'

'Sometimes. Did she tell you he could fly? I mean *really* fly? Judgement, navigation, touch. Had everything. She tell you that?'

'No.' When she'd mentioned flying, the word had been equated with escape. 'So he went *flying*,' she'd say, or, 'So off he *flew*.'

'They don't know, you see,' Ludlam said. 'Not their world. But you believe me, son, he flew like a pigeon, all straight lines and home James.'

'You liked him, obviously.'

He gave me a glance. 'Did I? Not sure. I'd a lot of time for him. Always have for real class when I see it, which isn't often.'

'Then inviting me here was an odd thing to do, surely?'

'Odd?' he repeated. 'Odd?' Then he gave a little cackle. 'No, not exactly odd. I could guess the kind of picture you had. So when I saw your name in *The Times* —'

'You decided the deserving lad ought to know?'

He scratched the tip of his nose with a finger. 'Sounds like rubbish, does it?'

'Well, the approach is a bit inconsistent. You tell me you're a friend of my father's, then say you're not sure you liked him much. You say he was brave as a bloody lion one minute and the next he had all the hallmarks of a cat burglar.'

Ludlam was nodding vigorously, grinning. 'He had, he had!'

I stared at him, and for no reason at all I said, 'What about the court-martial?'

He was suddenly motionless. 'What do you know about —?' Then he gave that grin. 'Told you that at the bank, did they?'

I grinned back at him, and he said, 'Exactly like him.'

We looked at each other in silence. I broke it by saying, 'Well, I'm here.'

Ludlam took a swig of rum, refilled his glass, then leaned across to top mine up. 'So you are,' he said.

'So?'

'Go and swim in the sea.'

I didn't argue. I collected my car and drove over the nightmares to the North Coast and lay on the sand for a while at Port Maria. I stayed there that night, at a little place the bank manager had recommended, spent much of the following day on the beach, and drove back to Ludlam's place in the late afternoon.

He was there, too, in that bare house, and when I went in, there were a bottle of rum and some fruit and water and ice and limes on the table. God knows where they came from, but he danced round tipping careful quantities into a jug and muttering an incantation that went:

> One of sour (the limes)
> Four of weak (water)
> Three of strong (rum)
> Two of sweet (sugar)

'The simple, classic one,' he said, with the stance and manner of an instructor in tactics at Sandhurst. 'Some would add grenadine, or even banana, but for a punch, this is the formula.' He pushed it over to me, and it was.

'You're patient,' he remarked suddenly.

'Thirty-six hours isn't long.'

He looked at his drink. 'I knew you existed of course, and your mother. But I didn't know where.'

'She ran off,' I said, 'with an Irishman.'

'So you were in Ireland? I never *looked*, mind you. I just wondered whether you were like him.'

'And I am?'

'That,' Ludlam said, 'is the question.'

And there the whole thing stopped. I was intrigued, naturally, and obviously he intended that. But he didn't mention it again and because he didn't, I didn't either. Perverse of me, perhaps, but I thought his behaviour childish and I hate that kind of daft guessing game. He'd invited me to Jamaica to size me up, and his first character test had taken place, but if there were others, I wasn't aware of them. After a couple of days I told him that if he wanted to tell me I'd listen, but in the meantime I proposed to enjoy my holiday, not ruin it with idle speculation.

He just nodded, and the day after that I moved out, telling him I'd be back before I left for England. It's my guess now that he was looking for indications of enthusiasm, or mad-headedness, or determination, or some combination of all three. But if he kept an eye on me, as he probably did, all he saw was idleness. I spent one Sunday at the bank manager's club and a lot of my time on the beach at Port Maria with a blonde American lady until – without either effort or intent – she'd reduced me to penury.

For me, then, it was either back to Ludlam or sleep on the beach, so on my last night I knocked on his door and said, 'Are you going to tell me?'

He didn't answer until he'd made the punch, then he said, 'I don't think so.'

'Okay,' I said amiably.

He took a long pull at his punch. 'What's it matter, anyway?'

But he woke me at one o'clock in the morning and told me he'd changed his mind. 'If you can just walk away, maybe you're fit to be told.' He handed me a wet, cold cloth. 'Face, elbows, wrists, back of the neck. When you've done, come down.'

Groaning a little, I obeyed. He had an enamel pot of coffee on the table and poured me a mugful, hot and black. I said, 'I really don't care very much. Do you mind if I go back to bed?'

'Sit down.' Spoken crisply. 'And listen. There's quite a bit to tell.'

I put my hands round the coffee mug and inhaled steam and thought resentfully that since he'd had two weeks to do this, it was a bit bloody unreasonable to wait until the last night, and then rob me of my sleep.

'Let me ask you a question,' he began, in his best instructor manner. 'When troops move into conquered territory, what's the first thing that happens?'

'Looting,' I suggested. 'Rapine, drunkenness.'

'Agreed,' he said. 'But on a practical level?'

'Legal code?'

Ludlam shook his head. 'Currency. Out with the old, in with the new, fast as you can do it. Puts power squarely where it needs to be, in the conqueror's hands. Ask me a question.'

'All right. Where's the money come from?'

'Now that,' he said, 'is a very *good* question. No doubt in Germany they moved in with notes fresh from the treasuries. In the east, no. We had to do it ourselves. Ask me another intelligent question.'

'Who printed it?'

'*Very* good. I did.'

'Oh?' I said, and repeated it with changing inflections as the possibilities rose, one after another, in my head.

'What they needed, you see, was a trustworthy senior officer with some experience of these things. Well, I'd been trained at Cravens. You know Cravens?'

'Vaguely. Banknote printers?'

He nodded. 'Can you guess what happened?'

I pictured the situation. War newly over. A thousand tasks to be done. 'You were in sole command of this?'

'Yes.'

I looked at him. 'You had a very good record.'

'And a red band round my hat. True enough. Go on.'

'Well, first,' I said, 'you thought about it. If you gave in to temptation, what would the consequences be? That kind of thing.'

He sat back. 'Take it through to the end. I won't be insulted.'

'All right.' I sipped coffee and tried to put myself in his place as it had been, then, in 1945. Big job, fine record, a lot to lose. 'First question. If I print one for them and one for me, and one for them and one for me, will I get away with it? The answer has to be "no". The army wants records kept. Detailed records. And banknotes have to be numbered. Was it possible to fiddle with the machines so they'd print more than one of each number?'

'No.'

'Okay. So in the end you'd get caught. Not immediately maybe, but sooner or later there'd be auditors and so on.

So the question is, how long had you got? And how much could you print?'

'Did you,' Ludlam asked mildly, 'ever get anywhere near a staff appointment in the army?'

'No.'

'I'm not surprised. You've an idle mind. *Think*.'

'You'd have to get it out.' He was watching me struggle as schoolmasters always watch thickheads. 'And you'd have to convert it, because there'd be nowhere else to spend occupation currency. So it's a four-part question: how long, how much, how is it converted, and how is it got out?'

No bravos, yet. Ludlam waited patiently. I thought some more. 'You had access to the facilities?'

'Jesus Christ! Is that the language you use in the army these days? Access to the bloody facilities! Lose a war while you're speaking that sentence, my lad. But yes, I had.'

'I'm thinking of transport.'

He nodded.

'All right,' I went on. 'It becomes a question of whether it's worth it. Can you turn enough money into enough suitable valuables *and* get them out, to make the game worth the candle. And what *is* the candle? What do they do to senior officers with distinguished war records when they catch them in criminal acts? Did you know?'

'No.'

I thought about *that*, frowning at him. 'All right. You need information. Legal knowledge. Precedent. You had – ?'

'Access to the facilities,' he said sarcastically. 'Yes, I had.'

'So you could get good legal opinion. Let's assume the lawyer says you'll be cashiered, and disgraced. Either that matters to you, or it doesn't. Did it?'

'No.'

I thought again, with Ludlam's little black eyes unwaveringly on the wrinkles on my forehead. 'You'd be out of the army, avoided by your friends. Cravens wouldn't have you anywhere near them. Only worth it if you can get a hell of a lot out.'

'Jesus wept. And – ?'

I looked at him humbly. There wasn't an idea in my head.

'And *keep* it!' he said. 'From what I know of you, my lad, I think I'd probably follow you into an attack. But only if somebody else had organized it.'

'I left something out?'

'You brought very little *in*! What about support? Do I need help? How much help? Who? With what specialist skills? If you're going to convert paper money into valuables, are valuables available? Can you get at them? How do you get them out? Where do they go? And how do they get *in* when they get there? Furthermore, how do *you* get in after them, because you're a criminal by then. My dear boy, I doubt if you could steal the doggie's dinner unless the kitchen door was open and he was chained up in the garden.'

We sat up all night, sipping at coffee and rum, while he talked and I listened goggle-eyed. He'd apparently decided it would be altogether quicker and a great deal less wearing if he gave up trying to thread the camel of my mind through the intellectual needle of the episode and simply told me.

'I'd twenty-four hours' notice of the arrival of press, paper and ink. Sealed packing cases, coming by aeroplane. The gentleman who gave me the job wasn't a fool. He'd been trusting me for several years in a lot of tricky situations, and I hadn't let him down. I began to ask myself questions. In my head, not on paper.

'First, support. I knew something about people. If the prize is big, they'll play. Your father was first in.'

I felt an obscure resentment on my father's behalf. 'Obvious, was he?'

'You,' Ludlam said, 'have a lot to learn. He was the boss's chauffeur and he flew the printing press and the plates and the paper precisely *because* the boss trusted him and had trusted him for years.'

'But there was that something in his eyes?'

He sighed. 'We'd got it all signed for and locked up and

we were having a drink, and your father said, "Imagine being able to print your own!" and began to ask me about banknote printing and security and in about ten seconds we both knew what the conversation was really about. So shortly after I started printing he took a suitcase full of paper and a jeep and a few days' leave and headed up to the Shan states. Know anything about them?'

'No.'

'Ruby country. Plus, at that time, some Japanese who hadn't heard about surrender, or didn't approve. Had its little hazards, that trip. But I'd heard from provost branch of a Japanese officer up there. Your father went to try and meet him. The Japanese officer had also worked a currency racket. He'd bought rubies from the governing families, more or less at pistol point, forcing his paper money on them when they'd far rather have kept the gems. But after the Japanese surrender he had no way out and we knew he was there. If we could get in touch . . .' Ludlam gave a little shrug and a little grin.

'And did you?'

'George did. He had a flag of truce on the jeep. He knew he was bound to be stopped – this was only days after the surrender and the country swarmed with Japanese – and when he was, he said he was there to negotiate with this Colonel Toshiba.

'George said he thought he was going to be bayoneted – the people he'd run into were infantry and tough and quite keen to add another round-eye to their tally. The fact that he knew Toshiba's name saved him. So the deal was done, on what terms I never knew. Never wanted to, either. George's business. His service for me was transport; mine for him was scrip. I know he got rubies, and a goodish quantity, but not how many or their value.'

'And the Jap, Toshiba. What was in it for him?'

'For the moment,' Ludlam said, 'we'll leave him. The rubies were George's and I didn't ask him to deal for me. I had my own source of valuables.' He grinned reminiscently. 'Gold. And furthermore I didn't have to go looking. It came to me. Or, rather, she did.'

'She?'

'Oh, it's novelette stuff here,' Ludlam said. 'Not just some local tart, I might tell you. This was an intriguing bloody beauty, the genuine article. Eurasian, she was. Father was a second generation German with a Chilean passport, mother Burmese. How about *that* for flags of convenience! Batted her eyelashes at my sergeant clerk to get in through my door, and then began pouring out a long tale about how her home kept being searched by the military police. She'd been the mistress of the local Japanese administrator, a colonel called Nakamura. She denied it, of course. He'd forced his attentions on her, you know the kind of tale. She was dressed in silk, full of crap and confidence, and she wanted to trade. What is it they say – takes one to know one? Well, she had me spotted after about twenty seconds. Out comes an American twenty-dollar gold piece, down on my desk top with a loud click. Her savings, she says, and could the army look after it for her? Wide-eyed innocence. Marvellous! You see, she knew, and I knew, and everybody else knew, that Colonel Nakamura had been a very smart chappie. About twelve months before the surrender he'd taken all the local pawnshops under formal military government control to regulate their activities. Pawnshops were doing excellent business, because food on the black market was sky high and everybody was pawning valuables. So, come the first atom bomb, Master Nakamura peers into his crystal ball and sees the end is nigh. What's he do? I'll tell you what he does. He's off with a couple of trucks and a load of packing cases, not to mention a squad of soldiers, taking all the gold and jewels into protective custody. Issuing receipts. Proper, formal, polite, straightforward theft. You can imagine, eh? Informal estimates at the time put the accumulated loot at about two million sterling. On the day of the Nagasaki bomb, the good Nakamura took off for places unknown, and to the best of my knowledge has never been heard of since.'

I said, 'But if he took the gold with him –'

'He didn't, not all of it. Couldn't because it weighed too much. One of those nice little flying equations where you balance range off against payload. Result was that the girl-friend has access, as *you'd* put it, to the rest. He'd said he'd come back for her one day, but she could see certain difficulties in his way. In any case, she was impatient by nature. What she wanted was to get out, and to take enough of the stuff with her to set her up for life.'

'She was taking a risk, surely? I mean, to walk in to a senior officer and tell him all this?'

'She didn't tell it all at once. It was done with great delicacy, I might tell you, and much oblique . . . look, she knew I was the currency man, and she'd seen the greedy gleam in my beady bloody eye. She knew what she was about. Took a while, of course, to get to a point of agreement, but in the end we had a deal. Her idea was to head for South Africa. If she liked it, she'd stay; if not, on to Chile, which she'd never seen, of course, but where her passport guaranteed not just entry but residence. It was all neat and tidy for her if she could get the gold out. So – in return for making it possible for her to leave with enough to set her up for life, I'd get enough to set me up.'

'Transport,' I said. 'My father.' Then a thought struck me. 'If he'd got his nest-egg in the form of rubies, was he still around? And if so, why?'

Ludlam said, 'If I say it was trust, you'll probably laugh, but that's what it was. We'd agreed we wouldn't let each other down, and neither of us would have broken the agreement. Thieves' honour. There was something we did disagree about, but I'll come to that later. Yes, he was still around. He was flying a good deal, too; the Old Gentleman was making inspection trips all over the place and George was chauffeuring him. Perfect situation, you see.' He sat there laughing at me. 'I mean, can you imagine anything sweeter?'

'You mean you just flew the gold out in the C-in-C's own plane?'

'*Just?* No, we didn't just. The old boy had a very sharp eye and an enquiring nature, and he disapproved strongly of smuggling in any form. There was no question of just shovelling the stuff aboard.'

'So how *was* it done?'

'By bringing in another specialist. The idea was George's, and very clever it was. Carrying it out was even cleverer. George had a mechanic who was a highly unusual chap: Malay-Chinese who'd been adopted as a nipper by some civil servant and his wife. Well, this feller had been taken to England and educated in sundry ways and ended up as an engineering apprentice with Vickers. Shouldn't really have been in the services at all: skills like his were much in demand in those days. But this chappie had done time – for bigamy of all things – and when he came out of chokey both wives were waiting at the gate. He went straight to the recruiting office and volunteered rather than face them. Unlikely, you may think, my lad, but such things happen. So this mechanic had many skills, among which was mould-making and casting. He also had two excellent reasons for not returning to Britain. You see that?'

'Yes.'

'It now became a question of selecting which part of a Dakota aircraft could be replicated in gold and substituted for the real part without making the plane unsafe. Didn't want to kill the C-in-C or ourselves. But George and his mechanic reckoned there were floor beams that were suitable, so they removed one during routine maintenance and a mould was made. Know the melting point of gold?'

'No.'

'A thousand and sixty-three degrees centigrade. This laddie had to build himself a furnace and get a crucible. And do it quickly. But the job was done, and in due course George flew five floor beams over into India. On separate trips. They each weighed about a couple of hundredweight, and sprayed with aluminium paint and bolted in position in the C-in-C's own aircraft, they weren't likely to be found. Nor were they. One for the mechanic, two for the girl and two for me. After that it was admin. Had to get her out, of course, but that was just paperwork and permits and none too difficult for me to fix. George took her off to Calcutta on a day he was flying empty. The mechanic went out the same way. Said he intended to vanish in India, which wasn't really too difficult, and he had a spare pay book in another name. I often wonder how many wives he finally acquired.

'But that left George and me, and as I said to you before, we had a disagreement. Not a fight. It was just that we didn't see eye to eye about the proper way to proceed. I was always a planner, you see, and George was like you, all anxiety to get moving. So what it amounted to was this: he intended to run for it. He'd just fly off one day taking the rubies with him, and vanish. That was how he wanted it. But I didn't like that idea at all. You'd spend the rest of your life wondering when somebody was going to recognize you and howl for the police. So I decided I'd have to give myself up. Confess all. Be court-martialled. Be cashiered. Then go away and spend the money. Once you've had the punishment you're free. But of course, it was essential to get in first. If the auditors set the military police on me, things would go rather harder than if I simply went to the Old Gentleman and confessed. I'm sure you see that.

'Upshot was, George and I fixed a day. His scheme was to take the aeroplane and fly off towards the islands: Solomons, Gilbert and Ellice, Fiji. Find somewhere he liked the look of, and sit back.'

'Easy as that?' I said.

Ludlam nodded. 'More or less. Papers, you see, were no great difficulty, or not to me. I'd kitted him out with the documents of a Canadian who'd died in hospital. Military documents carried no photographs and the general description matched. Once George got among the islands, nobody would even care, let alone investigate. So he'd commandeer petrol as far as the C-in-C's writ ran, which was a bloody long way. Then he'd dump the plane and take a boat. Nice white schooner bound for Tonga and taking a couple of months. It wouldn't have been difficult.'

'But?'

'Things intervene. Random events. Some bright spark cataloguing Japanese naval stores found a shed full of torpedoes, one of which was made to be dropped from aircraft and rather different from the rest. I don't know the technicalities, but there was some sort of primitive guidance system and everybody got vastly excited about it. Get it to Hong Kong for examination. No, better still, to Sydney. Didn't matter a toss, of course, with the war over, but the C-in-C got himself fascinated and said, yes, he'd have it flown down to Sydney right away in his own plane.

'So George set off with a somewhat complicated load. They'd taken the VIP seating out, so it was a straight cargo Dakota. But George had a torpedo and its bits and pieces in the back. Plus his collection of rubies. Plus his false documents. Plus Colonel Toshiba, from Shan, believe it or not, wearing khaki and a blue glengarry with a diced border and pretending to be the adjutant's batman from the Shanghai Volunteer Force on his way home on compassionate leave. Yes, you may laugh, but things were possible in those blessed days of chaos.

'So there we were. George in the air with a wink and a fortune. The girl and her gold safely away. My gold safe in a bank vault in Calcutta. I made an appointment to see the Old Gentleman, entered, saluted and said, "Sir, I have done a terrible thing. Succumbed to temptation, sir. Deep regret, squandered the money. Now realize what a fool I've been! And so on." And he looked at me without vast surprise and said, "Had to be somebody. There always is. Curious that it should be you." I remember wondering why he should think it curious, but I could hardly ask then and I never did find out.'

He looked at his watch. Outside it was becoming light, and before long I'd be on my way to the airport and home. I watched him as he stretched and yawned, and for once he looked old and sad and slow. I said, 'What happened at the court-martial?'

He blinked once or twice. 'Cashiered. Finished. And a year inside, which I served in Singapore. Not the full year, of course, because I was very well-behaved indeed. It wasn't until I came out that I heard about your father, though, because they'd whipped me off to Singapore as soon as I'd spoken to the Old Gentleman. But then, you know what happened.'

'Yes,' I said. 'He disappeared. But I don't know any details.'

Ludlam looked at me. 'Details? There aren't any, really. He took off from Changi for Kuching in Borneo. Refuelled there, took off and vanished. No more George. Never a word.'

'And you think – ?'

'I think,' Ludlam said, 'that George had planned to disappear, and disappear he did.'

We moved ourselves then. Semblance of some breakfast and off to the airport, and I kept wondering two things. The first was why he had told me this ancient tale. And the second was why I had *not* told him about Miss Franklin. Right up to the moment we shook hands and parted, I kept trying to make myself do it; but something stopped me.

CHAPTER FOUR

I'd been up all night, so I slept a bit on the plane, and then I woke up with my mind full of crooked fathers and missing rubies and distant jungles, all rattling round together like ice in a cocktail shaker. Plus Ludlam, of course, the bartender who'd put the constituents in the shaker.

Why, I asked myself, had he left it until the last night? Not for the reasons he'd given, certainly. Ludlam wasn't the hesitant type. Then it occurred to me that what he'd done was to send me off with everything sharp and fresh in my mind, where it could safely be left to fester. Nor had he just done it, he'd *contrived* to do it; *that* was why he'd waited so long. He'd said to himself, here's a fellow who's youngish, fairly fit, trained and can look after himself. Why don't I send him off to look for his father and cut myself in on the proceeds? On the other hand there weren't

– at least from Ludlam's point of view – likely to *be* any proceeds. Borneo, as I quickly discovered from the encyclopaedia, is not exactly small. Indeed it's the third largest island in the world, area 292,000 square miles, roughly three times the size of Great Britain. Furthermore, it's largely covered in primary jungle. Ludlam would know that any man setting off to find a lost aeroplane twenty years after it crashed would have his work cut out.

Next question? Yes, well, the same event that brought Ludlam out of his burrow had brought Miss Franklin out of hers. Two of them, both anxious that the orphan boy should know certain facts. Yet neither knew of the other's existence. I wondered whether either of them would have come anywhere near me if they'd met each other first. Miss Franklin knew where the aircraft crashed; Ludlam knew what was aboard. *But neither knew what the other knew!*

And I – now – knew both. More or less. If Ludlam was to be believed, a very valuable packet of precious stones was lost in the jungles of Borneo. If Miss Franklin was to be believed, *lost* was not the word. She knew where the aircraft had crashed, near enough . . . That cut down the 292,000 square miles quite a bit.

Two things came the day I went back to the bank. First, manager Birstall was waiting with the manacles, ready to fasten me for ever to his mahogany counter. He assumed I'd accepted the new job and he would go over my duties with me presently, but in the meantime . . .

'I have a, er, pleasant – ah – task to perform, Mr Tunnicliffe,' said Birstall. It was four-thirty and the staff had suddenly been summoned to his office. We all thought, or at least I did, that there was some major discrepancy, fingers in the till, or something roughly along those lines, and we were going to be working beyond the chimes of midnight, with Scotland Yard breathing down our necks.

But no. 'The directors, very generously it seems to me,' Birstall continued, 'have decided to reward your, er, ah, your – ' Words of approval come with extreme reluctance to Birstall's lips, but he finally found the one he wanted.

' – to reward your, ah, effort, in a, er, suitable way.'

He gave me an envelope and shook my hand very briefly, and said, 'That's all' to those assembled. I went to the Gents' to achieve decent privacy, and found myself staring at a cheque for two thousand pounds! I could live a year on two thousand pounds. Or buy a car: a Morgan with a leather strap across the bonnet. Or buy my flat.

Or . . .

One of those thoughts that comes trampling into your mind, elbowing everything else aside, and making guts churn in anticipation. Get out, I told it, and stay out. But back it came, full of aggression and alluring argument. Come on, old boy, said the voice in my head, think a little: look at you: fine young fella, fit, free and unattached. Know where there's a fortune in missing loot, and you've just been handed money and independence! The damned voice even quoted Housman. Poetry's not my territory, but an old army friend used to say it was the perfect philosophy for a soldier – and also an excuse for all the boozing and assorted nonsense a man could cram into a short life:

> Clay lies still, but blood's a rover;
> Breath's a ware that will not keep.
> Up, lad: when the journey's over
> There'll be time enough for sleep.

Like a bloody bugle blowing! On the other hand, there is a kind of cautious side to my nature, which busily offered the opposite counsel: good job, money in the bank, secure future. Et cetera. Et cetera. Et cetera. And very dull it sounded.

I didn't make a decision then, or for several weeks; not because I didn't want to, but because administration, as usual, got in the bloody way. I was firmly fastened down until the trial was over, and that would be weeks. If, in the meantime, I threw over the job at the bank, I'd have to support myself, nibbling away at the windfall. So I became number one man on Mr Birstall's counter and welfare officer to the young ladies, and it proved as bad as I'd expected.

But I kept at it, and worked, and went to the identification parade and picked out the lawless one. Shortly afterwards I received a brief phone call at the bank and was told that I would be taking unnecessary risks with my health if I gave my evidence of identification quite so firmly when the thieves came up before one of Her Majesty's judges.

The police, when I mentioned this, said : You seem to be able to look after yourself tolerably well, don't you, sir? And yes, they knew about the desirability of a whole skin, but there's the duty of the citizen, isn't there, sir, and after all it *was* a very positive identification. They'd keep an eye on me, though.

It was an uncomfortable few weeks and I took to walking round with a nice, thick ashplant walking-stick, just in case.

I also rented a car one Sunday and went to see Miss Franklin. It was an impulse, really, and I went by car rather than by train because if somebody intended violence, I didn't want to lead them to her. I was taking the threat fairly seriously. But the impulse meant I hadn't let her know I was coming, and when I stood on her doorstep at ten o'clock that Sunday morning, she answered the door with hat on head and prayer book in hand and said crisply, 'You should have written. I'm on my way to church.'

Wrong-footed again, I mumbled that I could come back later.

'I expect,' Miss Franklin said coolly, 'that morning service will be a novel experience for *you*, Mr Tunnicliffe. It might even do you good. You may come with me.'

So I went. She had a good, firm contralto voice, and when she saw I was barely singing she nudged me and frowned, and I heard my own voice raised for the first time in a lot of years. Afterwards, at the church door, she introduced me to the vicar who said he hoped to see me again.

'I wouldn't bank on *that*,' Miss Franklin said, 'but I'm sure Mr Tunnicliffe would like to make a contribution to the church roof appeal fund.' She fixed me with an eye.

That cost me a fiver, and as we walked away, she said, 'Five pounds may not buy a place in The Kingdom, but it's a beginning.'

Surprisingly, she produced a bottle of sherry when we got indoors, and with it a small smile. 'Don't look so startled, Mr Tunnicliffe. A little wine for the stomach's sake is permitted in scripture.'

That fiver had put her in a good humour. 'One of my sins is occasional impatience,' she said, pouring. 'I must not add lack of hospitality to it. You'll stay for lunch?'

It was chicken risotto and a half-bottle of white wine. I looked at the bottle and raised an eyebrow and she said, 'Occasionally, and only on Sundays.' There was a custard flan, also very good. She cooked well. Then coffee and, to my amazement, a cigar.

'I won them in a raffle, Mr Tunnicliffe. The vicar smokes one sometimes, when he calls. I do not understand why they give such enjoyment, but it seems they do. Please smoke it.'

So I did, and we began to talk, and this time I was very much on my best behaviour. She remained brisk. 'Now, you will want, I imagine, to know more about your father?'

'Yes.'

'I don't know how much I can help you. He was badly injured and I was unable to do much for him. I had very little morphine, and when it was gone, there was no way of alleviating his pain which, I assure you, was distressing. I also had a small quantity of sulfa drugs but not, as it turned out, enough to hold the infection at bay.'

I said, 'Forgive me, but why were you there? How did a wom . . . how did you come to be in Borneo? This wasn't long after the Japanese surrender.'

'No place for women? Let me explain. I was a medical missionary. Not a doctor. When I was young, there was no money for expensive education, so I became a nurse. I had tropical training, then went to serve first in India, later in Borneo. When the Japanese came in nineteen-forty-one, I was put into a detention camp.'

'Uncomfortable,' I said, and felt instantly foolish.

'It was certainly that. However, I survived, which is rather more than some were able to do, and then I succeeded in escaping from the camp.'

I blinked at her. 'Surely there was nowhere to escape to?'

'There was the jungle.' She said it matter-of-factly, imparting information, but I had some small idea what that little statement meant. I'd read enough by now about Borneo. There were headhunting tribes, dangerous wildlife, tropical diseases. And, of course, the Japanese army.

'When was this?'

'In nineteen-forty-three. August, to be accurate.'

'Two years before the surrender?'

She gave a little nod. 'I had good friends among the Sea Dyak and Iban tribes and I was taken in. I was in Borneo because I had never left it. I continued my nursing as best I could. Even without equipment and medicines there are always ways in which a trained nurse can be useful.'

Looking at her then, neat and cool and upright, a spinster in middle-age just back from church, it was difficult to credit. Two years hiding in the jungle, two years of murderous hardship, taking risks no commando would want to hear about, two years being hunted, because the Japanese were remorseless in tracking escapees. Difficult to credit, but not, somehow, to believe.

She went on matter-of-factly, 'In due course a small force came, to gather intelligence and to organize whatever underground action was possible against the Japanese. Some were British, some Australian, a few Dutch. I was put in touch with them.'

In touch, I thought. Long treks through primary jungle, with all that that entailed, and then contact with a bunch of desperadoes with Tommy-guns, explosives and radio sets. Hunted by every Jap in Borneo. I said, 'Tom Harrisson?'

'You know about him?'

'I know something.' Harrisson had organized the Ibans into a highly-efficient scout force. Blowpipes against modern arms and the blowpipes gaining ascendancy. 'How long were you with Harrisson?'

She frowned. 'I find war experiences very tedious, Mr Tunnicliffe, and all this is hardly relevant. What was important to us about Mr Harrisson's force was that they had some medical supplies, and were occasionally sent more, in aircraft drops. I was able to persuade them to let me have some small amounts, and so to do my work more effectively. But they *were* small amounts, and that is why, when your father was injured, I was not properly equipped to treat him.'

'But surely,' I said, 'that was *after* the war? Supplies must have come in.'

'You must understand the remoteness of the territory, the distances, and the difficulty of travel. I could hardly leave my little parish, you see, because if I did I would at once have been sent back to England, and the people who looked to me for help would have had nobody. Once replacement staff could be sent, that would be different, but until then I really had to stay where I was. Anything else would have been desertion.'

She was astonishing. After a couple of years of that sort of life, most of us would have been off like sprinters, heading for the hot baths and the heaped plates and the clean sheets. But she'd continued in hiding, this time keeping away from her own side! I said, 'Where were you?'

'Just a hut the Ibans had put up for me. I could visit several longhouses from there.'

'But where? That's where my father must have crashed.'

'It was at –' The name was a couple of grunts and a glottal stop. Into my mind crept the deeply unworthy thought that Miss Franklin just might be being evasive.

So I persisted. 'Where's that?'

'The area's scarcely mapped at all,' she said, grey eyes direct and frank, 'so you'd hardly be much wiser.'

'And he came to you?'

'Yes, he did.' There was a momentary, and wholly uncharacteristic hesitation, and she exhaled sharply in exasperation. 'I have never been quite sure what did happen, Mr Tunnicliffe. I had malaria. I may perhaps have been a little confused.'

'You didn't hear the crash?'

'I have never been sure. It may have been a dream. I was asleep when he – when he reached me.'

Confused, I thought. Always the word chosen with care. She had been rotten with malaria. High fever. Asleep was a euphemism for delirium. 'Was anyone with you?'

'I was capable of looking after myself. However, your father reached me, and I awoke to see him – ' she looked at me for a moment – 'on the floor, covered in mud. He was exhausted and in great pain, and unable to talk. I managed to lift him on to the bed.' She paused again. 'I'm not sure there's much point in detailing his injuries. Nor am I really sure how many separate ones there were. The most important, externally, were a broken thigh and a number of broken ribs. Deep lacerations. Probably internal injuries. In this condition, he'd had to crawl.'

'How far?'

'I don't know. I washed him and splinted his thigh and cleaned his wounds, and I administered the drugs.' She poured more coffee, frowned, hesitated, then said, 'I have never been sure that I acted correctly.'

'What do you mean?'

'It might have been possible to get him out. If I had gone to the Ibans, I might have persuaded them to take him downriver by canoe. But it was a trip of about a hundred miles, and I was about three miles from the longhouse and not sure of my own ability to reach it. Malaria is weakening.'

'So I'm told.'

'If I had set out for the longhouse, and had failed to reach it, your father would have been alone. If I had been stronger, and certain of returning, I think I would have gone. But one does not risk abandoning totally a badly injured patient. So I stayed. That decision may have cost him his life, and it may have been the wrong one.' She looked at me squarely. 'I have thought about it often, Mr Tunnicliffe.'

All the years thinking about it; all the years reminded

by the letter. I said, 'I'm sure you had no real alternative.'

'By the evening of the next day, the wounds were infected. If I had been strong enough, and quick enough, those two days would have seen him miles downstream.'

'Or dead already.'

'Perhaps. There wasn't much I could do for him and there would have been less in an Iban canoe. I stayed with him until he died.'

I said, 'He was lucky in that.'

She straightened suddenly. 'Lucky!'

'He might have died filthy and alone. He knew he was dying?'

'On the third day. I'm afraid gangrene is unmistakable.'

'But he could talk? In the letter—'

'He had periods of lucidity. He talked about you, and told me what to say in the letter, and made me promise to deliver it. As I told you, the promise was not easy to keep.'

'It was kept. I behaved badly that day. I'm sorry.'

She nodded. 'There is no more I can tell you.'

'One thing,' I said. 'There's a reference in the letter that I don't understand.'

'The number?'

'Yes.'

'I don't understand it either, but he was insistent. He repeated it several times, quite determined it should be given to you.'

'Without any hint of what it was?'

'He would not say. Only that the number must be given to you.'

'And that I would have to work out its significance for myself.'

'If you care to.' Her hand brushed something from her sleeve. 'You mustn't imagine I'm not curious. I have wondered about it, too. And about him.'

I gave her an edited version of his life story, leaving out the more slanderous of my mother's observations and also leaving out Ludlam and the dirty work. He came out as a man who'd found his métier in the air force, had been decorated and flew very well. 'I don't know,' I said, 'what happened to his good name. Did he explain?'

'No. He was dead. I had watched him die, and he was brave. I buried him myself. If he had secrets, they belonged to him. If he wished to pass a message to his son, then I owed him that duty. But that is all.'

I said, 'There was one thing more. You did not report his death.'

'He asked me not to.'

'Even so. There's a legal requirement, if nothing else. A duty.'

'We were a long way from the law, Mr Tunnicliffe. He told me that his death in a crash would bring his son distress, but not for long. Anything else might mark his son for life.'

'And you simply agreed?'

'Yes.'

I said, 'I wonder what it means?'

She rose. 'So do I. And I have no idea.' And then her manner altered and she said slowly, 'But, talking to you, I have begun to realize that you *have*.' Her eyes were on my face and after a moment, she said, 'Yes, I thought so.'

I felt myself colour.

'I think perhaps you should go, Mr Tunnicliffe.' There was a hard ring, now, to her voice.

I protested, but it was no use. She meant what she said. Two days later, a letter set out her feelings.

Dear Mr Tunnicliffe,

The parallel between you and your father cannot have escaped you. He was clearly a most admirable man in certain ways; so, and equally clearly, are you. You share his courage, as you have shown. He had fought and survived. So have you. In the end he lost his life, *wasted* his life, in some enterprise which I feel may have been criminal or close to it. That may be libelling his memory, but I don't think so.

I find now I regret the effort I made to find you and to pass on the letter. I expected that you would find its contents as mysterious as I did, but it seems you do not.

You have some knowledge I do not possess, and I am very much afraid that in giving you the letter, I have set you off on a course of action that will do you harm.

I have found in my life that Biblical precepts carry a great deal of weight and I am thinking now of the words: 'The sins of the father shall be visited upon the children.' There is no doubt in my mind that your father committed some considerable sin and I fear that I have been the instrument of its visitation upon you.

You will perhaps think this is insufferably pompous, and that I have no right to interfere in your affairs. But I feel that my part in this gives me such a right, and I must tell you that I feel responsible for what may happen. It would distress me greatly if the parallel between father and son were now to be extended. There are many prospects in life, superficially attractive, that are best ignored, if one can find the will. I feel strongly that you are facing one of them now, and that to ignore it is the course of wisdom.

The events of 1945 are history now. I beg you to allow them to remain so.

Yours sincerely,
C. Franklin

I read and re-read it. I thought about rubies and moral precepts, and I thought about the parallel. There were rubies, and my father had died for them. There was no knowing who owned them. They had been bought by a Japanese with occupation scrip (but from whom?), had been bought by my father with more occupation scrip – and were now lost in the vast jungles in Borneo. If I didn't go looking for them, they would never be found, or not for generations, by which time the question of ownership would be insoluble.

But Miss Franklin was right, too. I had absolutely no right to them. *And* she held the key. She alone knew where the crash had been; furthermore it was a racing certainty she wouldn't tell me. If she'd only known it, she could keep me on the straight and narrow simply by keeping her mouth shut.

I wrote back. Just a simple acknowledgement of her letter, intended to keep the channel open while I thought a bit more. Because by this time another factor had entered the calculation.

There was war in Borneo.

CHAPTER FIVE

Like most wars, it was the product of ambition; somebody dreams great dreams and puts soldiers to the job of making them come true. The dreamer in Borneo's case was the dictator Sukarno, who, having turned the old Dutch East Indies into Indonesia, was now intent upon adding to it. He already had most of the crescent that runs through from Sumatra to New Guinea, and, at the time, Malaysia was in the process of being created out of the former British-controlled areas of Malaya, Singapore, Sarawak, Brunei and North Borneo. Sukarno wanted the lot. The dream was Pan-Indonesia, with the Philippines dragged in for good measure, and the whole lot to be known as Maphilindo.

Malaysia, though, wasn't prepared to be gobbled up for Sukarno's dinner, so Sukarno, who had studied his Mao Tse-tung, decided to embark upon guerrilla campaigns. The first, in Brunei, was swiftly squashed by the British Army in a small but bitter war. At that point, in April 1963, Sukarno went after Brunei's southern neighbour, Sarawak, formerly the domain of the Brooke family, the celebrated White Rajahs of Sarawak.

I heard about that first attack on a radio news broadcast. It didn't sound much, at first: an attack on a police station, one dead and two wounded. The point was that it was the starting flag. Sukarno had attacked and things were happening: commandos and Gurkha troops moving in.

Helicopters and warships. The radio announcer said, 'There is speculation that a major confrontation with Indonesia has begun.'

That's how that particular war has been described ever since: it was Confrontation. I got out an atlas and tried to find Tebedu, where the attack had taken place, but the map was too small and I had to go to a library to lay hands on a bigger sheet. The attackers had come over the mountains from Kalimantan, the southern, Indonesian part of Borneo, and gone a mere three miles into Sarawak to strike. *The Times* went into it at length.

It would be a strange war; that was clear. There was a thousand miles of border. Nobody could guard it, not when it consisted of a high spine of mountains, with dense jungle on their slopes and all around. Abruptly I realized I was thinking like a soldier when the real question in my mind was whether, war or no war, it would be possible for me to move if *I* went to Borneo. At some point my brain had rejected Miss Franklin's approach. I *wanted* to go. But I couldn't without her help, and I was sure she wouldn't offer it.

That was the day before the trial began. In the afternoon there was another telephone call at the bank and a cold voice repeating its threat. 'We know where you live,' it said, 'and you can't be on your guard for ever.' Two sentences and the click of disconnection. I went to see the detective chief inspector in charge of the case that evening, a man called Henderson, who gave me some canteen tea and said, 'You're worried?'

'If they mean it.'

He lit a cigarette. 'We're dealing with big violent organized gangs. Comes of scrapping the rope. They make more threats than they carry out, but it can happen. Not the ones we've got, because they're all in custody, but they have friends, or somebody gets paid. But you *were* clear enough at the identity parade. Look funny if you changed your mind.'

'And besides,' I said, 'you want them locked away.'

'Better for everybody when the door slams.'

'Society with a capital S?'

'That's right,' Henderson said. 'I'm paid to defend it. As you were, once.'

'Not any more.'

'Look, you've taken risks. This is one more. A lot better chance than you had against the shotgun.'

'One risk seems to lead to another.'

He nodded. 'That's the way it works.'

'All right.' I was ready to leave.

'One thing before you go,' Henderson said. 'Just to cheer you up. They may have violent habits, but their memories are short. After a while it stops.'

'How long is a while?'

'Week or two. Month or two. Could you take a bit more leave?'

'Banks are frugal.'

He winked slowly, and gave me a grin. 'We go in for a bit of collusion sometimes. Especially with bank security people. On the same side, you see. I wouldn't be surprised if we couldn't fix something.'

'My manager wouldn't be very happy.'

'He might find he gets instructions.' Henderson held out his hand. 'You got a nice reward, didn't you? Take a trip. Leave it all with me.'

At the court hearing, I sat in the corridor waiting to be called, ostentatiously not discussing the case, while the preliminary statements were gone through. One of the counsel came out for a smoke after a while and chatted to Henderson, and when he went back, Henderson told me the judge now knew about the threats to me and had scowled in a very satisfactory way. 'Maybe put a year or two on the sentences,' he said.

'I doubt if that's good news for me.'

'It is for me, though,' Henderson said cheerfully. 'By the way, I had a word. Security chief at your bank used to be my divisional superintendent a few years back. He's all in favour. I'd start looking at the holiday brochures.'

I read *The Times* instead, to see how things were progressing out east. A Royal Navy assault carrier had sailed from Singapore for Kuching in Sarawak.

In evidence, I was asked about the threats, first by counsel and then by the judge.

'I take a very serious view of this,' he announced, and later, after I'd been examined and cross-examined, and pointed my finger at the dock, he delivered a few words about how thankful society should be for people like me. I averted my eyes modestly and found myself looking at Miss Franklin.

What the hell was she doing in court?

As I left the witness box, I jerked my head at Henderson, who was sitting at the back of the court. He followed me out. 'What's up?'

'There's a lady in blue in there. Second row of the public gallery. She's a friend of sorts. If somebody wants to get at me and she's seen talking to me – ' I stopped. Miss Franklin was just coming down the steps from the gallery.

'That the one?'

'Yes. I'll walk away. Could you explain to her?'

He nodded, and I moved off. Shortly afterwards a policeman handed me a note from Henderson: 'She wants to see you. Don't worry. I'll fix it.'

Late in the afternoon, the men in the dock collected twelve years each. All had records of violence and all gave me long looks of incandescent hate. The judge said that but for my action they would probably have got away with a great deal of money. They obviously saw it the same way, but their perspective was different.

I left the court in a police car, which went the wrong way up a one-way street in case anybody tried to follow, and was taken to a hotel where, for my own protection, I was to spend the night. In the car Henderson told me, 'My sergeant's bringing the lady. Meanwhile there's all sorts of little tricks you can try, you know. Dark glasses, trilby hats, have your hair dyed blond.'

'Thanks. I was thinking of a swordstick.'

'Can't do that. Offensive weapon. You're not allowed one,

even for self-defence.'

He dropped me off and when Miss Franklin arrived I took her into a quiet corner of the lounge. She would, she said, like some tea. She watched a little frostily as a large Scotch was delivered to me.

I said, 'Why did you come all the way from Birmingham?'

'To see you in court. To listen. When I had your note, I found it rather unsatisfactory.' She sipped at her tea. 'You were impressive in court today. The more so, now that I know about the threats made to you. That is the curious thing about you, Mr Tunnicliffe. You *are* impressive, in certain ways. But not, I'm afraid, in others.'

'Don't you think you're presuming? I'm grown up. Blameless. If you want a testimonial, I'm sure the judge –'

'The judge,' she said, 'saw only Jekyll.'

'And you think there's a Hyde?'

She said, 'When I told you about your father, it seemed to me that you reacted oddly. Not in the way one might expect.'

'Not enough grief, you mean? It was a long time ago. I'm used to the idea that he's dead.'

She shook her head. 'It was an unpleasant thing for me to tell you. But less so, in some way, for you to hear.'

'Miss Franklin, I have seen death and wounds. Men who were friends.'

'Not that,' she said. 'I sensed excitement in you. I felt I was adding to a store of information. You knew something and I was telling you more. That was the whole direction of your questions.'

'You're imagining –'

She held up her hand. 'Please. Dishonesty does not become you. It is not natural to you and you do not conceal it well. Nor do I like having my intelligence insulted. I have the usual female memory for the detail of a conversation. You asked whether he knew he was dying, but not whether he suffered. Doesn't that strike you as a strange response from a son?'

'You told me what the injuries were. I knew he was suffering.'

She said quite sharply, 'You are dissembling again, Mr Tunnicliffe. I find this conversation quite as uncomfortable as you do. And if it continues like this I shall end it.'

'That's your – '

She interrupted. 'And if I end it, let me tell you that I shall not, in any circumstances, speak or write to you again.' She sipped her tea, watching me over the cup. 'Another of your questions also struck me as odd. You asked where your father had died. I told you that it was in the middle of nowhere, an unmarked spot in the jungle. But you persisted. It was important to you, to your stock of information.'

I said, 'The ability to recall conversations doesn't belong only to women, Miss Franklin. I can remember it too. And for some reason you didn't want to tell me. Why was that?'

'Because I was already concerned about your behaviour and your actions. As I am still. I believe your father had done something very wrong. I had no idea you knew it. But you did, didn't you?'

I looked at her. I was hanging from all sorts of hooks, practical and moral. Miss Franklin would always mean what she said. If she cut off contact, it would stay cut off. And then there would be no chance in the world of ever finding the place where my father crashed. On the other hand, she wasn't the sort you talk to lightly about things on the fringes of the law.

She put the cup and saucer down and it clicked on the tiled table; she slipped back her sleeve and looked at a small, old, gold watch. 'I shall not wait. Make up your mind, Mr Tunnicliffe. If I leave in two minutes there is a very convenient train.'

'You play rough.'

'Are you going to tell me?' She was pulling on her gloves, smoothing the thin leather over her hands in compact movements.

'I'll have to,' I said.

She listened quietly, without interruption, self-contained as a Brazil nut. She showed no surprise, nor even disapproval, and her eyes never left my face. I'd have made a bet that she'd be able to repeat it all word for word at the end, and match every facial expression to every nuance.

When I'd finished, she said, 'And you are hoping, of course, to go and find the aircraft?'

'I've thought of it.'

'And also of your father's grave?'

I winced and she said, 'That's it, you see. Your priorities are rather curious.'

'Not as curious as all that,' I said. 'I never saw him after I was seven. He hasn't been very important in my life!'

'Until now.' She let the words hang in reproach and my temper began to fray.

'Damn it! How much filial piety do you expect?'

'These rubies, if they are there, are not yours.'

'They're not anybody's. And they're not doing any good where they are.'

Miss Franklin looked at me. Then, 'That, at least, is true.'

'Furthermore,' I said, 'they –' Then the meaning of what she'd said hit me and I stopped and blinked. 'You *agree*?'

'It's self-evident. How could they be doing any good?' She began to peel off her gloves again, finger by finger. 'In your possession, would they be put to better use?'

'Of course they would!'

She put the gloves neatly beside her bag. 'Oh yes. You could live like your friend, the ex-brigadier, this man Ludlam? Idling in a warm climate.'

I said, 'Have you ever worked in a bank?'

She gave a sudden little smile that lit up her face, as her rare smiles always did. 'Let me offer you a thought. I agree the ownership is probably untraceable now and it would be manifestly absurd to think of going to Burma to ask people if they have lost rubies. The fact remains that, in the old phrase, those stones are ill-gotten gains.'

'So?'

The smile was lively now, a trace of mischief in it. 'There's no reason, is there, Mr Tunnicliffe, why good should not emerge from bad?'

'What do you mean?' Though a suspicion was dawning.

'I was a missionary nurse in Borneo.'

I nodded.

'My employer was the Sarawak Medical Missionary Society.'

'I thought,' I said, 'that you always took up strong moral positions.'

She laughed, then, actually laughed; the first time I ever saw it. 'The Society does a great deal of good and I assure you their moral position is quite unassailable. And like all such charities, they are permanently and chronically short of funds.'

I looked at her grimly. 'Why me? A chance of a fortune and you want to use it to buy Bibles and bandages. It's not even a division of labour! You give me directions, I go and get, and you hand it over to somebody else.'

She laughed again, happily. 'You must see it's wonderfully appropriate.'

'No.'

The mischief showed again. 'I'm prepared to compromise a little.'

I said, 'Half.'

She shook her head. 'A third.'

'For you.'

'Oh no. Two-thirds for the mission. A third for *you*.'

I sat and thought about it, while she took in tea through what, on another face, would have been a grin of delight. After a moment it began to be infectious and I found myself responding to it, until we sat there grinning at each other.

'Done?' she said.

I found myself putting out my hand and having it shaken. 'Done.'

'There's just one more thing, Mr. Tunnicliffe. You'll never find it alone. I'm afraid I shall have to come with you.'

CHAPTER SIX

Yes, she knew about the war and the hazards it presented. She pointed out that war meant more for medical missions to do, not less. That was the first of my arguments to be knocked down. The others were ruined just as briskly. She had lived for years in the Sarawak jungle, for two of them as a fugitive. She had friends in the administration and friends in the tribes. She knew the area where the crash must have taken place and intended, thank-you-very-much, to keep it to herself because that knowledge represented her claim to two-thirds of what was found. 'It's not that I don't trust you, Mr Tunnicliffe. I am merely being prudent.'

'I still think it's crazy.'

'No, I have my little secret. You have yours.'

'Have I?'

'Of course you have.' She was smiling. 'The stones are concealed in some special way, and Mr Ludlam has told you about it. That knowledge represents your contribution. I think you have *probably* told me everything else, but you carefully did not describe the means by which the gold was taken to India, or how your father concealed the rubies. Correct?'

I sighed and nodded and played what I hoped was the trump. I didn't want her with me. When I have been in tricky country, I've always been there with well-trained men, properly equipped, and the prospect of dragging a middle-aged-to-elderly woman around dangerous country wasn't one I fancied. I said, 'I know it's not done to ask, but – '

'But how old am I?'

'Yes.'

'I retired two years ago.'

'Sixty-two, then? Surely you must see!'

'I retired at fifty-five. I drink rarely and smoke not at all.

I'm extremely healthy.'

'Even so.'

She laughed again. The whole thing delighted her; more so with every passing minute. Everything about it appealed. Retirement had her champing at the bit. The prospect of a return to Sarawak was a dream come true. She'd be of *use* again, putting funds to a valuable purpose.

I lit a cigarette and frowned at her through the smoke and she watched me with amusement for once, instead of disapproval. 'Your real trouble is that you object because I'm a .woman, but you can't use the argument, can you, because it doesn't work. I'm far better in the jungle than you are. So one prejudice is not valid and you fall back on another : my age.'

'I'm being wholly practical.'

'Of course you are, and you are entitled to your doubts. Many people of my age could *not* cope. I can. And I'm prepared to prove it.'

'How?'

'Do you know Yorkshire?'

'Not really. My father came from up there, but I never lived there.'

'Very beautiful. The best walking country I know. I thought we might walk together.'

'Walking's not enough,' I said.

'I think you'll find it is. I'm not talking about a pleasant little hike. There is a rather famous walk which is quite demanding.'

'How demanding?'

'More than you imagine. Three mountains: Ingleborough, Whernside and Pen-y-ghent, forming a triangle. In one day you climb them all, and cover about thirty miles.'

'And you think you can do it?'

'I know I can do it, Mr Tunnicliffe.'

'And if you don't manage it?'

'If you insist, you will then get the information and go to Sarawak alone. But what – I must phrase this delicately,

I think, or your pride will be hurt – what if *you* don't manage it?'

'Oh no you don't! *You're* not going alone.'

'Indeed I'm not. I was thinking of another five, no, *ten* pounds for the church roof? Would that be agreeable?'

She sat there in her hat and her neat suit, with handbag and gloves beside her : she was small and grey-haired and she looked like a tidy housewife out for a day's shopping. Yet behind it lurked a will that drove on like a battle tank, plus any number of surprises. I was going to have to walk over those damned mountains, and I had more than a suspicion that at the end my feet would be the ones with blisters.

Feebly I tried one more ploy. 'Are you sure,' I said, 'that it's quite proper for a single lady to travel alone with a man?'

'That is altogether too general a proposition,' she said. 'But in the case of you and me, I think it entirely suitable.'

Game, set and match to Miss Franklin.

I told Henderson I was going off to Yorkshire for the week-end and he was kind enough to have me taken to my flat to pick up some gear. More out of sentimentality than because I ever expected to use them again, I had kept an old pair of army boots, comfortable enough to keep the blisters at bay for a while, though the skin of my feet was certainly very soft. I shoved the boots and some old trousers and pullovers in a bag with my shaving kit and took it to the bank on Friday morning. Birstall wanted to know where I was going and I told him with a certain pleasure. He had just been given the news that I was to have some extra leave and was predictably tight-lipped and shirty, but since the instructions came from on high there wasn't much he could do beyond saying it was 'most inconvenient, Mr Tunnicliffe, *most* inconvenient!' At the end of the day, just to be malicious, he pretended to discover some minor incongruity in the day's balance and insisted on a re-check. It meant that everybody's week-end was delayed by an hour and a half and that the bank would have to pay out some entirely unnecessary overtime. I suppose he got some satisfaction out of it.

I was picked up by Henderson in a police car and taken to collect a little Ford I'd rented and he pulled another trick in case we were followed. This time, his car had a rendezvous with a second one that faced in the opposite direction and we stepped out of one and into the other and roared off with bells ringing and blue light flashing. The traffic made way, then pulled in again behind us, and Henderson grinned and said he had fifty-seven variations.

Once in my own car and clear of London, I kept my foot down on the motorway to Birmingham, collected Miss Franklin, and we set off for Yorkshire. I'd made a booking at a pub in a village called Settle, and it was bolted and barred by the time we got there and we had to beat on the door to be let in.

Next morning : breakfast, and off with a very different Miss Franklin. Practical days and practical clothes. She wore a strong modern pair of hiking boots, with grey socks showing over them, lisle stockings, tweed skirt, a jacket of Grenfell cloth, and a woollen bonnet. A small haversack on her back carried sandwiches and a flask. I doubt if she'd weigh eight stone wet through, but she looked rangy and energetic, and she had one of those easy hiker's strides that adapts itself to rough ground without variations in pace.

The weather was magnificent : spring sunshine and the sky dotted with small cumulus clouds drifting their shadows across the great brown-green faces of the fells. Bright bracken shoots were pushing through everywhere and the moorland turf was springy underfoot. The sort of day that fills you with energy, and just as well, because I was trying to remember the last time I'd done thirty miles in a day, even without the mountains thrown in. Miss Franklin read not just the thought but the words themselves, and asked me how long it had been.

'About ten years, I think.' And, felt an obscure need to glamorize it. 'That was in army kit, rifles and ammunition, run, walk, run, doing it fast. What about you?'

'On Christmas Eve. When I was young, I used to do this walk with my father every Christmas Eve. Then we'd go to the Watch Night service and sing the carols. For the last two years, I've done it again.'

'It must make quite a day.'

'For me it's a religious experience, Mr Tunnicliffe. Perhaps you can see that.'

'I think I see what you mean.'

'Then perhaps there's hope for you.'

The first few miles went easily, but as the climb up Pen-y-ghent went on the steepness started dragging at my calf muscles. I told myself I was healthy enough, and the squash I played three times a week had kept me fairly fit; but long uphill marches make particular demands on particular muscles, and they're not the ones you develop playing ball-games.

We stood on top of the mountain for a minute or two, admiring the view and enjoying the breeze and I wanted coffee and a cigarette. I mentioned only the coffee.

'Oh no,' she said. 'That's not the way at all. Coffee in the valley, before we tackle Whernside. There's a routine to this.' So I didn't get the cigarette either.

Muscles stretched on the ascent were rested on the descent; the strain came on to another set altogether. But it was a good feeling to be moving easily down those long slopes and as we sat on a boulder the coffee tasted wonderful and the cigarette better, though I looked at the next two-thousand-foot climb a bit warily.

She went up it like a fifteen-year-old, legs moving in that tireless, even, pendulum rhythm that comes from being taught as a child and staying in practice. Her breathing stayed level and deep, no puffing, no panting: in through the nose and out through the mouth and keep on doing it, taking oxygen and using it. I, on the other hand, was beginning to grunt a bit, and my left foot, with the three toes missing, was starting to ache, as it does occasionally under stress. But if she could cope, fifty-seven years old, then I damn well could.

We ate our sandwiches and drank spring water on the far slope of the mountain and she pointed out Ingleborough with its distinctive flat top in the distance, and said we were going well and we mustn't stop too long or the muscles would stiffen and it would all become that much harder.

And my God, but it did become hard. The cheerful walk was changing character, and so was the weather, and it was doing so to match. Blue skies and cumulus had gone : the sky was darkening, big drops of water were beginning to spatter out of rain clouds, and the faces of the fells lost their springtime gleam and looked dark and demanding.

We saw the occasional hiker here and there, but nobody close enough to speak to; those moors are big and empty and they can swallow a lot of week-end walkers. It was several wet miles on, as we were sloshing, soaked, up the base slope of Ingleborough, in steady rain, that she saw two men coming down from the top. I'd seen nothing. I'd reached the stage of walking with my head lowered, watching my feet, the mark of fatigue.

'Silly men !' said Miss Franklin. 'Look. Up there. Rain-coats. Won't people ever learn to wear proper clothing !'

I raised my head, looked and suddenly began to wonder. Halting for a moment, I stared up towards them.

She turned to look at me. 'What is it?'

'Let's change direction for a bit.' I turned to look round through three hundred and sixty degrees and there was nobody else to be seen in the whole wide sweep of country.

She plainly thought I was mad, but for once was prepared to be indulgent. We continued climbing, but moved to our left towards the corner of the next shoulder of the mountain.

They changed direction at once, moving purposefully: our paths would meet two or three hundred yards up the hill.

I stopped again. It was still possible I could be wrong, but both instinct and logic told me I wasn't. They weren't dressed for hiking, and the town of Ingleton lay on the far side of the mountain, therefore they were walking away from it, into wide stretches of open country, and in heavyish rain. They were coming down the mountain, and I knew from the map that the town was visible from the top, so they weren't coming towards us to ask the way.

Miss Franklin said presciently, 'You think the threat is materializing, don't you?'

I nodded, watching them. 'But how the hell did they know I was here?'

'Somebody told them. *I* told the innkeeper in Settle that we were doing the Three Peaks, but I told nobody else where I was going this week-end. Did you?'

'Henderson,' I said. 'I told him, but he wouldn't . . .' And then I remembered. 'Birstall, the bank manager. I told him, too.'

They were coming unhurriedly towards us, slipping a little on the wet slope, and Miss Franklin said, 'Then we wouldn't be difficult to find, would we? If we're doing the Three Peaks, they need only wait on one of them.'

'Easy,' I said grimly. A telephone call to Birstall : somebody posing as a policeman, maybe even as Henderson. Where's Mr Tunnicliffe this week-end, sir? 'He's doing the Three Peaks walk in Yorkshire,' Birstall would have said, hoping in his nasty little heart that my week-end would be ruined. Not difficult after that to find the names of the Three Peaks. I thought briefly about the secret hotels, the tricky work with the cars. Very clever-clever, and security as strong as wet tissue paper.

The two men had stopped. In the rain and at a distance it was difficult to see clearly what they were doing, but they seemed to have sticks. Or maybe not sticks !

'Down. And round,' Miss Franklin said. She didn't point, just moved.

I said, 'Those things could be shotguns.'

'Yes, we must use the ridges.' Her hands were under the shoulder-straps of her knapsack, gripping, her body leaning forward a little, and she was setting a pace. Where she got the strength, I don't know, but it was almost light-infantry stuff, a walk that was almost a trot, and keeping up wasn't easy.

We went hurrying down and across. She said evenly,

'Ingleborough's an odd mountain when you know it; a series of ridges, almost like big steps in the landscape. If we can get behind one . . .' I glanced over my shoulder. They were coming after us fast, stumbling and slipping a bit, but with a downslope to help them. The classic pattern : dominate the high ground. They were about three hundred yards away.

'How close do they need to be?'

I said, 'With shotguns, up to a hundred yards. At that range shot would hurt but not kill. Over that they're not effective.'

'Over there,' she said, 'about a quarter of a mile, it steepens.'

'We're going to have to run!'

She shook her head. 'We walk quickly. They're not dressed. They'll tire.'

'I doubt it.'

'We'll see. I'm not a runner, I'm afraid.'

We were moving on to rougher ground. When the idea had been merely to climb the mountain, we'd taken the good route, the easier walking; here there were small rocks in the heather and it was hard going, at a brisk pace.

Another glance back. They were gaining, but we were coming nearer to the lip of the ridge. Another couple of hundred yards and for a few moments we might be out of their sight. But a couple of hundred yards was the extent of our lead, and it was being cut back. She glanced over her shoulder. 'I think I *am* going to have to run. Just a little.' She ran awkwardly, without balance, and after no more than fifty yards, gave up. 'It's no good. I can't.' But she could, and did, slip straight back into that metronome walk of hers. 'I'll try once more as we reach the lip.'

I was wondering how I could delay them, without being killed in the process. If I could do that, she'd walk away from them, no doubt about it. Give her half a mile start and nobody who wasn't a practised fell-walker would get near her in this kind of country.

We came over the lip and she ran again, swinging us left, closer to them, but briefly out of sight. When we saw them again they were no more than a hundred and fifty yards away.

But hardly any higher.

'Now,' she said, 'we climb.'

A shotgun banged. Terrifying, but they weren't close enough. There was a little scatter of pellets to our left, almost indistinguishable from the rain, as we turned and began to go upward, fast. This was the most dangerous part; they were frighteningly close as they swung and began to hurry after us. Another shot, and the rattle of pellets was nearer. I copied her walk, hands on knees, pushing down with each thrust of the leg. She must be tiring now; I certainly was. And they must be, too, I thought, but they hadn't twenty-odd sapping miles behind them.

No, but they'd had to climb a mountain, and *that* wouldn't be standard exercise for urban gangsters! My legs ached. How would theirs feel?

For a minute they stuck to the flat, cutting across behind us. What was the distance now? We were perilously close to being in range.

In front of me, Miss Franklin was stamping her feet into the ground, driving upwards with astonishing stamina. Another shot, and a feeling like bee stings as a few pellets hit my windcheater. Not damaging. Not yet. But if they gained a few yards more, we were in trouble. I risked another glance back, trying to measure distance. They were scrambling on the slope and the distance was hardly more than a hundred yards.

Ahead of me, Miss Franklin was edging left again, picking a steep route. Another shot and again I felt the impacts on my back and legs, but at this distance heavy material offered some protection. A little pain but no injury. But Miss Franklin gave a little grunt and I saw flecks of blood on her calf where one lead shot had gone through her stocking, but she said quickly, 'I'm all right,' and moved determinedly on.

Two more shots, and the scatter all around us, the little stinging impacts there, but not, thank God, any worse. And behind me a sliding sound and a man's voice swearing.

I looked round. One of them had fallen and was struggling up raising his shotgun, levelling it, firing. I actually glimpsed the scatter-shot flying at me in a little dark cloud as I swung my head away. One caught me on the ear, and when I put my hand to it there was a trace of blood. Nothing serious, but a pain sharp enough for straight fear to ram adrenalin into my bloodstream.

We stamped on up the slope. The next shot told me they were not gaining, now. And the one after that was either inaccurately aimed, or we'd moved out of range.

'Are you all right?' I gasped at her back.

'Don't talk.'

We fought to gain height, and advantage with it, and when I glanced back again we'd also gained distance : not much, a few yards, but vital. The next ridge was roughly two hundred feet above us and we ground towards it, my legs now beginning to feel heavy, muscles full of twinges on the back of the calf and the front of the thigh. We were slowing a bit, but so were they, behind us. Mountainsides make demands. We gained a few yards more, and there were no more shots. We'd moved out of range and perhaps they no longer had enough cartridges to want to waste any. They concentrated on following, knowing there was a lot of country, and that one of the people they were pursuing was a woman with grey hair. In their book, that must have meant they were on to a winner; they had only to wait for her to tire. They were men, after all, and younger. If they'd known her, they might have played it differently, expending energy quickly to make a quick gain; but they probably hadn't met too many Miss Franklins. For that matter, neither had I.

Ahead of us, as we came over the ridge, she moved left again, beginning to traverse the face of the slope towards roughly the ground they'd been on when we saw them first. I didn't know what she intended and didn't ask. This wasn't familiar ground to me, but it was to her, and she clearly needed no lessons in how to use it.

All the same, it couldn't go on for ever. Miss Franklin was a small, ambulant miracle, but there were a lot of miles, as well as a lot of years behind her. I glanced at my watch, saw it was just after six, and tried to remember at what time darkness had fallen the night before. About eight, as far as I remembered. I'd switched on my headlights on the motorway up to Birmingham. But we were farther north now, so there'd even be an extra minute or two of light. Two hours was a long time: well beyond me, at this pace.

Looking back, I could see them tramping grimly upwards. We'd gained a little more: they were about a hundred and fifty yards back. We were out of range but far from out of trouble. Nor could we continue climbing upwards for ever and it was there that our thin advantage lay: in boots that gripped the slope where shoes did not. Once we were on a wet downslope they'd slip and slide as fast as we did; faster, probably.

And I hadn't an idea in my head. Without surprise to help, there's no way an unarmed man can take on two with shotguns. Nor could I see where safety might lie. Even if we could be safe in a small town, it was a couple of miles away, on the far side of the mountain, and something told me the two behind us wouldn't give up just because a few houses came into view. I'd have to think of something soon. But what? My little backpack had nothing in it but a Thermos and some empty sandwich wrappings. There were cigarettes and matches in my pocket, and a bit of loose change.

We came towards boulders jutting from the slope and I realized Miss Franklin was cramming on the pace, somehow picking up an extra little bit of speed. I strained after her, gasping now with effort, and suddenly she was dodging among them, nimble somehow on the wet rock, then falling. I thought she'd tripped, and moved to pick her up, but she whispered 'No!' sharply and wriggled forward. 'Follow me!'

The hole was tiny – just an aperture, hidden up under a little overhang. She slid into it like an eel, and I watched her feet disappear into darkness, and flung myself down and crawled after her, but I was too big and my backpack jammed me in the entrance.

'Hurry!'

I retreated a foot or so and ripped it off and passed it through to her, then wriggled myself frantically forward, scraping knees and elbows on the stone. Once inside, in the grey light, I looked round the tiny cave. It didn't go anywhere: a small fault, not a passage. If they found it, we were trapped.

A minute later we heard them blundering by, grunting and breathless. We crouched, still and silent, as the footsteps moved past, died away.

And came back.

And a voice. 'In here somewhere. Bloody must be!'

'Can't be. There's nowhere to hide.'

'Christ, I'm bloody soaked!'

'And me.'

'They've got to be somewhere. You can't just vanish.'

'Must be a gulley somewhere. Can't see one, though.'

They moved about, now nearer, now farther away.

'Go on up a bit. See what you can see.'

'Christ, I'm knackered.'

'Never mind that. Move!'

Footsteps scrambling away. A pause, then close by a voice shouting, 'Well?'

We couldn't hear the answer. After a while a second sound of movement, growing fainter. The minutes dragged by. Five became ten, then twenty. And the footsteps returned.

'They've got to be here!'

'They can't be. We've bloody looked. There's nowhere to hide.'

'We can't have lost 'em. Christ, it's bloody open country. Look at it!'

They went away again. More slow minutes. Again they came back.

'It *has* to be here, there's nowhere else!'

'Look, they aren't going *down*, are they? We'd be able to see them. And they aren't going up, either.'

'It's half an hour, now. We've bloody lost 'em.'

'Look, it's not far up to that flat bit. We can watch the

whole bloody area from there. Well, can't we? Right, then, come on.'

Once more they moved away, and we stayed motionless in the limestone fault. We ought to have been on the far side of the mountain by now, with a feeling of pleasant achievement and the prospect of a hot bath ahead. Instead, we were wet and cold and beginning to shiver, wedged in cramped positions in a damp little hole, waiting for a darkness that was a long time away, looking at our watches and at each other, saying nothing because one of them might have returned, or the sound might carry. We'd been an hour in that hole when cramp hit and the calf muscles in my right leg had begun to twist and knot. She understood at once what had happened, and dealt with it with swift professional competence, taking my heel in one hand, pushing my toes upward with the other and then, when the spasms had gone, kneading the muscle fibres into quietude with hard fingers.

There were a lot of questions. We couldn't discuss them, but they hung in the air. How dark would it be? There'd been a bit of moon last night, but then the weather had been clear. The sky now was heavy with dark rain clouds which ought to blank off a lot of the moonlight. There were two other important questions, as far as I could see: first, how long would the two men be prepared to wait? They were in the open, in heavy rain, and not particularly well-dressed for it, either: they'd be as miserable as we were, and, I hoped, as full of apprehension. I tried to put myself in their position. They were already afraid they'd lost us and an hour's absence of movement would have done nothing to reassure them. Yet they knew that we couldn't really have vanished off the mountain, that they'd have seen us, at some point, crossing those wide stretches of open slope. So they'd know we were waiting for darkness. The second question was where they'd be. One of them had mentioned a bit of flat ground higher on the slope; but how much higher? If they were sitting within range we'd be finished the moment we moved out of the shelter of the rocks.

It was a stalemate, of a kind likely to make pneumonia cases out of all of us, pursuers and pursued. Miss Franklin and I were both shivering intermittently, in that bone-cold hole in the rocks; they, out in the open, would at least be able to keep circulation going with movement. It was a nicely-balanced problem. If we didn't act early we'd be in danger from cold and damp. People must have died out here from exposure before. But if we moved too soon, the chances of being spotted were much higher.

And the most dangerous time would be shortly after darkness fell. That would be when they'd expect us to move.

I gave it half an hour, then leaned across to tap the point in the darkness where Miss Franklin's shoulder was, and began to try to straighten myself out. My legs had stiffened so much they felt as though they were set in concrete. I heard a very soft, whispered, 'Not yet.' Another half-hour, and I was aching with impatience, watching the little luminous tips on the hands of my watch as they dragged themselves round the face. Again I made to move. Again the negative. She was right, of course, patient where I was impatient, calculating the moment. Up above us they'd be saying to themselves; an hour of darkness; this is when they'll come. Seventeen minutes later, she tapped my shoulder, and I almost smiled to myself. No sort of milestone in time, concentration perhaps beginning to slip.

I turned awkwardly on to my stomach and inched forward to the aperture. There must be no scraping sounds, no scratches of boot on stone.

I got my head out beneath the little overhang and listened to nothing but the steady hiss of rain. On knees and elbows I crawled slowly out, stopping every foot or so to listen, afraid always that the tiny noises I made would be enough to alert them. We had disappeared in the rock patch and that's where they'd expect us to reappear. Clear of the hole, I stayed crouched low, hidden from above by the rock, and waited for Miss Franklin to follow. Every minute scrape of movement seemed hideously loud, but I suppose the hiss of the rain must have made a kind of deadening blanket of sound.

There was precious little light. She was inches from me, and not much more than a dim outline. The clouds that were spilling so much water were shielding the moon, too. It would work two ways, one helpful, one not. They'd have a hell of a job to see us; but equally, we'd find it difficult to move quietly over rough ground we could barely see.

I took a cautious step. A hand on my arm stopped me. A second later Miss Franklin slipped past me. Well, it was her mountain, I thought, and she'd already shown she could make use of terrain. She glided away from me, bent low, silent on her moulded rubber bootsoles. I followed stiffly, conscious of my clumsiness of movement, of the lack of suppleness in my muscles.

A dozen yards took minutes of concentration with every step a separate operation : the slow lifting of the foot, the slow lowering : so slow that it came into contact with the ground without sound, and took weight only gradually in case of invisible hazard beneath. That dozen yards took us successfully to the edge of the rock patch and we crouched there, bent and tense, listening. We'd had luck: there had been no awkward footfall, no momentary loss of balance; and we'd had the shelter of the rocks.

From above us came the sound of a cough and impulses slid across my scalp. They were there! And not too far away, either. The cough had been a clear, unmuffled, recognizable sound. How close? No way of knowing, but certainly well within shotgun range. I turned my head slowly, hoping to find the answer; maybe they'd be silhouetted against the dark-grey sky.

But they weren't. We stood hesitantly. The next movement was commitment to open ground and sooner or later it was inevitable we would make some sort of giveaway noise. Then, even if they couldn't see us, there was no guarantee that at some point there wouldn't be a brief break in the cloud, or a moment when our silhouettes might show. The man coughed again; they'd be drenched and miserable, but the fact that they were there at all proved the extent of their determination.

We had to move, and now we were edging on to scrubby land, patches of low, tangling heather mixed with the moorland grass. There'd be rabbit scrapes here, and stones to rattle or trip over. Once do that and we'd have to start running, and once we began running they'd have a trail of sound to pursue. We moved one step, another, and halted. Everything dead slow, when fear demanded flight. I ached to charge off down that hill, into the darkness, away from those damned shotguns that had menaced us now for so many hours. Staying low, praying we looked like rocks rather than people, we crept on, counting the steps.

We'd gone something like forty yards when her foot slipped and she was momentarily unbalanced and there was a sharp rattling scrape as small stones clicked together. They'd have heard that! They would know now that we were moving somewhere below them, and be alert as dogs for the next small indication of where we might be. For minutes we stayed motionless, shivering with cold and fear, listening as hard as they must have been.

There was no sound from them except, minutes later, another cough. Now we had to go again, somehow reach the magic point beyond the range of either sound or shotgun. We hadn't made another ten yards when I suddenly tripped over my feet and fell full length. I must have grunted loudly enough to be heard in Ingleton! Certainly it was loud enough to be heard on the slope above us; enough, too, to give them a good idea where we were, and set them moving after us.

'Throw this!' Miss Franklin said quietly.

'What?'

She was wrestling something out of her knapsack, handing it to me. A Thermos. I threw it as hard as I could, farther down the slope, and it landed on something hard and shattered loudly. We heard them crashing down the hill towards it, and moved off again, uphill this time, still taking every step with slow care.

They must have stumbled on the Thermos, though God knows how in the darkness, because the sounds stopped.

And so did we. But the trick had worked. We'd gained distance. Very soon we'd be out of range. They must have been standing there, baffled, in the rain, as afraid they were losing us as we were that they'd find us. We paused and moved on and paused again. Then they moved too, and towards us. Why had they found that bloody flask! Having done so, they must have understood our intention. We'd gone uphill before; we'd go uphill again. And we were doing exactly that.

But not for long. Miss Franklin, ahead of me, was changing direction on to a suddenly steeper slope and beginning to descend. She was also going faster, with less caution, and I realized the heather was behind us, and our feet were silent on moorland turf. A little later I heard the sound of a stream, swollen with all the rain, water rushing noisily over rocks.

Still we could hear them behind us, and moving in the right direction in some uncanny way. We crossed the stream, climbed a little, swung left. Another twenty yards, and Miss Franklin halted abruptly. I turned and saw them for a brief second, darker shapes against a dark sky.

She said softly, 'Lie down.'

'What on earth – ?'

'Down!'

We lay full-length on the grass.

And suddenly, startlingly, crazily, she was screaming at the top of her voice. 'Go away. Go away. Leave us alone!' I rolled towards her and clamped my hand over her mouth, but she struggled and yelled again.

She'd gone mad!

I heard one of the men yell, too, and then grunts and heavy footfalls as they hurried towards us. I grabbed her by the arm to drag her to her feet. She'd *have* to run now, we'd both have to run and we'd have to run impossibly well to have any chance at all of escape. We were pinpointed, and in a moment we'd be in range.

'Stay still!' she said sharply, and bafflingly too, because the tone was totally *un*hysterical. Then, only a second later, she was screaming again: 'Go away. Leave us alone!'

'Come *on*!' I grabbed her again, ready to throw her over my shoulder and carry her, fireman style, for as far as I could run.

She pointed. 'They're there!'

I saw them again, dimly; shapes, but coming directly towards us.

She yelled, 'Please, please, please!' her voice rising madly.

I tried to drag her. She resisted fiercely. The whole world was suddenly, lethally, whirling into madness.

I heard other sounds mixing then: a sharp kind of yelp-and-grunt, impossible to describe, a couple of thuds, a bang as a shotgun fired. A despairing voice yelled 'Christ!' Then yelled again, but not words, only despair. It was all quick. The yells, the tumbling, rolling, noise, then the weirdly-vanishing shout.

Then silence.

I didn't know, couldn't guess what had happened, but there'd been something grisly and final about that strange sequence of noises.

Beside me, Miss Franklin began to weep and then to murmur something indistinctly through the tears. It took me a moment or two to understand that she was praying. I said stupidly, 'What? Why?'

'It's a pothole,' she said. 'A very deep pothole.'

I looked at the by-now kneeling figure beside me, at the pale shape of the uplifted face. They were dead deep below us; and she was praying for their souls. Also for her own.

CHAPTER SEVEN

She was grim and silent as we picked our way round the flank of the mountain, along the dark track and down to the town. Still shocked by the suddenness, the release, the extraordinary, deadly ruthlessness she had shown, I tried once to ask questions, but she said only, 'Not now. *Please*, not now.'

It was after eleven when we reached the road, together yet somehow detached. Miss Franklin, exhausted in mind and body, moved almost in a trance, and as we came to the first street lamp I could see that she was crying still. Soon there was a telephone-box on the other side of the road and I made to cross. She put her hand on my arm.

'We have to tell the police.'

'No.' She shook her head slowly, full of despair.

'But we must. Those two—'

'Are dead. I know. I killed them.' She gave me a look that blended defiance with deep sadness, then seemed to stagger and all the strength went out of her as she lurched against me, burying her face in my soaking windcheater. If I hadn't held her, she'd have fallen.

We must have looked very odd, standing there like that in the rain-washed street. Certainly the taxi-driver who came along a few minutes later gave us a funny look, when what he'd probably taken to be two lovers turned out to be something more like mother and son. He cocked an eyebrow at me, and I nearly hit him, but he was too precious for that: finding a taxi there and at that time was almost miraculous.

'Settle,' I said.

'Long way.'

'Just take us.'

He shrugged. 'Got enough money?'

I asked how much and he told me. It was robbery and I paid it happily and forgot about it as the warm car carried us smoothly away from the nightmare. She wept all the way and either I'm not good at offering comfort, or comfort was no use to her. At one point, the taxi-driver turned his head and said, 'What's wrong with the lady?'

'Not much,' I said. 'Not much at all. But she's had a nasty shock.'

She wasn't the only one, either. What an astonishing woman she was! First, I thought, you meet what seems like a prim, if strong-willed, middle-aged woman. Plenty of them about. A type. Then you discover she's more than that, far more than that; you discover she has an extraordinary history, and come to realize there are depths and reserves you could not have suspected. You begin to appreciate her strength and resource, mixed in with an irritating rectitude and manifest compassion. And then – well, the way she'd dealt with those two, the coolness, the self-containment, the calculation: *nothing*, I thought, could prepare one for that!

And now she was drained, conscience-stricken. I kept glancing across at the small, weeping figure with the grey hair who, with nothing more than her own brain and inner toughness, had just defeated and destroyed two armed and determined men. I was the trained soldier, the experienced fighter, the supposed toughie. Yet from the moment they appeared, she'd taken charge. She had naturally led: I had as naturally followed. Now she intended to break the law. Two men were dead, and she didn't want to report it, just as she hadn't reported my father's death, all those years ago.

A confusing set of values, Miss Franklin's: to me, at least, and probably to her, too; ever-ready with starchy disapproval, but just as ready with puzzling switches. For me to contemplate going after the rubies was selfish and wrong; for her to blackmail herself along, in order to give two-thirds of the proceeds to a mission, was not just acceptable, it had set her eyes sparkling with fun and her mouth widening with laughter.

I had never previously quite been able to believe that thing about the female of the species being deadlier than the male, but sitting in the back of the taxi on the way to Settle that night, I began to give it credence. Up on the mountain *I* had thought only (and ineffectually, too) about trying to escape. At some point, *she* had begun to think about killing. She thought about it, planned the means, and carried it out; and never for a moment gave the slightest hint of what she was doing. Why? No confidence in me? Total confidence in herself?

The tears had dried at last, before we reached the little hotel, but she was pale and red-eyed and suddenly far older. She went off to lie in hot water, and then to bed without a word, and I followed her example, feeling the heat taking the aches out of me, and thinking about that calculation of hers: the one that went: 'If I get to one side of the pothole and scream, they'll come running towards me and fall down it, and be killed. So I'll do that.' Christ!

I woke next morning to a knocking at the door of my room and surfaced blearily, and a little painfully because every muscle seemed to have its twinge.

She came in, and there wasn't a trace or a sign of the previous night's disintegration. She was smart, crisply-pressed and groomed and that sudden ageing that had rolled over her had rolled straight back again. She didn't say, 'Good morning,' or 'Wasn't that a difficult moment yesterday?' or even 'How do you feel?' She said, 'I think we should leave as soon as possible.'

'Okay. Soon as I've had breakfast.'

'You misunderstand,' said Miss Franklin. 'I mean, for Singapore.'

'Whoa,' I said. 'Wait a minute. There are some details. To begin with, we'll have to tell the police about yesterday.'

'No. It would be wrong.'

'Wrong! We're obliged by law.'

'Mr Tunnicliffe, two men with shotguns fell down a pot-hole. They were evil men. If they hadn't been engaged in something thoroughly evil it would not have happened. There is such a thing as natural justice.'

She did one of her fast switches, this time to straight practicality. 'Think,' she said, 'what it would mean. There would be statements, there would be enquiries, there would be inquests, there would be publicity of a most distasteful kind. A coroner's court is a court of law. You would be asked, on oath, whether it had been accidental. You would be asked whether you knew the land sufficiently well in the dark to dispose of those men deliberately. To both those questions you would have to answer no. It would become apparent that it was I who was responsible. I'm sure you can imagine what would follow. Headlines in the popular press.'

I said, 'Hold on.'

'Please allow me to finish. I should become a grotesque, which is ridiculous. We would both be hounded, endlessly. And there is also the possibility, *only* a possibility perhaps, but it is there, that some kind of charge might be brought against us.'

I said, 'Rubbish!'

'It is *not* rubbish. While I do not pretend to be expert in the law, I *do* know that there are limits to the lengths to which you may take self-defence. If, for example, a burglar breaks into your house, you are not entitled to shoot him.'

'I know the phrase. You're entitled to use sufficient force to restrain. Now look, these were two armed men with shot-guns, and the police and everybody else knows threats were made.'

She looked at me steadily. 'There is one more matter which may not have occurred to you, and it is this. You are known to be capable of taking a shotgun from the man who holds it. You have demonstrated it recently and to public acclaim. Some people, including the police, may think that you have repeated the trick.'

'Ridiculous!'

'How many people have you killed, Mr Tunnicliffe?'

'As a soldier, a few.'

'Yes. As a soldier you're accustomed to it. You see how their minds will work? But if we do *not* report it, none of these things arises. There will be no publicity, no inquest, no suspicion, no delay. At some future time, potholers will find the bodies. There will be an *inquest* then, of course, but it will be simple and the verdict will be accidental death. One thing more.' She paused.

'Go on.'

'If those men have families, it is far more desirable that this unpleasant affair should not be visited on them. Children should not have to learn that their fathers died trying to commit murder. You know my views on the visiting of sin upon succeeding generations.'

I said, 'This is called rationalization. They may not have had children. You're weaselling out from under.'

'Pragmatism is the fashionable word, Mr Tunnicliffe.'

For a second there was a trace of amusement about her, but it vanished at once, and she went on. 'I have prayed, and I believe I am right in this.'

No doubt about it: I was putty in her hands. And the arguments *were* very attractive.

We left for Singapore a few days later and busy days they'd been : a lot of the time I seemed to have been spending money. My two thousand had a very sizeable puncture in it by the time I'd bought air tickets, and there were a variety of other punctures on my arms and bottom, made by syringes intended to protect me from a wild variety of tropical bugs.

In London I was using my little flat with a certain confidence on the grounds that there wouldn't damned well be anybody else on my track seeking vengeance until the avengers discovered what had happened to the first assault wave. And probably not then either. The thought of them lying at the bottom of Gaping Ghyll (which, I discovered, is the deepest pothole in England – Miss Franklin did nothing by halves) came into my mind from time to time, but did not seem to trouble my conscience. Henderson, however, did just a little, the day he came knocking on my door, concerned about my welfare.

He took one swift look at me and said, 'You're looking pretty chirpy.'

I was feeling it too, at the time; enjoying all the preparations and the prospect of faraway places with strange-sounding names.

'Not worried any more?'

I took a deep breath and told a heavy lie. 'Well, nothing's happened.'

'Good. Where are you going?'

'Far East.'

He gave a little whistle. 'Last of the big spenders, eh? I thought you'd be off to Majorca or Torremolinos, not the other side of the world. When do you go?'

'Friday.'

'We'll keep an eye on you till then.'

'Thanks,' I said, feeling guilty. 'But you don't have to worry too much.'

'Policy,' he said. 'We've got a vested interest in looking after witnesses. Encourages the public. If you see a fellow with big feet and a raincoat hanging around, don't worry: he's ours.'

Outside the rain was lashing down. 'He'll get his death. Better not bother.'

'No? I'll change the word. You're not chirpy, you're positively cocky. All the same, we'll watch discreetly, in case somebody does have a go at you.'

One more try: I was thinking of the unfortunate coppers more than anything. 'I'll be away one day. Probably the night, too.'

'Where?'

'Thought I'd go see my old colonel. He sent me a telegram in hospital, and I haven't seen him in years.'

Henderson wandered to the door. 'I suppose you'll look after each other moderately well, two old soldiers.'

My mad old colonel lived in Suffolk, near Bury St Edmunds, and I drove up and took the precaution of booking myself in at the Angel. He'd want me to stay overnight, no doubt, and I wasn't having any, having had a great deal already. The colonel's nights consisted of talking till about two, sleeping three hours, then rising to a brisk session of calisthenics and a two-hour walk. He might have mellowed in retirement, but I doubted it. My purpose was two-fold: I wanted to see him again, out of sentimentality, and I wanted to pick his brains and use his friends out of practicality.

A sign nailed to a tree said 'The Sutherland Pedigree Goat Herd', and as I went through the gate, it occurred to me that the sign wasn't necessary: the goats did their own advertising. Hector McLeod Sutherland opened the door himself, saw me trying politely to unwrinkle my nose and said, 'They're fascinating beasts, young Tunnicliffe, and eventually you don't notice. Come in, come in.' And when I was in, 'You're a good excuse for some gin, aren't you? Eyes all right?'

'They're fine, sir, thanks.' I knew the weight of his touch with the gin bottle, and said, 'With lots of tonic, please.'

He snorted and said, 'Faddy.' He was an old Eastern hand and diluted *his* gin with water, when he diluted it at all. Drinks poured, he sat opposite in a creaking old armchair, stretched out long legs and crossed them at the ankle, nearly blinding me with the shine on his shoes, and looked at me sadly. I knew what was coming and there was no escaping it : I was one of Hector McLeod Sutherland's very few failures and he blamed me, without any justice at all, for it.

We took a good ceremonial pull at our drinks, without raising them to each other or saying anything fatuous like 'Cheers' or 'Bottoms up' or 'First today'. In our regiment that was never done.

'Trouble with you, young Tunnicliffe, is that you're a bad judge of a railway train.'

'Yes, sir,' I said. 'A dreadful judge.'

'Yes.' He stared at me above his vast beak of a nose. 'Tell me again.'

He knew the story perfectly well, but he didn't enjoy failure much and he liked to pick the facts over and see whether, if I'd shown proper soldierly initiative, things couldn't have been made to work.

I'd come back from Korea as a young lieutenant, minus my three toes and plus a Military Cross, and the army was about to boot me out, because I was a conscript officer and had been turned down for a regular commission. Sutherland, disagreeing with the verdict of his superiors, had set about some scheming behind the scenes, involving the current Chief of the Imperial General Staff, who happened to be colonel-in-chief of the regiment. As a result, I found myself seated opposite the CIGS one night at a mess dinner – the purpose being to let the old gentleman run his tough gaze over me. I must have passed inspection, because a considerable fiddle was then worked on my behalf.

The army was governed according to Army Council Instructions, and the CIGS presided over (and it's reasonable to imagine he dominated) the council, which duly issued a Special Instruction. This, formulated with extreme care, said that National Service officers who had lost three toes in the Korean fighting, and who were holders of the Military Cross, could apply to the Army Council for regular commissions. Nor was that the end of it; that Instruction might have let in other deserving cases, too, but since impartial justice was not intended, there was a rider to the effect that any such application must be delivered in person to the CIGS's office between the hours of eleven-thirty and eleven-forty-five on 18 February 1953.

The colonel had done his work and was full of bonhomie and satisfaction, and all I had to do was to be there with my envelope on the appointed day. That was where the train made its entry. We were stationed at Aldershot at the time, less than an hour from London, and I stepped aboard with plenty of time to spare.

I thought.

But somebody up there – in Heaven, not at the War Department – had outschemed Hector McLeod Sutherland, and the train halted. I thought at first that it had merely stopped at a signal, but as time passed I began to get nervous. I climbed down to the track and walked to the front. The train had broken down, and the problem was major, both for the train and for me: we were in the middle of the picturesque countryside, no train could or would get past the crippled one, and so on.

I belted off across country, knowing none of it, found a minor road and ran along that until I found a signpost which indicated that I should have been running the other way, doubled back, and then, on the main road, began hitch-hiking, a practice not approved for young officers. For twenty minutes nothing stopped. The smooth limousines, the little cars, the lorries, all swished past me, and then a lorry stopped. It was loaded with aggregate and had to stay in second gear at eight or nine miles an hour on any kind of incline at all.

In the finish I arrived, dreadfully sweaty and dishevelled, seven minutes late.

The CIGS's office wouldn't even accept the envelope.

The Instruction had now been withdrawn. Et cetera.

Hector McLeod Sutherland pulled moodily at his gin. 'Y'know, I think you should have stood in the road so they'd have had to knock you down, then commandeered a car. Told 'em you were chasing Russkies with snow on their boots.'

And so perhaps I should. But I hadn't, and the years in the bank had followed inexorably.

'Been what now? Major, I shouldn't wonder,' he said, rubbing it in. 'Pity, pity, that's what it was, a pity.'

I said yes and changed the subject. I changed it several times before arriving where I wanted to be. Had the colonel any friends at the War House who'd be able to turn up the file on Ludlam?

He frowned at me, but responded absolutely characteristically. 'Personal thing?'

'Yes.'

'Important to you?'

'Yes.'

'See what I can do.'

There was also the question of whether he knew anyone in Sarawak. He would find out who was there, he said, and be in touch soonest.

'And for all this, young Tunnicliffe, you may buy me some game pie at the Angel.'

'Delighted,' I said, and I was.

I knew it wouldn't take him long, and it didn't. I'd promised to telephone him the following evening, and when I did he launched straight in. 'Funny friends you're making, young Tunnicliffe. Markedly subdued responses to the name of Ludlam.'

'Were there?'

'They didn't want to talk at all, which usually means — well, you know what it usually means. Strange chap, though. He is, isn't he?'

'Strange? You could say that, sir.'

'Un-army.' A favourite word of his: it was meant to indicate undue flexibility, of which Hector McLeod Sutherland theoretically disapproved. He liked to think of himself as a textbook soldier, yet his own flexibility was a byword. He was rumbling on. 'War throws them up, of course, these bendy chaps : in peacetime they're weeded out. What is it you want to know?'

'Well, whatever you –'

'Everything. Yes. I haven't got everything, young Tunnicliffe. But here's what could be safely passed to a discreet, if ageing gentleman. This Ludlam of yours was officially a staff officer of outstanding ability, and if *that* goes down in black and white, it's true. Joined as a private in August of 'thirty-nine, and damn me, he made Brigadier, and then, damn me again, he was court-martialled. You knew that?'

'Yes.'

'Hm.' He was disappointed I knew. 'Don't know why you bother to ask.' I heard paper rustle. 'Banknote printer before the war. By Jove, you don't want bendy people as banknote printers, do you, eh? Look where it led to. He was grammar school. Not Sandhurst, obviously not university. Had a diploma in printing technology, whatever that means. Art of theft must have been self-taught.'

'Anything else?'

'Not much. Except one funny thing. He was a damned Red once.'

'What?'

'Red as Stalin's bloodshot eyes. Early 'thirties. Unreliable. Mark this, young Tunnicliffe: if a man got to Brigadier with that in his background, he must have been good.'

'Also he must have changed a bit.'

'You think so?'

'I don't know, sir.'

'No more do I. In the matter of Kuching, I understand Freddie Taylor's there. He's a Gurkha. Father was rather a chum of mine, killed at Imphal, poor old lad. Freddie's promising, I believe.' He paused. 'You're going?'

'Perhaps.'

He sighed. 'There was a day when young men answered yes, sir, and no, sir.'

'Then, yes.'

'Better,' he said. 'Comes of contact with the shifty world of money. Teaches young subalterns to be evasive. Briefing ended. When are you off?'

'In a day or two.' I corrected myself hurriedly. 'Friday, sir.'

He chuckled. 'You see, I'm mending your sloppy ways already. Well, have a good trip, whatever you're up to.'

'Thank you, sir.'

'Goodbye, then. Oh, did I tell you I saw Pilling a year or two ago? He's keeping very well, it seems.'

On that note he hung up, and I grinned ruefully to myself and thought, you devious old sod, Hector McLeod Sutherland! Because the devious old sod was telling me something: he and I both knew that Pilling had left the regiment to join MI6 and the name wouldn't have been spoken without reason. We'd spent yesterday talking about more or less everybody we knew, and Pilling of Intelligence hadn't been mentioned. Ergo, mention of Pilling of Intelligence had meaning, and the meaning must be that Freddie Taylor was something along the same lines. Odd, that, for a serving Gurkha officer, but then it's an odd kind of world these people seem to inhabit.

At any rate, Hector McLeod Sutherland had produced. It would be very useful to have that kind of contact in Kuching.

On Friday morning I met Miss Franklin at the West London air terminal and we rode out to Heathrow on a BEA bus. I'd bought our tickets from the same obliging, Indian, cut-price operator who'd sent me to the West Indies. This time we were part of a different affinity group. We had little cards showing us to be paid-up members of something called the South-East Asia Religious Studies Society. The others were bound for the wide-open city of Bangkok allegedly to count the temples. We landed there rather wearily sixteen hours later, then flew on, on yet another fiddle-ticket, to Singapore.

On the way, I sat and thought about things in general, and puzzles in particular. There were several more each day, it seemed, but the worst of them was still that damned number. I'd thought about it all round, up-and-down and across and not produced so much as a sensible guess at what it could mean. The world is full of numbers; dozens of them attach themselves to all of us, and that one could have been anything; a speed, a distance, a height (very precise in all three cases, but why?). It could be the number of, say, a bank account or the balance of cash in it (unlikely); it could be a telephone number (even more unlikely with the decimal point) or the number of carats of rubies. It could represent a debt, or ... The fact was that it could be anything. Or almost anything – the one thing it couldn't be was a map reference, damn it! But nowhere was there hint or clue. I took my father's letter from my pocket and read it again and stared resentfully at the number for a bit. Then my eyes moved on to the next sentence, equally baffling : 'Charity could have nothing to do with it.' Just ramblings, or what? Here's the number and charity could have nothing to do with it? Well, Miss Franklin might know; after all, she'd written it.

I said, 'Have you any idea what this bit means? Here.' I pointed. 'It says charity couldn't have – '

As ever, she interrupted. 'Yes, I have.'

'Then what?'

'I suppose he was anxious not to involve me in his larceny.' While I was attempting to digest this, she opened her handbag and handed me her passport. *Name of bearer:* Miss Charity Franklin.

'I absolutely forbid you to use it,' she said. 'I dislike it intensely. But he was wrong, was he not, that I could have nothing to do with it?'

CHAPTER EIGHT

'What a bloody man he is!' Maillart said with mixed anger and contempt. He was a staff captain, Headquarters, Far East Land Forces, Singapore, an ex-member of my old regiment, and I'd managed to meet him by the simple means of telephoning Farelf and asking if anyone from the regiment was in Singapore.

He was talking, like everybody else in and around the Malay Peninsula at that time, about Sukarno. We were sitting in Maillart's car more or less at the top of Singapore's highest hill, looking out over the Malacca Strait to where Sumatra sat low and dark on the horizon.

Maillart raised a hand and pointed. 'Just about there. A place called Tanjong Sekupang; you can see it just across the water. Well, Sukarno has put a training camp for Indonesian commandos there. Calculated, of course. Have it in full view of Singapore, then make a noise about it and people come up here to look and wonder. Psychological warfare.'

'Successful?'

He glanced at me. 'No. Not yet. But he's trying. Trying all those tricks of Mao's: confusion, minor bloodshed like that bomb this morning, followed by bigger disruption and major bloodshed. Show me an ambitious politician and I'll show you an evil bastard.'

We sat there, looking across the dark water, until the sun vanished almost abruptly and the velvet black sprung lights below us, and Maillart went on talking. Earlier that evening we'd driven past the Indonesian consulate and he'd said bitterly, 'If there's one place in Singapore that needs a bomb, that's it. Do you know about Koesto?'

I shook my head.

'The consul,' Maillart said. 'That's the theory of the job. But he never did much consular work and now he does none at all. Full-time agitation these days. That building's the centre of the spider-web here, and Koesto squats inside it manufacturing trouble. Who's behind the bombs? Koesto. Who's behind the agitators? Koesto. He sits there counting the khaki berets in the streets, counting the ships in the harbour and the aircraft coming in to land. Diplomatic immunity, too, the bastard.'

'What are his chances? Sukarno's, I mean.'

Maillart thought about it for a moment. 'If he were as good as he is ambitious, they'd be first-class, but I don't think he is. Malaya was saved once, and it can be done again, especially with Tunku Abdul Rahman in charge. He'll give Sukarno no ground at all, short of full-scale invasion, and that's a long way off, at least I think so. And here, in Singapore, Lee Kuan Yew is twice as clever and three times as resolute . . .'

'Which leaves Borneo,' I said. 'What about Borneo?'

He sighed. 'Well may you ask.' And added suddenly, 'Look!'

Out on the water a scatter of fishing boats had been at work. As darkness closed down, they'd lit their lamps. Now something long and dark was driving fast among them.

'What is it?'

'Destroyer, probably. Sukarno's, of course. Part of the process of harassment. Regular practice, as a matter of fact. They crunched a fishing boat ten days or so ago. Whole family wiped out and profuse apologies of course and the next bloody day they were at it again. One trouble is, the man has a hell of a big navy. Fourth biggest in the world, so they say, and all that steel plate goes crashing round the strait and the South China Sea spreading mischief.'

'You were talking about Borneo.'

'Well, that's the crucial bit.' I sat back and smoked while he told me a great deal of what I knew already, about the thousand-mile frontier, the high spine of the range, the passes through the mountains, the absence of roads and dependence upon rivers for transport and communication. He said that at the moment the war was small-scale, but vicious, and that there had already been minor successes on our side : terrorist leaders caught among the Brunei mangroves and so on.

And then, surprisingly, considering the almost-depressed tone in which he'd been speaking, he gave a sudden chortle and as I glanced across at him I could see the white of his excellent teeth. 'What's the laugh for?'

'The big Gurkha and the little Gurkhas. No, I'm not being obscure. The Gurkhas are in Borneo already, and Master Sukarno is going to get a nasty surprise when he encounters them in primary jungle. The little decapitators; one flick of the kukri and your head's on the floor.'

'And the big Gurkha?'

'Walker. Know him?'

'He's in command?'

Maillart nodded. 'Major-General Walter Walker. Gurkha officer himself. Learned the rough stuff up on the north-west frontier in the 'thirties. Learned a great deal more in the jungle campaigns in the war. Learned more still fighting under Templer in Malaya in the emergency, and if you remember, that's the *only* war against insurgents that's been won in the last twenty years. Well, Walker has two mottoes. The first is : Win the hearts and minds of the indigenous populations, and *that's* the one he talks about. He talks about it all the time, except when he's asleep, and I'd be surprised if he stopped even then. The second, which he talks about a good deal less, is : Kill efficiently. It works roughly this way. You use your helicopters to airlift sick children to first-class hospitals, you use your technicians to build bridges, you teach, you inoculate. If you've an officer who knows about pedigree goats, he goes round advising on goats. You bring in experts on fowl pest and rice-growing. That's the Hearts and Minds part. Mean-while, your signal people are handing out radios and the locals love you so much that when the insurgents steal by in the night, they let you know all about it. At that point: Kill efficiently.'

'It works?'

'It did in Malaya, and my bet is Walker will make it

work in Borneo, too. But it's going to be a long, mucky business.' He turned to me. 'Why the hell are you going there, anyway?'

So I gave him my cover story, about Miss Franklin the retired missionary going back to visit old friends, and me going along because I had honorary nephew status and happened to have had a lucky windfall.

'What surprises me,' he said, 'is that they'll let you in.'

'Blundering amateurs, you mean?'

'More or less.'

'To tell you the truth,' I said, 'I think Miss Franklin may have a bit of pull in useful places.'

We drove past the Indonesian consulate again, on the way back to Orchard Road, where we were staying in an excellent and far-from-expensive hotel. Maillart gave Koesto's lair a look of loathing and then asked if I'd tried a Singapore Sling yet, and when I said no, turned the car round and drove smartly to Raffles Hotel, that monument to Kipling and Somerset Maugham, and we sat in the long bar there and sipped expensive nectar. One thing led to another, and we made a night of it, plunging finally down a dark alley into a seedy-looking kind of square lined with restaurants, where I ate one of the best meals of my life. Miss Franklin, who had been out visiting old acquaintances, was in bed and probably asleep by the time I returned; there was a brief note from her waiting for me, saying that I should spend the following day kitting myself out and suggesting both suitable equipment and the various emporia in which it could be found.

I took myself off to bed, too, and lay in the cool of the air-conditioning, expecting to drift easily off to sleep on the tide of relaxing alcohol. And failing.

Failing because Ludlam reared up in my mind and demanded examination, as he often did. Ludlam grew more puzzling with the passage of time: in that old epigram of Churchill's, Ludlam was a puzzle wrapped in a mystery inside an enigma, and he kept twinkling through my head on his little bandy legs with his flowered shirt and his sharp eyes. The rat on its way to the carnival, I'd thought that first day I met him. And more and more I kept asking myself what, and where, the carnival might be.

I lay there staring at the ceiling and going over him with a mental magnifying glass, from that first bluff letter (bluff, I thought, *bluff*?) which had been so entirely out of character. The beautiful credentials : old friend of your father's, my boy, to the confession of thievery and the swift tests of my own debatable moral rectitude, right down to the final act – pointing me in the direction of missing loot. Why? He'd never said, and I, damn it, had never really asked. But now, thousands of miles away and weeks later, the question wouldn't leave my mind. Ludlam knew my father had vanished into the great green yonder of a million square miles of jungle; he knew that nobody knew where, except Miss Franklin, and he wasn't even aware of *her* existence. He knew that going to look for a wrecked plane after it had spent twenty years in primary jungle was as futile as going into the Matto Grosso to look for Colonel Fawcett. And yet he'd taken a lot of trouble to push me that way. Why, why, why? Well, it certainly wasn't because Ludlam was some kind of bottomless benevolent society; whatever his motives, they'd wear the perfume of dubiety.

All right, the obvious one : he wanted the stones – all of them, or some of them. But the little so-and-so was umpteen thousand miles away, had no possible way of keeping track on me, and no reason to suppose I knew any more than he did. Indeed, he knew very well that I knew less, because in theory I knew only what he'd told me plus what the Air Ministry had told my mother all those years ago, and *that* was precious little.

Ergo, Ludlam knew something I didn't. He'd told me some but not all. But what could he know? If he knew anything about the location of the stones, why bring me into it in the first place? He'd had years and years to slip into Borneo and pick them up; and given his attitudes and capacities would undoubtedly have done so long ago, if he could. So he couldn't. Well, why not? Perhaps because he was *persona non grata*? No, that was rubbish ! *Persona non grata* he might very well be, anywhere where British forces were engaged, but that wouldn't have stopped him for ten seconds. Anybody who could orchestrate the movements of divisions with the clarity of mind Ludlam had frequently demonstrated wouldn't have much trouble with minor administrative matters like identity papers.

Perhaps, then, he had friends. Conspiracy theory. The trouble was that Ludlam wasn't the type: he was the solo type, who'd trust his own brain and fingers and nobody else's, and his essentially solitary approach was apparent in his whole life-style in Jamaica where, as far as I could tell, he seemed to exist without much in the way of friends and acquaintances.

The only bit of speculation about Ludlam that could possibly hold water was the idea that he might be running short of funds. He had, after all, been living on the proceeds for a longish period of time, and it might be that the dam was low and that he was using me, sending me off into Borneo, in the forlorn hope that (a) I'd find the rubies, and (b) when I did, would be generous enough to say thank you in a tangible way. But if that was the way he was thinking, then why on earth had he gone to such trouble to show me what a crook I was, before telling me the tale?

There came a time, in the wee small hours, when I switched on the light and took the phone book out of the bedside cabinet, and looked up the number of BOAC, because it seemed to me then that the only way to find any mental peace would be to blue more money on another trip to Jamaica to tweak the rat's whiskers in the rat's nest. But I gave that up, too, in the end.

I slept though, eventually, and next morning ventured out into the sticky heat to start buying things. Change Alley, Singapore's celebrated market, seemed the logical place to begin, and I plunged cheerfully into its shadowed mysteries in search, first of all, of boots. I'm not a man who likes shopping. Hell, when eventually I get there, will consist of spending all eternity in a rainswept Oxford Street, traipsing from one crowded store to another, being told by bored assistants that there's no call for it, sir, and meantime being shoved out of the way by determined dowagers burdened with parcels and greed and entirely unburdened by manners.

But Change Alley was fun. The traders were Indian, Malay, Chinese, possibly Indonesian, too, and they were dedicated to the proposition of making sales. You have cash? An accommodation will be reached. Bush shirts? But yes. My brother-in-law makes the most beautiful shirts, made to measure, of course, in two hours including a fitting. Second alley on the right, third stall along. Ask for Ali, tell him you've come from Haroun. So you go, and Ali isn't away at lunch. Not likely. Ali's there with a business-like air and a tape-measure and a hundred and fifty bolts of fine quality materials if the gentleman would care to make his selection. As to cost? Well, Ali's eye measures you even more carefully than his tape-measure as he judges just how much of a mug you are, and makes his bid. He grins, you grin, and a pleasant few moments of haggling begin. You finally settle, knowing you've got something of a bargain, but suspecting from Ali's demeanour that he thinks he's got one, too. Two hours later you have the shirts and they're beautiful. And if the gentleman wants anything else, Ali has a range of brothers, brothers-in-law, uncles, cousins and aunts wide enough to make the late King David look like an orphan, and they cover, between them, every conceivable area of merchandise and service.

I got some formidable calf-length *veldtschoen* boots, among other things, was given cups of coffee while I made up my mind, and broad smiles as new wonders were unfolded, and when I'd finished small boys were sent with me to carry my parcels and find me a taxi. I went back to the hotel with two tents (unnecessary weight, it's true, but the prospect of showing Miss Franklin one tent, with all that it implied, was too daunting for me), a small cooking stove, assorted camping equipment, and a sense of achievement. I'd been told to leave the ointments and insect repellents, the assorted bead and bangle gifts, to her.

Miss Franklin was due to spend the evening with some more of her friends from the heathen-conversion business, and I'd been invited by Maillart to dinner in his mess, but we'd agreed to meet and talk for half an hour or so beforehand. I had a stiff gin first, by way of preparation, and then went and knocked on the door of her room. The door was opened by a Chinese hung about with cameras. He wasn't a tourist, though : Miss Franklin was being interviewed by the *Straits Times*. I tried to excuse myself and failed and found myself being interviewed, too.

Some publicity-conscious character in the mission organization must have tipped them off, and I suppose it was a perfectly legitimate thing to do, but if I'd been Miss Franklin I'd have booted them out on sight. Considering why we were in that part of the world, advertising our presence didn't seem the most sensible thing to do.

But the interview was under way, and she was clearly quite happy about it, thinking, no doubt, that she was helping to spread the Great Message.

The result was that next day we were able to look at pictures of ourselves and read: WAR HEROINE RETURNS TO SARAWAK.

It was all there: Miss Franklin's wartime adventures, her devotion to her medical missionary work, her jungle expertise, and the fact that it was due to the kindness of her companion, ex-Captain George Tunnicliffe, that she was able to make the trip. And Tunnicliffe was a hero himself. Et cetera, et cetera. The only thing missing was the fact that the said Tunnicliffe's father had disappeared with a load of gem stones in the territory to which we were returning.

Reading it sent shivers up and down my spine. It had been announced to the world at large that we were on our way.

But compared to our next appearance in the newspapers, that one was relatively painless. I'd spent the day trying to buy maps, and Borneo is not especially well-mapped : the big sheets are in pretty colours and look as impressive at first sight as anything else published by the Defence Survey; but really they show little more than principal towns and villages, some spot heights, and large areas of green. That green is primary jungle, and is not disfigured by anything so sophisticated as contour lines. But the maps show watercourses, and if you're proposing to travel in Borneo, it's those you must travel along, so maps are important. Better maps would be in course of preparation, as they always are when war's afoot, but meantime we'd have to use what there was. I also had a small list of extras Miss Franklin had made: things like fish hooks and lines and clear filament. I asked her if she intended to turn her Dyaks and Ibans into match anglers, but she wasn't in a mood for small pleasantries at the time and instructed me fairly brusquely to do as ordered.

So I had a pleasant day, one way and another, mooching round that pleasant city, watching ships move and buildings grow, by no means sure which went along faster, because they were slapping up steel for the high-rise buildings at a rare old pace. I ate, and strolled and watched a game of cricket beside the statue of Sir Stamford Raffles overlooking the harbour. Then I strolled back to the hotel.

By chance, Miss Franklin was just getting out of a taxi as I arrived. She had various parcels with her and I, with very little in my mind but the thought of a nice cool beer, was compelled to delay it and help her carry her purchases upstairs. We collected our keys from the desk and rose up in a fast, silent lift that should properly be called an elevator in deference to its American origins. She put her key in the lock, opened the door and said, 'Bring them in, George.' And I bumped into her back because she took one step and stopped dead.

The room was in ruins: everything turned over and pulled about, drawers emptied on the floor, cushions ripped, suitcases torn apart and thrown on the floor. All that was bad enough, but as our eyes moved over the chaos, there was something else, something that caught and held our gaze. A long jungle machete was embedded in her pillow on the bed. And on the wall above, somebody had written with paint from a spray can, 'Beware 10598.' In blood-red letters.

I suppose the same words must have begun to run

through our minds at the same moment, the pointless who-and-what-and-why litany that is the invariable human reaction to this kind of invasion. I know I stood there, mouth hanging open, for long moments trying to comprehend what it was all about. She recovered faster and picked her way across the mess on the floor to the telephone. It had been ripped from the wall.

We went to my room, wondering whether it, too, had had the same treatment. It hadn't, and the telephone worked, and before very long we were swarming with managers and under-managers and floor managers and hotel detectives and cleaning supervisors and anybody else who might have something to offer in the way of information. The police arrived very shortly afterwards and began the inevitable process of questioning and taking statements, and not long after *that*, the *Straits Times* was once more on the scene, hung about with flash equipment and the latest in Japanese cameras. We turned the photographer out as soon as the first flash announced his presence, but it was too late by then, of course, because the photographer had his picture and didn't mind at all.

It was a long, trying evening, because the police couldn't believe we'd no ideas about who-what-why. They could see, as we could, that it wasn't the usual burglary.

'Anything missing?'

'Doesn't seem to be.'

'Please check.' And a check wasn't easy with everything thrown around.

But finally, 'No. Apparently there's nothing missing.'

'Malice, then. Why?'

'No idea.'

'You must have some idea. These things don't happen for nothing.'

And so on.

And then a miserable dinner in which Miss Franklin and I went over the same ground again. And again. And again.

We couldn't find any rational answers either, except that we both knew the real significance, and didn't want to face it. But it was there, and faced it finally had to be. The only logical reason was that somebody knew why we were in Singapore, why we were going to Borneo, what lay there, and was warning us off.

Who?

Ludlam knew, but Ludlam was in Jamaica. And the room that had been broken into was not mine, but Miss Franklin's, and Ludlam didn't know she even existed.

More and more we were forced back on a premise that seemed, at first, crazily unlikely. I brought it up first, perhaps because I'd disliked the idea of the press interview from the start. I said, 'Somebody here, somebody in Singapore, must know about my father.'

'Nonsense!'

'Why nonsense? It isn't twenty years yet. There must still be people around who knew him.'

She said, 'It would be far too much of a coincidence if the people who knew him were in Singapore now.'

'Why would it?' I argued. 'There are people in the army who've spent their whole service lives in the Far East. General Walker has for one.'

'You mean this is his work?' she said, with heavy sarcasm.

'If he's here, there are others. And I imagine stories of lost treasure have a long life!'

It was very thin. And nothing else linked up with it. In particular that damned number painted on the wall didn't link up. Nor could we begin to understand what the number was. The police had demanded to know its significance and had looked a bit sour and disbelieving when we told them we hadn't the slightest idea. But we hadn't, then or later, as we picked over the details.

We just kept coming back to the possibility that the story and picture in the *Straits Times* had alerted somebody to the fact that one George Hawke Tunnicliffe was in Singapore and Borneo-bound, and that somebody must be aware that there had once been an identically-named Tunnicliffe who'd disappeared over Borneo with a fortune in rubies.

In my mind that led by devious paths to matters of rank and nationality, though Miss Franklin didn't go along with this at all. She listened, though, as I said, 'No pongo private who was in the Far East in 1945 is still a pongo private. Second lieutenants have become captains and majors, and captains and majors if they're still around have become colonels and brigadiers. So if that business in your room *is* connected with the rubies, and with Borneo, we're up against somebody who's British, somebody who's army or air force, and somebody with rank.'

But by this time, another thought had occurred to Miss Franklin and she took refuge in it. 'Don't you think it's far more likely,' she said, 'that it's the Indonesians? They're trying to cause chaos, both here and in Borneo, and they don't like the kind of influence the missions have in Borneo, so they're using me as a threat to other missionaries there?'

'What about the number?'

'You think it matters?'

'Of course I think it matters.'

'I don't. I think the whole thing is just a way of getting the picture in the papers. Another piece of mindless terrorism, with the number adding a bit of mystery.'

Next morning, when the *Straits Times* appeared, there was some slight confirmation of her argument:

MISSIONARY'S ROOM RANSACKED
MYSTERY NUMBER PAINTED ON WALL

She said, 'You see. It's all part of Confrontation.'

Meanwhile something else confronted us: the decision whether to go ahead or not. It seemed to me we'd been warned clearly enough that somebody was on to our little scheme, and was prepared to be violent about it. That machete embedded in the pillow said clearly enough, 'You're unprotected. Next time your head will be on the pillow.'

'Stuff and nonsense,' said Miss Franklin.

I chewed morosely at my breakfast, thinking almost with longing of the bank and its quiet routine, and she probably read my thoughts because all of a sudden she said, 'Remember the shotguns,' then smiled at my frown. The decision, I could see, was mine alone. Miss Franklin, having got this far, was going to Borneo, thank you very much, and anything as inconsequential as my over-reaction to an incident designed for publicity wasn't going to get in the way of her purpose and the Lord's work, particularly when the two coincided so happily.

There was no fighting her impossible combination of determination and optimism, and I suppose that, though my own lust for a large lump of unearned wealth was waxing and waning by turns, it was really pushing me in much the same direction.

I was still worried and frowning as we walked up the gangplank that afternoon, to board the ship that was to take us across the South China Sea to Kuching in Sarawak. But Miss Franklin wasn't worrying. There was a cheerful spring in her step and an anticipatory glint in her eye as she marched across to the rail and looked out to the southwest. The deck was crowded with soldiers, on their way to reinforce Walker's forces, and Miss Franklin's gesture took in the lot of them as she said, 'You see. With all these soldier friends of yours, we're bound to be safe!'

I don't think I replied. Those soldiers were from a regiment my old lot had never held in much regard. There'd been something a century or two ago, at Oudenard or Malplaquet or somewhere, where they'd broken and we'd stood fast, and while Miss Franklin stood listening, presumably to the voice of the Lord, I was hearing the soft tones of my old mad colonel saying, 'If you have to go into battle, just make damn sure it isn't with *them*.'

Not the best of spirits in which to set off, and the cheer they set up as the ship moved away was not echoed in my heart or head.

Borneo, I knew, was going to be a bastard.

CHAPTER NINE

Nor was the bastard far to seek. I'm not the best sailor alive, and there are those who describe the South China Sea as the nastiest stretch of water on this or any other planet. We ran into rough water as soon as we were clear of Singapore's sheltering harbour, and before we were an hour under way the ship's rails were so thick with vomiting soldiery that it was next to impossible to find a gap to be sick through. The air was full of the hiss of the sea and the groans of the stricken. The happy grins and the parting cheers were somewhere in the limbo of things forgotten. Men staggered up and down the lurching deck, delivered their lunches to the guardians of the deep, and then made way for the next sufferer. I skated and lurched and groaned with the best of them, occasionally tempted, like some of the others, to roll with that bobbing bloody ship and keep rolling when it stopped, and let the sea finish off what it had begun.

Need I say that Miss Franklin was entirely unaffected? That while I kept clutching at my voided guts, she was taking tea below? That when she came up on deck again and took in the sight of the suffering mob, she was unsympathetic, and said to me, 'It's a matter of self-control, you know. You must simply take a grip on yourself.' Because that's what she did say. And she followed it up with the suggestion that, having taken the appropriate grip, I should go below and regale myself with ham sandwiches and toast and cake. Did she understand that what she was saying was, on your mark, get set, go? I know I was white-knuckled at the rail before the word cake had left her lips.

It got no better, either. If anything, it got worse: though it's difficult to be sure whether it actually was worse, or simply seemed so, because sea-sickness at night is even fouler than sea-sickness by day. It was the night of the green faces, that one, green faces, and sleeplessness and empty, voided guts: a misery lessened not at all by the knowledge that Charity the Uncharitable was sleeping like a babe somewhere below.

When I had a moment to think about anything, I thought about her: with incomprehension, with curiosity, occasionally with black bloody hate. I'd sit there on one of those slat-seats they provide on ships, seats devised, designed and built by Torquemada or one of his apter pupils, and try to work out what influences life could possibly have provided to turn out somebody like Miss Franklin. Compassion was her profession, or so she'd said once; but you'd look a long way and never catch a glimpse of it. Maybe she saved it all for the Borneo tribesmen, particularly the ones who did as they were told, but she didn't have much left for anybody else, me for instance, or the two she'd dropped to the bottom of Gaping Ghyll without either compunction or a word of warning to me in case I stopped her. Not that I would have stopped her; I was too scared that day to stop anything that would have saved my hide, but I was in no doubt that was *why* she'd done the whole dirty deed all by herself. I remember thinking, as I sat shivering in the wind, with the sweat of sickness cold on my face and neck, that there was something pretty terrifying about anybody so permanently convinced of his or her own rightness. Hitler, for instance. Most politicians for that matter. And Miss Franklin.

But the weary night did eventually end and warmth came with the sun to ease the shivering and I managed to gulp some hot coffee and, for the first time, to keep it down. I still felt like old slipper, thoroughly chewed by an enthusiastic mastiff, but I knew that the worst was over, both in misery and in time. The day was bright and we'd end the crossing in a few hours. During the darkness, there had seemed no end in prospect; now there was and I felt a shade less foul.

Miss Franklin appeared on deck finally, spruce and in order, and in spite of all the rolling and pounding, seemed to feel no need to hold on to anything. She came over to me, ran her eye disapprovingly over the wreckage, and asked if I felt better.

'Not so you'd notice,' I said.

'You would, if you spruced yourself up.'

She virtually ordered me down to my cabin to wash, shave and clean up, and I suppose there was something in it, because I did feel better when I'd finished. Not enough to face food, which had been another of her recommendations, but better.

I don't recommend a combination of Miss Franklin and roiling innards as a way to make time go swiftly, but the second hand of my watch revolved slowly, so the minutes must have been passing, and the moment came, finally, when there was the celebrated dark smudge on the horizon, and not an eternity afterwards we came into more sheltered water and began to ease our way into and up the Kuching river to our anchorage. Sea-sickness is like all the other aches and pains and miseries: it's wonderful when it stops. When that happened there came a miraculous return of balance, optimism and appetite. I even managed to get some food into my aching stomach, and quieten its rumbles and grunts, between the time when the sea flattened and the restaurant closed, and it was quite an achievement because the interval could have been measured in nanoseconds. I wondered if the man who ran the restaurant had some mental rule about selling only to the hardy, and shutting up shop when the weak came calling.

I stood beside her at the rail, with the newly-sluiced deck beneath my feet, watching the land as we went upriver, and she was all guide book and an almost girlish enthusiasm, now. Here was the beloved country, and she intended to describe it.

What I could see was all very low-lying and damp, mangrove swamps in places, and the river sluggish and brown, but for her it was the land of romance. I got the whole thing, from the first appearance of James Brooke, later first White Rajah of Sarawak, through his systematic destruction of pirates and headhunters, right down to the wise decision of his descendants to hand Sarawak over as a colony to the Crown, and its final and recent transfer into the youthful Federation of Malaysia. A long story of wisdom and enlightened rule, said Miss Franklin, and I didn't say, though I thought it, how come all that wisdom leads to shiploads of soldiers?

She was still chattering on as we came alongside and tied up. *There* was the Palace of the Rajahs, known as The Astana, and *here* . . . and *there* . . . and this and that is . . . and everybody else was standing at the top of the gangplank before we were, which probably meant all the taxis would have gone when our turn came. But finally I managed to persuade her to stop pointing her finger and collect her luggage and we began, belatedly, to get ourselves organized.

I was wrong about the taxis, the last one hadn't gone. Indeed, there was a queue of them and Miss Franklin gave me a little smirk of superior knowledge as we loaded it and climbed in.

'Odeon,' she said.

The driver grinned and nodded.

'Are they showing travel films today?' I enquired politely. In Britain Odeons are cinemas.

'The Odeon is a hotel,' she said. 'A nice one, and not over-expensive, and I have made a booking for us.'

Freddie Taylor, Gurkha captain, son of the colonel's late chum, was expecting my telephone call, having had airmail advice, probably on goat-scented writing paper, that I would shortly be in his vicinity. He sounded bright, sharp and good-humoured, which was more or less to be expected; if the colonel approves of young officers it's because they're bright and sharp, and good humour enters any conversation centred upon *him*.

'Can you give me a briefing?'

'I can do my best,' Taylor said, 'for what it's worth. What about breakfast tomorrow?'

'Breakfast?'

'We tend to be kept rather busy just now,' he said. 'I

can't be sure I'll be free any other time. Where exactly are
you intending to go?'

I told him, wrapping my tongue awkwardly round all the
-ongs and -ings, and he gave a little tut.

'What's the matter?'

'Been a bit of activity thereabouts, I think. Still, I'll go
over the sitreps and make sure it's all up-to-date. Breakfast,
then. Seven o'clock all right?'

I hung up with a grin on my face, half sympathy, half
envy, guessing what things must be like for Taylor. It was
an odd kind of war they were fighting: small incidents over
a vast area about which nobody knew half enough; a
general in command who'd probably come storming in like
Christ into the temple, turning out, turning over, and
demanding, demanding, demanding . . . Maillart had told
me about Walker's phenomenal energy, and if Taylor had
the job of keeping the general informed, Taylor would be
a very active fellow with a boot permanently embedded in
his behind. I'd have given a good deal, including my share
in the rubies, to swap places permanently with Freddie
Taylor.

I had an early night that night, having slept not at all
the previous one, and made sure of a solid rest with a
couple of largish whiskies taken slowly and with pleasure,
because Miss Franklin was elsewhere discussing His Work,
no doubt, with some old cronies, and I could enjoy the
drinks without her disapproving gaze upon me.

I slept like a giant sloth, awoke feeling marvellous, and
was almost as bright-eyed and bushy-tailed as Freddie
Taylor as we shook hands in a corner of the dining-room
at five minutes to seven. Almost but not quite. Everything
about Taylor gleamed, including both eyes. Razor creases in
the tropicals, boots and belt you could shave in, and a mind
to match, I hadn't the slightest doubt. We talked colonel
until Miss Franklin joined us on the stroke of seven. She
took one glance at all that peacock militarism and was
prepared to be disapproving – I was beginning, by now, to
be able to detect the various shades of her disapprobation –
but it dawned on her very quickly that Taylor was probably

as good as he looked. He'd been six weeks in Sarawak, and seemed to know almost as much about it as she did, right down to pronunciation of place names.

'What I'd like to suggest,' Taylor said, crisply taking command, 'is that we eat as quickly as digestive safety will allow, and then perhaps go to Mr Tunnicliffe's room. You have no objection, Miss Franklin?'

'No.'

'Splendid.' So the bacon and the toast and marmalade disappeared and we talked colonel a little while longer, then went upstairs with Taylor and his polished briefcase. With the door closed, he opened the case and numbers of things began to emerge: maps, wax pencils, even drawing-pins to fasten maps to walls. Setting up took about ten seconds, including the placing of two chairs facing him.

'Now,' he said, 'you're hoping to reach Lobang Nibong, is that correct?'

'Yes.'

'Right. I know Tunnicliffe is new here, but you are not, I believe, Miss Franklin. Four years, is it not? Well, there have been changes.' His finger traced the snaking line of the Nibong river. 'This will be as you remember it, no doubt. Well here –' a plastic overlay emerged from the briefcase to be held over the map – 'here, you'll see that the river has taken a new course. The old channel's still there, but it has also found itself a new one. This loop is roughly sixteen miles long. Depth, I'm afraid, is as yet unknown. Survey very soon, but not in time for you. You have this map?'

I nodded.

'Fine. Then I'll let you keep the overlay. It's the only topographical change of any significance so far as we know.' He paused. 'Now, I am given to understand that the purpose of your trip is to visit the places you worked in. Is that correct?'

'I told them that in Singapore,' Miss Franklin said, 'when I asked permission and it was given.'

'In my opinion,' Taylor said, 'it is a mistake. However, the authorization has been given and will be honoured. I feel, though, that I ought to advise you to put off your trip.'

Miss Franklin said 'No', quickly.

'For this reason,' Taylor continued. 'I'm aware you know the area and the people in it. You also know, therefore, how remote it is, and how difficult the country. It would be our wish to offer you as much protection as possible, but I have to tell you that in that region we are unable, at the moment, to do very much. We are still under-manned here, and still having difficulty in covering such a large terrain. We do not yet know the size of the force facing us.'

Miss Franklin said, 'I'm prepared for risks, Captain Taylor.'

'Though we have just met, Miss Franklin, I know enough of you to know that. I am anxious only that you should know what the risks are and take appropriate – ' he meant sensible – 'decisions. Lobang Nibong is very close to the border, and it is in the border regions that infiltration is beginning to take place. Small groups are entering Sarawak from Kalimantan and are beginning to fight a guerrilla campaign. It will inevitably follow the accustomed pattern of harassment of the indigenous population, ambushes of patrolling troops, and so on.'

'There aren't too many places where they can cross the mountains,' Miss Franklin said. 'Surely those can be watched.'

Taylor wasn't the man to be called a fool to his face, but patience he certainly had. He smiled, but I was glad I hadn't said it.

'You see,' he went on, 'we have a programme of building small fortified areas close to crossing points, but it takes time. We have men there now, but they're not properly protected so they're vulnerable and the watch we can keep is as yet inadequate. We're heavily dependent upon helicopters, but very short of landing pads, and having to operate at longer range than we'd like. But we'll get there, Miss Franklin. Now – I told Mr Tunnicliffe last night that I thought I'd seen a report of an insurgent group in the Lobang Nibong area. I have checked that report, and last night I made further enquiries.'

'And?'

'It is not much better than rumour. No actual observation, but a *belief* there are intruders in the area.'

'A belief?' Miss Franklin said. 'Who believes it?'

'I do. More important, so do the locals.'

'At Lobang Nibong longhouse?'

'No,' Taylor said. 'We have no communication with them.'

'Then where?'

Taylor smiled. 'I'm sorry. I'm sure you understand, but I am not at liberty to –'

She interrupted. 'Local trackers?'

Taylor said again, 'I'm sorry. I'm happy to provide what information I can, but not to divulge sources.'

She didn't exactly sniff, but it was that sort of reaction.

'As I say,' Taylor continued smoothly, 'my advice would be to call it off, unless the journey is absolutely essential. Having come out from Britain, no doubt at considerable expense, I can understand you would be reluctant to do so, but the advice stands.'

I said, 'I'm afraid it looks as though we *are* going. What's your advice about the journey?'

He shrugged. 'Very little I can say, except to warn you that we anticipate there will be guerrilla action on the rivers. As you know, they're the only really effective means of communication outside the immediate Kuching area, so they're an obvious target for disruption. I can only suggest that you be very cautious.'

'These infiltration groups? What size?'

Taylor shrugged again. 'One or two have been up to fifteen men. Not very efficient, by which I mean it's a less than ideal size, and they're learning that and cutting down. Fours and fives and sixes, probably.'

'Radio?'

'Difficult. Jungle cover goes to two hundred, sometimes to two hundred and fifty feet, and very solid, and they're very large trees to climb. Most of the time, with our own patrols, we operate timed rendezvous points.'

'Even so. Could you provide one?' I tried to give him

a persuasive smile, but he wasn't to be persuaded.

'Sorry. Still a shortage, for one thing, and the radios we have tend to succumb to jungle fever rather quickly. It's another thing we're working on.' He fished in his briefcase again, and produced a sheet of paper which he handed to me. 'We've been running an amnesty on privately-held, unlicensed arms, hoping to clear up as many as we can. I'm going against that, just this once. This is a permit for rifles and shotguns. One each. Probably as much as you can carry, anyway.'

He turned away and began to take out the drawing-pins and fold the maps. 'If you're going, when?'

'Soon as we're ready,' I said.

Things were disappearing into the briefcase and in a moment or two he was packed and ready to move, brushing at his uniform with his hands.

I walked downstairs with him, out through the doors and across to his gleaming Land-Rover, and as we shook hands, he said, 'The colonel's letter said your father disappeared over here during the war.'

My stomach gave a little lurch as I corrected him. 'Not during, just after.'

He gave me a sympathetic glance. 'You're hoping to find his aircraft?'

'No,' I said. 'There's no chance of that.'

'Glad you realize that. Can't you talk her out of this trip?'

'No,' I said. 'I don't think I can.'

He smiled. 'Tartar, I can see. I had an aunt like that.'

I said, 'Not like her, you didn't.'

He swung himself in behind the wheel. 'I suppose I ought to say "Look after her", but I won't. I rather think the boot's on the other foot.' He grinned as he swung the Land-Rover away.

I gave a little relieved whistle to myself. I didn't like Taylor knowing about my father, because Taylor's job was to find out what was going on and if he began to wonder about something, he'd chase very hard. But at the moment, it seemed, he wasn't wondering.

There was a boat to be found and I went hunting for it that morning, and for an outboard motor, too, after a brief argument with Miss Franklin who thought it unnecessary. Having a motor meant carrying a large quantity of petrol, which was the basis of her argument. My side of it was that I was satisfied with my body weight as it was and didn't want to shed two or three stones paddling a hundred miles and more upstream.

She said, 'I'll do my share.'

I said, 'Will you?' and went shopping.

What I bought was a medium-sized rubber dinghy with a wood-reinforced transom and a little Seagull motor to mount on it. The motor wasn't powerful, but it wasn't heavy either, and it didn't guzzle fuel. When the time came to lift the boat out of the water to carry it past rapids, weight was going to be important. I bought ten five-gallon jerricans for petrol, and filled them up. Then a footpump, some rubber solution and patches in case of accident, one rifle and one shotgun and ammunition for both. While I was in the chandler's I saw the reels of rope, counted my diminishing balance of money, and invested in a hundred fathoms of half-inch nylon line. I didn't know quite why, even as I was buying it; it was an impulse purchase, something to do with the height of the trees, perhaps; I don't know.

The whole lot was left under lock and key at the chandler's and I walked back to Padungan Road and the Odeon Hotel, arriving damp with sweat. The temperature was in the eighties and humidity high and I felt the need for a cooling beer, or perhaps two, just as I had that day in Singapore.

Perhaps there's some kind of natural law that says: when you stand in greatest need of a cool refreshing beer, you won't get it. A barrier rose between me and the bar. It was quite a small barrier, but not the kind you can walk past, or clamber over.

This barrier had stopping power.

CHAPTER TEN

Ludlam was dressed in worn, ancient and rather baggy tropical uniform, 1944 vintage, still with little holes in the epaulets where rank badges had once been. He also wore a little grin and a pleased look, and was holding out his hand for shaking. I was tempted to shake his scrawny throat.

'It would have saved trouble if I'd known where you were staying, my lad,' he said. 'Didn't say where your base was.' And then, diagnosing from my expression that I wasn't gushing with happiness at the sight of him: 'Something the matter?'

I stared at him angrily. I imagine my jaw was working, and my forehead creased, and I probably grunted a bit trying to hold back the fury I felt, and he patted my shoulder with his ratlike paw and said, 'Stop giving this impersonation of Neanderthal Man and tell me all about it.'

I said, 'Singapore. That's the matter.' Ever since the break-in to the hotel room I'd been trying to work out who in Singapore could have known why we were heading for Sarawak. Not Ludlam, I'd told myself, because Ludlam was a million miles off, in Jamaica. Only he wasn't. He must have been in Singapore too!

'Singapore? Always thought it was the nicest spot in the whole Far East,' he said. 'Changed a bit, so they tell me. Why's Singapore bothering you?'

I resisted with difficulty the impulse to pick him up and dash him down again, and said, 'What the bloody hell brings you here?'

He looked at me almost pityingly. 'Surely, son, you can guess? After all, you wrote me a letter.'

'I didn't send you an invitation!'

'You didn't get my cable?'

'What cable?'

'When I got your letter, I thought to myself: why not go along? Bit of an adventure, you know. Old for it, perhaps, but fairly spry. So I sent a cable to London to tell you I'd meet you in Kuching. You didn't get it?'

'I didn't get it.'

'All right, you're surprised. But why this imitation of an incendiary bomb?'

'Who,' I demanded, 'did you talk to in Singapore?'

'Not a soul. Don't even know what makes you think I was there, because I wasn't. I flew to the Philippines, then to Jesselton in Sabah, and then on here. Never touched Singapore.'

'Show me your ticket!'

Ludlam looked at me severely. 'You're a bag of nerves, young man.' He pulled out a wallet stuffed with airline tickets and showed them to me. Los Angeles, Manila, Jesselton, Kuching. 'So simmer down, eh? You had trouble in Singapore, did you?'

'Yes,' I said, 'we had trouble.' I was still glaring at him, still somehow certain, with the rat in the neighbourhood, that the initial smell of rat was now justified.

'*We?* Got somebody with you, or is that the royal we?'

I took his arm in what I fancied was a steely grip and began to propel him towards the bar. The beer could wait no longer; refreshed I might be able to hammer at him harder.

But I didn't reach the oasis. Miss Franklin must have been sitting in the lounge, which offered a view of the bar, waiting for me, and she came bustling out, halting when she saw I was accompanied.

I said very formally, 'Miss Franklin, allow me to introduce Mr Ludlam.'

She frowned; a frown that kept deepening.

'From Jamaica,' I said.

Ludlam extended his hand, bowing a little from the waist. 'Good afternoon, Miss Franklin.'

She ignored them all, him, his hand and his little bow, turned to me with a face like a sharp frost, and said, 'And what is Mr Ludlam *doing* here?'

'He's come to join us.'

'Has he indeed?' Now she gave Ludlam the benefit of that bleak gaze. 'At whose invitation?'

'Invited myself,' Ludlam said. He gave a little smile intended to be either charming or disarming and succeeding at neither. Its failure bothered him not at all. He glanced over her shoulder. 'They serve tea in there? You'd enjoy some tea, I expect, Miss Franklin.'

He slid away into the lounge and she glared first at his back, then at me.

'Tea,' I said.

'I require an explanation.'

'He'll be giving you one.'

'From you.'

'I can't explain anything.'

She emitted something very close to a snort of impatience, then turned abruptly and marched after him.

The room was nicely Edwardian, and so was Ludlam's manner. He was taking control in a very neat way, fussing her into a seat. 'Now – would you rather sit here, Miss Franklin, where you can face the door?'

'I don't care where I sit. What I –'

'Some ladies do, you know. China or Indian?'

'*Mister* Ludlam!'

'So nice, I always think, tea at the end of a hot day. Our young friend was heading for the bar, but tea is so much more refreshing, isn't it? Ah, here's the waiter. Did you say China or Indian?'

She said, 'Indian,' through gritted teeth, sat simmering as Ludlam ordered, then: 'An explanation, please, Mr Ludlam.'

He looked at her mildly, and it occurred to me then that in a way they were not unlike: same generation, both on the thin side, both positive, both accustomed to getting their own way.

'I don't know how much young Tunnicliffe has told you about me, Miss Franklin. He certainly told me nothing about you. So we're both a little surprised, eh? Well, I always think that in those circumstances the best thing is just to talk quietly, preferably over some tea. And here it is. Will you be mother?'

Watching the byplay, my anger had gone and I caught myself grinning and stopped before she caught me, too. A fair amount of the wind was out of her sails for once and she wanted it back. 'It doesn't matter who pours, Mr Ludlam! I –'

'No?' Ludlam said. 'Oh, but it's so much nicer for the lady to do it. Reminder that the world is still civilized. Would you, please?' And that please held the tiniest trace of command.

She stiffened slightly, but she took the teapot and the initiative with it. 'Yes, of course, Mr Ludlam. You must have had trouble finding us?'

'I just telephoned the Kuching hotels until I found the one that had your booking.'

'And how did you know we'd be in Kuching?'

'Young Tunnicliffe sent me a note from London. Did you know? No, I can see you didn't.' He could see because she'd turned to glare at me. 'Well, I'm sorry, of course, that I was unexpected. I hope it doesn't make me unwelcome?'

She handed him his cup. 'When Mr Tunnicliffe said you had come here to join us, Mr Ludlam, what did he mean?'

'I just told him; when I got his letter it seemed to me just the ticket. Bit of an adventure, that kind of thing. At my age I won't get many more, but I'm still fairly fit. So you see how it was : impulsive, perhaps, but I thought it would be fun to come along. Couldn't see young Tunnicliffe minding, and of course, I didn't know about you.'

'You know now.'

He sipped his tea. 'Well, now that I'm here, yes, of course I do. And I must say it's a great pleasure to meet you. I knew Tunnicliffe's father, you know.'

She handed me my cup, much as though it were hemlock, and said crisply, 'A pair of crooks.'

Ludlam gave a curious yet polite little laugh. 'There are more than two now, wouldn't you say? And after all, I have a part in all this.' He paused. 'Do you, Miss Franklin?'

She smiled coolly. 'An indispensable part, Mr Ludlam.'

'Ah?' He turned his head towards me, raised eyebrows asking the questions.

So I explained. I told Ludlam that Miss Franklin had nursed my father until his death. Ludlam beamed at her. 'That should narrow down the search area a bit. Let me see: you know where it is, I know what's in it, and young Tunnicliffe is the heir, if a slightly illegal heir, to it. It seems to me, Miss Franklin, that we all have similar rights.'

There was a certain amount of argument after that. Miss Franklin disputed his use of the word rights, and he conceded politely that it was perhaps ill-chosen and talked about fairness. What it all boiled down to was that only he had known about the rubies; only she had any idea where the wreck of the aircraft was, and but for me these two valuable pieces of knowledge could not have come together. There was haggling about whether he should come with us or not, but Ludlam was as determined as Miss Franklin. Finally I surprised both of them by telling them to stop, that we were stuck with one another, and that all that remained was the question of the split.

Here, of course, she was on the high ground. We'd already agreed on two-thirds to the mission, one-third to me. It now had to be renegotiated and Miss Franklin was powerfully disinclined to budge. Only she knew where it was, she insisted, cheerfully ignoring the fact that I knew it must be somewhere in the Lobang Nibong area and presumably relying upon me not to introduce that fact. Not that I did. Sense is sense, and Lobang Nibong was only the start for the search, and I knew it. But the point was there in the air between us and she finally – with tremendous reluctance and very little grace – gave way and began to talk fractions. One-third each she ruled out absolutely: the mission must have the lion's share. One-half to the mission and quarters for Ludlam and for me went down the same plughole on the same grounds: more for the Lord than for the sinners. The bottom figure of the fraction kept rising as we sought an accommodation.

In the end, five-ninths turned out to be the Lord's (or

lion's) share, and Ludlam and I were to have two-ninths each. My share kept dwindling. I hoped it would turn out to be two-ninths of something substantial!

We'd intended to start next morning; now we had to put it off while Ludlam bought suitable gear in Kuching; in fact we were delayed two days after that because the coastal trader I'd chartered to take us to the river mouth wouldn't now be available and I had to find another, which entailed something of a search and a good deal of haggling. Meantime Miss Franklin was keeping her beady eyes on Ludlam. She trusted him about as much as I did and had imposed regulations. First, he did not know, and was not to be told, the name of the area we were to explore. Secondly, he was at no time to be out of sight of one or the other of us. So when he went shopping, she went with him; at night, he and I shared a room. We took our meals together. It was far from foolproof, and I suspect her main purpose was to underline her disapproval of Ludlam's general character. It didn't make for a particularly cheerful three days, but Ludlam seemed unworried by our suspicions, even laughing at us occasionally. I continued to brood about Singapore and Miss Franklin reminded Ludlam fairly frequently that the way of the transgressor is justifiably hard.

At the end of the week, we paid our bill at the Odeon Hotel. I made an early-morning telephone call to Freddie Taylor to enquire if there had been changes in the situation on the ground and was told there had not. Then, dressed for adventure, we set off in search of fortune. I think it's fair to say that there was a nice air of anticipation about us, if no song in our hearts.

The grubby little coaster took us out of the Kuching river, past the swamps of the delta, then turned east on a smooth South China Sea to follow the coastline of Sarawak. The skipper had several calls to make, before and after he dropped us off, and he didn't hurry things, tying up alongside ramshackle jetties and drinking tea with the local traders, chatting and generally taking his time as we fussed with impatience because the day was wearing on. We kept asking how long, and he kept saying: two more calls, one more call, and finally it was little more than an hour before dark when the coaster halted. The dinghy was taken from its position on the dirty deck and we began to load first our supplies and then ourselves into it. The tide, happily, was running with us, a fact the coaster's captain pointed out with some pride, as he gazed down loftily at the little rubber boat with its Seagull outboard. If the tide had been against us, he said, the motor would not have been sufficient to run against it. The offended Seagull snarled its answer at the first tug on the starting lanyard, and pushed us smartly away towards the first of the river's countless bends.

Here, as we began, the banks were far away, but the wide mouth narrowed quickly as we headed towards the great wall of forest dead ahead. On either side lamps were beginning to flicker in the stilted houses scattering the shores. The water was brownish green, thick as cough syrup with silt washed down from the interior. Looking back, I could see that the little coaster already had navigation lights at her masthead, and with every passing minute the vastness of the forest ahead grew darker. Overhead the sky was heavy with cloud, whose effect would be to hurry the always speedy onset of darkness. It was no longer a question of how far we'd get up the river while daylight lasted, but whether there'd be enough light to seek out a suitable camp site on the shore and get the tents up.

We came puttering into that first long bend, the ship now out of view behind us, and the river narrowing as we headed for the trees that seemed to grow down almost to the water's edge. With the sun already low, high foliage was blanking off the dimming light. We were beginning to be anxious now; it was essential to get clear of the soft, silted banks before we ventured to put a foot ashore. Essential, too, when we made camp, to be sure where we were making it. Borneo's animal and vegetable life is highly varied, as are the menaces it presents to the careless, and I knew it was all too easy, for instance, to give offence to large colonies of armed and organized ants, not to mention problems of the occasional snake or even crocodile.

Anxiety faded at the sight of a light ahead, shining out from the dark shadows at the forest foot. As we came towards it, the sound of the outboard across the smooth water alerted somebody; the light became larger and square as a door opened and a figure stood silhouetted inside. The man waited at a little improvised jetty as we motored thankfully towards the bank, and an unmistakably Australian voice called to us.

There were three of them as it turned out: botanists from Melbourne University engaged in the apparently endless task of classifying species and sub-species and sub-sub-species, that has apparently been going on for a century and a half and is still far from complete. We were lucky in several ways: first that they were glad to see us; secondly, that they had space and to spare in their hut; thirdly, that they were extremely well-equipped and prepared to feed us; finally, that they were nice people, and very interesting.

I don't know how much Miss Franklin learned that night as we sat in the hut after dinner, drinking coffee and a little Australian brandy, and listening to them talk, but I know I learned a good deal. Borneo is young, as this earth goes; it didn't even rear out of the ocean until long after the age of the dinosaurs. Then, some time during the ice ages, the sea became shallow and for a while dry land connected it to the rest of Asia, and migration after migration of animals took place. When the sea rolled in again, turning Borneo into an island, its immensely diverse variety of animals and plants remained there, and was barely affected by any other major changes in the earth's development. All it had to do was develop and diversify.

They told us there were thousands of species of trees, all mixed together seemingly at random. Not like England with a line of oaks here, and a stand of elms there: examine ten trees and you're likely to have nine or ten different species – and quite a job to identify them unless the bark is very characteristic, because getting your hands on a leaf is tricky unless you're about a hundred feet tall.

The Australians were delighted both by the mammoth job they were undertaking, and the presence of an audience. Their hut was full of slides and specimen bags and microscopes, and an unspoken ambition to make discoveries important enough to have their names attached to them. I could have stayed on there, very happily, for a while.

But Excelsior was the watchword; at least, it was Miss Franklin's. Onward and upward and follow the flag. She had us up and about before dawn and the first starting rasp of the Seagull outboard went echoing across the water well before the sun clambered up, surprisingly suddenly, to gleam golden off the surface of the river.

We estimated about forty miles before the first portages, and hoped to reach the rising land before nightfall, and now as we moved deeper into the forest, the life of both land and water began to teem around us. Birds of brilliance and birds of prey, monkeys racing about the branches, secure in their height above the ground, beside themselves at our presence.

A few times there were small communities by the riverside; two small longhouses with a little white-block school between them, and what looked remarkably like a pair of goalposts set up in a long low space fronting the water. Pigs grunted below the longhouses and children waved from the balcony above. I grinned at them and waved back; I was beginning to enjoy Borneo.

But as the sun rose, all this simple enjoyment began to wear off. Every insect for miles seemed to want to inspect and, if possible, to sample us. We were smothered in repellent creams, but that didn't stop them coming up close to have a good look or make an investigatory landing: and some of them were startling: one dragonfly came zooming in like an attack helicopter, low over us and menacing as only a great insect can be. Its wingspan must have been a foot across! I waved my hat at it, and it went away, but uncles, cousins and aunts of various kinds continued to haunt us.

Still, we were making distance smoothly enough. We didn't expect any problems on the water until we were well clear of the coastal plains and beginning to enter the higher ground, and it was a pleasure to sit in the buoyant little boat, watching the life that teemed in the forest on either bank; like a little group of wild pigs, frightened by the sound of the motor, taking off into shelter at high speed, but in careful single file. Brilliant kingfishers dived like darts, and occasionally a huge, dark hornbill, with its great down-curving beak, slid over us, mooching round its territory. There were no reptiles, apart from one monitor lizard I spotted that lay basking on a rock watching us go by. Five feet long, he must have been!

About eleven o'clock, as Miss Franklin was pouring coffee from a Thermos, a helicopter chattered over, like another and larger jungle insect, crossing the river, not following it, but flying so near the sun in the brief seconds it was visible that I couldn't tell whether it was the army or not. It came back about half an hour later, bumbling obliquely across us, but at fair range. I began to appreciate Freddie Taylor's point about the difficulties of patrolling, and tried to imagine what they'd have seen from the helicopter. Would they have seen us, for instance? Perhaps . . . but from a seat several hundred feet up, the river would be a shadowed canyon in the endless green canopy, glimpsed only for a moment. I know from experience how easy it is to miss things on patrol.

We didn't talk much. I sat steering with the outboard, handle in one hand, coffee cup or cigarette in the other. Miss Franklin, immobile as the monitor lizard, sat gazing rapt at the river banks, smiling occasionally and clearly happy. Ludlam, for some reason, fidgeted endlessly.

He'd shifted his position for about the hundredth time, rocking the boat a bit in the process and causing coffee hot enough to be uncomfortable to fall on my leg, and I said irritably, 'Is that St Vitus's dance?'

'Sorry.' He shifted again, to look back downriver, and it occurred to me that he'd been doing a good deal of that. I wondered why, and said, 'Something the matter?'

Ludlam shrugged. 'Always jumpy in places like this.'

'I thought you were used to the jungle.'

'That was Burma, and it was a long time ago.'

He couldn't keep still at all, and though everything else was so tranquil, the combination of the insects and the fidgeting began to irritate me. Ludlam's head swivelled constantly and his eyes searched restlessly over every little sandbank, every bare patch of shoreline. Most of all, though, he stared back over the stern.

He got me doing it, too, but I saw nothing. The back view was like the one at the front: high trees and water; the only difference was that behind us the water was busy re-forming itself after our passage.

'Beats me what you're looking *for*,' I said.

He shrugged. 'Nothing. Jungle's like this. Always so much of it and always the bloody same.'

He seemed to have changed altogether since we'd set out that morning. The old, perky, confident Ludlam had vanished and in his place sat this twitching little man, and his twitches gradually communicated themselves to me, so that suddenly I wasn't comfortable for more than a few seconds together, and the dinghy began to behave like a trampoline as the pair of us bounced about. It even disturbed Miss Franklin's daydream, and she turned her head and said, 'Keep *still*, for heaven's sake, the pair of you. You're fidgeting like schoolboys!'

I confirmed the resemblance by saying, 'It's him.'

She shifted her position and turned to watch us. 'What do you mean, it's him?'

'It's infectious, like yawning. He can't keep still, so neither can I.'

'Ridiculous!' Miss Franklin said. She turned away, then a moment later turned back.

'You see,' I said, as the boat yawed again. 'You're doing it now.'

'Yes, but why *can't* he keep still?'

'Damned if I know. But he can't. Why can't you?' I said to Ludlam.

'Lot of fuss about nothing,' he said.

She stayed as she was, half turned. A minute or two passed, and then she said, 'Are we being followed, Mr

Ludlam? Is that what's worrying you?'

The thought hadn't occurred to me, but it should have done. All that staring over the back of the dinghy. I said, 'Well, is that what you think?'

'No, do you?'

'I have no cause to think so, Mr Ludlam,' she said.

'Neither have I.'

She was watching him now like mongoose watching snake. 'Because if you do, there's a way to find out.'

'Let me be clear,' Ludlam said, suddenly brisk again. 'I have seen nothing to suggest we're being followed. What I'm doing, for God's sake, is looking round! Something wrong with that?'

She looked at him for a moment more, then addressed herself to me. 'Pull into the bank, just over there.' She pointed. Low trees reaching for the sun leaned out over the river. 'Go in close, upstream of those trees.'

I steered the dinghy over, pulled in beyond the overhang and cut the outboard.

'Now we'll see,' Miss Franklin said. 'Give me the machete.' She stepped ashore and began cutting low branches, draping them over the dinghy until it was hidden, then returned, burrowing beneath them with practised competence. She could have been an instructor at a jungle warfare school.

We sat there, waiting. Ludlam protested once that it was all unnecessary and she told him she hoped so but it was worth being sure. Out of habit I reached for a cigarette. I should have known better – I'm supposed to be trained, after all – and was sharply reminded of it. I looked at my watch and kept looking. Minutes drifted by: two, three, five, ten. As she looked at me I shook my head. Nobody. She shook hers by way of answer, and put her finger to her lips. We were silent, but nothing else was. The jungle shrieked around us, and no doubt a lot of eyes observed us: insect eyes; animal eyes; reptilian eyes. We'd been there about twenty minutes when half a dozen large, revolting leeches looped over the side of the boat on to us, bent on dinner, and one unfortunate found itself on the back of

Miss Franklin's hand, where it was instantly and thoroughly squashed before it could even lay its three horrible teeth against her skin. But those leeches had relatives, and they kept coming in divisional formation, and all the stick-waving in the world did nothing to undermine their blood-lust.

We kept fighting them off, and listening and watching too, at intervals. It seemed to me the noise we made was likely to carry across water and inform any followers of our presence, but Miss Franklin was in command; she intended to endure and we simply had to endure with her, trousers tucked in socks and hats pulled low and careful eyes on such skin as was exposed.

Nothing went by, and watching nothing, in conditions of discomfort and revulsion, is a very slow business. At the end of an hour, I'd had enough. It might be foolish, it might even be insubordination, but I reached for the lanyard, tugged the Seagull into life and, with a little shudder of relief, pushed us away from the bank and the leeches.

As we came out into the middle of the stream, I said, 'Are they always there?'

'Leeches?' Miss Franklin said dismissively. 'You just have to deal with them quickly.'

At least we weren't being followed. 'You can simmer down,' I told Ludlam. 'Nobody's there.'

'Didn't think there was,' he said.

Either Miss Franklin wasn't quite so sanguine, or she preferred to be certain. After only a very few minutes, at a point where the river reached a small arm into the bank, she again told me to pull over. It wasn't so bad, this time, because the little arm was surrounded by drifted silt and the leeches were fewer in number, and handicapped by lack of concealment. We still had to fight them off, though, from time to time.

Again we let an hour go by. Again nothing happened. If anybody was following us upriver, they were doing it with such monumental caution that we were a good two hours ahead. They'd never know which tributary we turned into.

I suppose it was because we'd been busy battling the leeches, and busy watching when we weren't, that we hadn't noticed what the water had been up to. If we'd been on the river, instead of parked to one side, we might have noticed because we'd have been moving faster. But we'd noticed nothing. The river had seemed smooth, and we'd been moored away from the stream. None of us had even noticed that the dinghy was higher in relation to the surrounding vegetation than it had been. Or if anybody had, it had not been mentioned.

As a result, we were completely unprepared as we motored out of our little hiding-place; we may even have been a little smug at the knowledge of our privacy. The Seagull engine sang cheerfully and I took the dinghy out into the middle of the river, swinging her round the next, slow bend.

It was Ludlam, eyes busy as ever, who saw it first. 'Look! What's that?'

It didn't look particularly alarming, then. Two or three biggish waves, following one another, some distance ahead of us, and surprising only because the river had, until then, been so quiet. But the sight of them certainly alarmed Miss Franklin.

She turned in her seat and made a frantic gesture. 'Get in to the bank, quickly, for God's sake!'

CHAPTER ELEVEN

There are a great many things I know nothing about, and tidal bores used to be one of them. Not long ago, I looked up an encyclopaedia to find out a bit more. To get a bore on a river, you need a combination of factors. First a heavy tide, then a river with a wide mouth but narrowing sharply; then you must have no natural block to the water, no rapids or waterfalls, so that there's thirty or forty miles of narrow river. Then, when the tide sweeps huge quantities of water before it, the water can gather far upstream, gain strength, and then pour back as the tide wanes. Simple, really, and apparently they happen all over the place. I'd just never come across one . . .

I did that day. She yelled to me and I, obedient but as yet unworried, swung the dinghy in towards the bank we'd so recently left. I did that first, then asked why.

'Tidal bore,' she said. 'Hurry, you *must* hurry.'

I don't know how quickly it all happened, but it was murderously fast. One moment there was the quiet river, the next the dark, but not threatening lines across it. Then, almost before you could blink, the great, escalating roar of sound as the waves gathered themselves into a vast wall of water that hurtled down on us fast as an avalanche. There was never a chance that we'd reach the bank, though it was no more than thirty yards away; the bore thundered down on us, gobbling distance at unbelievable speed. Height? I don't know; it must have been eight or ten feet, but that's a guess dredged out of an imagination already distorted by surprise. I only know what I did, and even that is confused because everything happened so damned fast. The bore must have travelled half a mile in a few seconds; that, at any rate, is how it seemed.

All I had time to do was turn the dinghy's blunt nose hopefully into it and yell, 'Hang on!'

The wave towered over us now, a great wedge-shape, clean-lined as concrete. If I'd expected anything, it was that it would smash down on us; instead the forward slope drove beneath the dinghy and tossed us high in a contemptuous little flick of power that cartwheeled the dinghy horizontally, spinning it, filling it with water, drenching everything. The thought flashed through my mind at that second that the Seagull was turning behind me, and flapping, too, and that when we were spun over the side, its propeller would be damned dangerous. Still spinning, the dinghy sat perched for a moment on the wave's high back; momentarily I glimpsed another behind it, before we glissaded down the dark, glistening back of the ridge of water.

Instantly the second was driving under us, and lifting,

and because the dinghy was already half-tipped, it was flipped upwards on its side, turning slowly in the air to fall, inevitably, upside down. I was hanging grimly on to the thin line that looped round the rim of the dinghy's side. A lot of our gear was tied to that line, too. It had seemed a sensible precaution, when we'd set off: but what now happened was that the jerricans, the food cases and water cans, the rifle cases, everything was swinging with gravity and centrifugal force, smashing me in the same second in a dozen places.

I thought of nothing but keeping my grip. Totally disorientated, with no idea which way was up, down or sideways, I was simultaneously being spun and buffeted, crushed and bruised. The thin cord bit into my hands, but among the other pains it was a minor one. I was waiting, and hoping and praying, too, that there were only two waves, that when they passed, calm water would lie behind them. The dinghy was lifted, turned, smashed down again. The waves spun it and flicked it; eddies of power drove beneath it to try to pluck me away. A second or two more, surely, and the wave must pass by! What I forgot was that we were being carried along on the bore; that as the rock-hard ridges of water boiled along, we were stuck in the middle, bouncing helplessly with every movement of the water.

Seconds of held breath, held with a struggle as the water and our own captive equipment, now turned into flails and hammers, tried to bounce the breath out of me . . . I was beneath the dinghy as, buoyant as a cork, it floated upside down . . . Suspended by the arms, my body was treated like a whip, now lifted clear as the inflated boat leapt upwards, now plunged deep as another unpredictable surge of force thrust down on it.

I was drowning, by now. My mouth had been forced open and the river had driven its way in, past the throat and down into the lungs. Coughing opened my mouth again to more water and the retching combined with all the other blows from the merciless thrashing of our tethered equipment to try to drive the life out of me. Somehow, in desperation, I dragged enough of the line loose to make a loop and twist my wrist into it. I remember doing *that*, and it's the last thing I do remember . . .

What happened, then, I don't know, and never will. The dinghy was carried a long way, and I went with it, unconscious and uncaring. But, having wrecked me, the river must have decided it could save me, too. The dinghy must have flicked over in the tail of the last wave, and been guided towards the shore by tricks of the current. I became aware, inside the darkness of my own half-consciousness, that the world was still again. I opened my eyes, looked clean into the sun and, half-blinded by it, shut them again, and turned and began to feel with my free hand. It touched a tree root, and I grabbed it and held on and after a moment opened my eyes again. I lay cradled in roots, with the dinghy tilted over them beside me. I began to cough, and it went on for minutes, searing and painful, the brown water coming up thick, sticky and reluctant from my lungs. I moved my legs a little, and they moved well enough, bruised but serviceable. My arms. One was free. The other . . . the other had the rope looped round it, and I couldn't feel my fingers. Panicked more by that than anything else, I hoisted myself painfully clear of the dinghy and began to try to free it. The rope had cut deeply into my wrist, and blood seeped steadily down over hand and arm, where three of those horrendous leeches stuck feeding. You're not supposed to tear them off: a cigarette end, so they say, or some salt: a touch with either and the leech releases its grip. But my revulsion was too great for patience; I simply ripped them away, and rinsed the arm in the river, hoping that whatever was left in the little triangular wounds wouldn't fester.

There were others on my chest, legs and back, feeding happily through the material of my soaked clothing, and I pulled them away, one by one, sickened by their greedy battening, and flung them from me with a kind of shuddering disgust.

I suppose, though, that they did me a favour in a way.

By the time I'd got rid of the loathsome things, I was at least thoroughly conscious, and as the last of them popped into the water, I also began to think.

And then to look around.

There was no sign of Miss Franklin. Nor of Ludlam.

I didn't sit and think long, but I had to try to work things out. They must have been whipped off the boat by the waves. I'd been saved by the dinghy's buoyancy; but if they had had no buoyancy to protect them, they'd have been helpless against the giant forces of that tremendous onslaught.

I must now search, hopeless as it seemed. Upstream or down? It seemed to me, after brief consideration, that the waves *must* have carried the dinghy along more efficiently and faster than they'd carry two half-submerged bodies. Stood to reason, I told myself. Less drag. And the dinghy would have moved downstream *after* the waves had passed, whereas Ludlam and Miss Franklin . . .

With feeling returning to my right hand, I struggled to pop the boat on the water again, then to make enough order out of the chaos in the bottom to give me a place to sit. The next job was to start the Seagull and I looked at it doubtfully. It was a mercy it *had* stopped, but that wasn't much consolation: dousing small engines with water and then waving them about isn't exactly recommended treatment. A few pulls on the lanyard produced nothing. *Damn!* Where, in all the chaos, was the tool kit? Probably on the bottom of the bloody river. I hunted for it for a moment or two, until the thought crept into my fat head that the engine had ended up upside down; that it might even have been low on fuel. With the filler cap off, I looked into the little tank and gave a shake. Nothing swishing about. I untied one of the jerricans, still mercifully attached to the line, and sloshed petrol in, then began tugging again. The first five pulls produced only frustrated grunts from me; the sixth drew a grunt from the outboard; the seventh brought it to smooth, even-running life! It sat there singing at me as though saying: all you have to do is treat me properly. I gave it a friendly pat on the petrol tank and pushed away from the bank.

Downstream first. Three or four hundred yards ought to be enough. I watched the banks as I went, hoping to see something, anything, that might mean they had survived, but there was only the water and the green. The jungle was its unchangeable self. I thought grimly that a small matter like a death would leave no marks here.

There was nothing to raise a flicker of hope. Kingfishers still dived, monkeys still leaped about the high branches, the treetops waved unconcernedly above. After a quarter of a mile, I turned the dinghy and began to motor back upstream, torn between the need to hurry and anxiety to miss nothing. I came to the point where the tree roots had trapped the dinghy, and went slowly past. How far had the wave carried me? It was hard to tell. I was on a bend in the river, but the damned thing was all bends. The waves had moved so fast! How many seconds to cover how much distance? No way to make that calculation. I could be searching in the wrong place entirely. I puttered slowly, steadily upstream, hoping every second there would be something to indicate what the river had done to them. Several times, heart thumping, I drove in close to one bank or the other to look at a something that had seemed, momentarily, to be human; it never was. One big patch of pinkish fungus had my hopes high until I was only yards away, then dashed them with its stink as I came close.

A little sandbank jutted from the right-hand bank and I tried to remember whether I'd seen it before. Torn branches and mud clothed it now, dumped there by the waves, and it was a second or two before I realized that one of those branches, waving a little as I passed, wasn't a branch at all but an arm! I whipped the dinghy's nose round. The arm reached up out of a little mud pile that heaved slowly upwards until it was a torso. I jumped on to the bank, carrying the boat's line, and scraped mud away from Ludlam's face.

There was mud in his mouth and in his nose; it was a

wonder he had been able to breathe at all. I dragged him towards the water and began to sluice it all off him as he spat and choked and retched and grunted. I flicked him over on his belly, then, and began to apply artificial respiration, to push water out of his stomach, too. A few pushes and he sputtered, 'Christ!' Not long after that he mustered a little grin. His next word was 'Thanks', and shortly afterwards he said, 'Disgusting bloody filth!' and began to sluice water over himself. I picked him up bodily, dumped him in the dinghy and pushed off again. I'd found *one*. Was there a chance of a miracle – a chance I'd find them both? As we inched upstream again, he told me, as far as he could recall, what had happened to him. The first wave had simply ripped him out of the boat. He'd managed a single breath as it drove him deep into the river: how deep, he'd no idea, but 'I was pushed through the mud on the bottom like the blade of a plough, and fetched up with a bump against what felt like a bloody great rock. I was crushed against it. All my breath came out in a horrible whoosh and I couldn't move. Just held there by the pressure. Then, just as I thought the pressure was going to crush me, it disappeared, and I gave a shove with my feet. Must have inhaled a hell of a lot as I came up. But that's all I remember.'

Obviously the rock had saved him, holding him fast while the waves tore by above, and once he reached the surface, the current had pushed him on to the bank.

As he sat, coughing and slowly recovering, I kept searching those damned river banks, hoping and praying that Miss Franklin had had comparable luck, but as time meandered on, I began to be afraid that that tough little body, and the tough little spirit that inhabited it, had been broken at last in her beloved Borneo. It was, in a way, what she'd have wanted, though I'm always wary about people who say that kind of thing about the dead. Oh yes, they say, he'd have wanted to go like that. Heart attack at the golf-club, bullets in action, there's always somebody ready with the platitude; but in my experience nobody wants to go at all, and the ones nearest the exit are the most reluctant.

In my mind, now, she was dead already. There'd been one piece of magic for me and another for Ludlam; to expect a third was to expect altogether too much. But I might have known, really: the Miss Franklins of this world make their own miracles, and when, finally, we came level with the spot where she'd cut the branches to shelter the boat, there she was on her own two feet, yelling across the water at us: waving with one hand and fighting off the leeches with the other. As we came to her, she nipped smartly aboard and took a swift look at the dinghy, then began issuing instructions. 'Go straight to that little arm of the river where we waited before,' she said. 'We *must* do something about all this!'

She'd been the practical one. Seeing the wave coming, she'd dived deep, trying to get under, and succeeding in part, staying down, trying to face into the onrushing water. She'd been somersaulted over and over, and forced down, and had accepted it, rolling with the strength and finally trying to swim with it. She surfaced just behind the third wave and used its power as best she could to fight her way across the bend, bobbing in the turmoil, but making it finally to the bank. She made very little of it, characteristically making it sound more a matter of sense than survival, and at the finish offering a brisk little prayer of thanks on behalf of the three of us. But she was irritated with God at that moment; her thanks might be humble, but her tone wasn't.

We began, then, to get ourselves in some sort of order. Astonishingly, though we were all bumped and bruised, we were in reasonable working order, and the same was true of our equipment. The jerricans were bashed and dented, but only one had been opened. The supposedly waterproof bags holding our equipment hadn't kept the river out, but they had kept the kit in, which was more important. We built a fire on the sandbank and set about drying clothes and heating water for a hot drink. Ludlam and I laced our coffee with whisky and were reproved for doing so at that time of day, but need overcame disapproval and I for one drank boldly and defiantly.

Then, tired and aching, we were off again. 'At least,' Miss Franklin said, 'we can now be reasonably certain we're not being followed.' I didn't quite see how she reached that conclusion, but she seemed happy with it, and soon had resumed her serene survey of plant and animal life.

After a bit I disturbed the serenity. 'How come,' I asked her, 'that you didn't tell us about that damn great wave? I thought you knew this country.'

She turned to stare at me, detecting facetiousness in honest enquiry. 'I have travelled this river only once,' she said, 'and the bore must have been small that day. It must have been a low tide.'

'Only once?' I said, puzzled. 'But you must have been up and down several times.'

She shook her head. 'After 1945 this was not my area. I told you that.'

And so she had. She escaped from the Japs over on the Dutch side of the mountains, and walked. Looking at the jungle beside us, I thought about that walk, and about the years of living in hiding, the long, hard war she'd had. I sat looking at her narrow, straight back, and the guardsman's set to her head, and I thought: it would take more than a river bore, wouldn't it, Miss Franklin?

One way and another, we were still on the big river at nightfall; we'd hoped to turn into the first tributary on the route to Libong, but too much time had been lost and about five o'clock we started to look for a place to set up camp. First thing we needed was a good smoky fire to keep the local livestock at bay; after that we put up our nice, sophisticated tents, with their sewn-in ground sheets and long zips on the openings that would exclude anything short of a rhinoceros. We ate, I smoked, Ludlam and I had another medicinal whisky, and then we went to bed.

Ludlam dropped off at once; I don't know about Miss Franklin, but probably she did, too. But sleep was not for me. Every bone seemed to ache, and my mind too, but it wasn't that which kept me relentlessly awake so much as my own thoughts and the sounds of the jungle outside. I stared up at the thin, nylon ridge of the tent, knowing that all around me there was teeming activity. In the daytime the jungle looks vast, it looks formidable, it looks deep and secret. But it's green and brown, friendly colours, and above all, it's possible to see. That night I was preternaturally sensitive to every sound, and they came thick and fast upon me, many of them strange, sudden and indescribably eerie. There was a background, constant and almost as loud as traffic in a big city, of humming, pinging insect sounds. There were strange rustlings in the trees, and from time to time a cry, a shriek, close yet ghostly, as though some lost spirit yelled outside the tent. A snake seizing a monkey? A nightbird? Swarming millions of creatures were outside, hunting each other, killing each other, eating each other, replacing each other. For hours I lay with a profound sense of my own lack of importance in this world. Die at home, and somebody grieves, or at least knows. Die here, and neither the forest nor its creatures is affected, or even notices anything except a new food source, a little more decaying matter.

I must have dropped off eventually, though with fear in my throat, lonelier than I've ever felt. We'd come very close to death that day, and survived. Would it come for us again, somewhere in the remoteness ahead, and this time irresistibly?

I woke to frying ham. Miss Franklin, of course, busy and practical, up for hours already and with our wet kit spread on bushes to dry in the morning sun. There weren't any eggs to go with the bacon – they were casualties of the bore – but there was something else, an edible fungus that looked awful, smelled odd, yet when one finally managed to get it past one's nose, tasted delicious. She told me its name, but I've forgotten it. It was marvellous though, like mushrooms flavoured with sweet tea, and if that sounds revolting, let me assure you it wasn't. There was steaming coffee and a cigarette to follow, and by then the night's ghosties had crawled back into their cupboards. By the time we'd packed up and were ready to move off, optimism had begun to reign again.

At mid-morning we seemed to have come to the first major tributary, the one we wanted. Ludlam and I checked it on our maps, then I swung the boat into it, past a long brownish-yellow sandbar. The waterway was narrower here: not much more than twenty-five yards or so, and the great trees on either side met overhead in a thick mat of foliage that excluded direct sunlight. It was light enough, but with a strange kind of light that seemed to throw no shadows and offered no reflections on the water. That ran more swiftly, too, with rocks breaking the surface here and there, and the current streaming from them. But the Seagull pushed us cheerfully forward, more slowly now that it had to cope with a stronger stream, but with the healthy roar of bright confidence.

We hit the first rapids at noon. And it was then that the real torture began. First they had to be reconnoitred, and for much of the time we had to cut our way yard by yard along the bank; or rather I did, because Ludlam seemed not to have the strength. Three hundred yards sounds little enough, but it took nearly two hours to clear a track through. There were creepers and thorns, high, clinging grasses in places, and underfoot the earth was made of soft, decaying vegetation that slung slimily to our boots.

The path had to be cleared properly, too; we'd a lot of stuff to carry up past those rapids, and it would be taxing enough on a clear path, without the added difficulty of fighting a way through undergrowth. So I laboured and sweated with the machete, careful always where I put my feet, and careful, too, to see what was on a branch before I hit it, because once, early on, only Miss Franklin's shouted warning stopped me slashing close to a small snake which lay, curled and camouflaged in a fork, watching us. It stayed still for a few moments, then unhurriedly slithered to the ground and off into the thick mould.

'Krait,' Miss Franklin said.

'How dangerous?'

'As you see, it got out of the way.'

'But venomous?'

'Oh yes, its bite is lethal.' She seemed entirely unconcerned.

I wasn't, though. If I'd struck, and it had struck, one of us would have died, probably me. 'Do they always get out of the way?'

'Yes, as a rule. Unless you tread on one. Except the cobra. The cobra *is* aggressive. You must keep your eyes open!'

I did. Sweat might be running down into them as I slashed and ripped at branches and foliage, but my eyes scarcely closed long enough to blink. A complex world of insect and lizard life lived among that thick, luxurious plant growth: some of it beautiful, some of it not. Butterflies lifted fluttering ahead of me, lizards darted, leeches looped, and I hacked my increasingly weary way forward, yard by yard.

When at last we reached a small, clear patch on the river bank just above the rapids, I was exhausted, aching all over, my arms a mass of small scrapes and cuts, my neck and face bitten a hundred times by vengeful insects. I sank to the ground and stretched out. It was blissful, but brief. Miss Franklin's forebears must have included Arab slave-drivers and she was urging me to my feet again before I was half-way down my cigarette.

We had to march back the way we'd come, and begin the long slow business of hand-hauling our equipment. If you'd care to imagine what it was like, imagine picking up a five-gallon jerrican in either hand and carrying them most of the way round a running track, an uphill one, with the temperature in the high eighties, and then going back and doing it again. And again. And then, finally, with everything moved except the boat, going back to deflate it, and then carrying a good hundredweight of black rubber.

Even then it wasn't over, because the dinghy now had to be pumped up again. I was more or less taking a bath in my own perspiration by this time, stamping rhythmically on that damned footpump and apparently making no impact at all. The collapsed dinghy lay there, limp and unenthusiastic, and I forced air into it, until finally my calf muscles exchanged one sort of agony for another by coiling into cramp.

Miss Franklin, naturally, knew the answer to that. She found salt from a plastic container and poured some into my hand as I writhed in spasm. 'Eat that, it will help' It didn't, though, or not for a while, and I treated myself to the pleasure of observing Master Ludlam's spindly leg at work on the pump. He didn't enjoy it half as much as I did, cramp or no cramp. There's not much fun in being the strong young man, it seemed to me, and I was determined to savour what fun there was.

He didn't have a seizure, but I reckon it was a close thing. By the time the dinghy was inflated again, he looked like a small, greasy spot; face purple, clothing soaked. Towards the end, as I sat massaging my calf muscles and trying to suppress my grins, I noted that he kept glancing at Miss Franklin. One big question was whether he'd have the nerve to ask her to take her turn; a second was whether she'd offer. The answer to both was: no.

Eventually, though, we were out on the river again. Mid-afternoon by this time, and only Miss Franklin in anything approaching decent nick. I rested my aching bones against the resilience of the rubber, smoked as I steered, and said very little. Miss Franklin sat forward, giving the passing forest the benefit of her full attention, and said nothing either. Ludlam lay collapsed, more or less, beside me. He grunted and groaned occasionally, but those were the only sounds he made.

We were due to make another turn a few miles up that first tributary, but it was clear we weren't going to make it that day. As the gloom beneath the trees began to intensify, we looked once more for a place to camp.

The night was very much like the one before, except that I did not lie awake so long. Sheer weariness shoved me under the velvet black as soon as I crawled into my sleeping-bag, and though one ghastly shrieking wail right outside the tent brought me bolt upright about three in the morning, even the roar of the jungle traffic wasn't enough to keep me conscious and philosophizing for more than a minute or two.

I felt better in the morning: stiff and aching, but full of energy, and it was just as well, because if I'd known what lay ahead, I'd have pointed the dinghy in the opposite direction and headed back downstream at full power.

CHAPTER TWELVE

I looked at the second run of rapids, when we encountered them about mid-morning, and thought that they didn't look anything like so bad. But they were – my God they were! That first sight was of a short scatter of rocks, rising almost like a stair up the middle of the river, with green-brown water turned to white round the rocks themselves, but running smooth between them. There looked to be a fall of sixty or seventy feet, steep but short, and I tackled the tangled scrub along the bank with early-day energy and a sense that the job would soon be over. If I'd been able to see the shape of the surrounding ground, I might have known better, but there was no way to get a picture of the topography: to left and right the jungle streamed towards the sky, matting across it two hundred feet above the river. From the bank it was possible to see a few feet into that extraordinary mass of tree and creeper, shrub and bush, but only a few feet; after that the sheer bulk of everything turned into a wall. The lushness of the vegetation hereabouts was quite unbelievable, the size of the monster trees almost overpowering, and they were closer together than one would have believed possible. The unique Borneo combination of endless water, masses of decaying matter for food, and the days of hot humidity, produce perfect growing conditions. I swear those trees stood close together as spectators at a football match.

At the beginning I hacked away hopefully. The ground rose ahead in the only place we could see it, and even in the steamy heat there was a kind of mental cool in the proximity of rushing water. And there was a rock, high in the middle of the river, to act as a kind of measuring post. Every time I stopped to wipe away the sweat it came a little closer, immobile but encouraging. It took me an hour of hacking and chopping to get near, and when I did I felt like yelling a greeting to it. But it had encouraged only to deepen despair. When, with a sense of triumph, I came level with that blasted rock, it was to see that although behind it lay a short stretch of flat water, not far away the rapid continued, straight and climbing, for an awful long way, in an expanse of creaming white water tearing between jagged rocks.

It was a hell of a day: I never want to see another like it, and don't expect to. There was no question of Ludlam or Miss Franklin taking the lead in cutting a track for us. Both tried, but neither any longer possessed strength or endurance to fight hour after hour at a green tangle that seemed to be growing as I looked at it. Gradually and a little crazily I got the impression that if I stopped for a moment it would swarm back over me like some science-fiction nightmare.

Nor was the vegetation the only thing to fight. The ground here was thick with leeches, the air humming with stinging insects, and there was no let-up in their attack. Every time I stopped for a few moments' rest it became harder to start again. Fatigue tightened my muscles and increasing weariness ate into such reserves of will as remained. Hack one way, hack another: forehand, backhand, up-stroke, down-stroke, and every swing of the machete in a different direction. No chance here to slip into the rhythm a man can achieve with axe or scythe.

After a couple of hours, close to exhaustion, I flung down the machete and asked Ludlam to return to the dinghy and get a rope. I was utterly immune now to the beauties of the things around me: the flowers, the insects, the multi-coloured fungi, the great trees. The only thing attractive to me here was the rush of water, and I was going to give my aching body the benefit of contact with it. The rope was a precaution. The river raced so fast between the rocks that I knew I'd be swept away without it, so I made a running loop round my chest, told Ludlam to hang on tight, and slipped into the river in a narrow little eddy where water slid fast and smooth between a rock outcrop and the bank. For a moment there was that exquisite pleasure cool water gives to a hot, tired body. It lasted only an instant; the water's power was enormous, sweeping me immediately to the limit of the rope, tightening it round my chest, spinning me spluttering in its grip. I had no more control than a twig would have had, and a lot less buoyancy, and something in the way the water swept at me seemed to drive me under. I managed to get to the surface, and get a swift glimpse of the bank, where Ludlam and Miss Franklin were hanging on to the rope, leaning steeply backward, trying to haul me in. Yet the power of the current was clearly too much for their combined weight. After that there was no clarity to my thoughts at all. I only knew that if the rope slipped from their hands, I'd be swirled away into that mass of boulders below, crashing from one to another, overwhelmed in a second or two, drowned in a few more. In the meantime I couldn't breathe. The rope round my chest was tied in a running loop, a big noose that seemed to be cutting into my chest, tightening until it was squeezing the air out of me. I was fighting and thrashing, but my head broke the surface only occasionally.

It was Ludlam who saved me, though at the time I didn't sense it. The next glimpse I had of the two of them, leaning back like an old, tired tug-o'-war team, showed that they were farther away than they had been before, so their grip must be slackening. They couldn't hold me any longer against the appalling strength of the water's flow! It meant there could be only one end : the river must win. Its strength was endless, constant, unyielding.

I panicked terribly, smashing at the water with my arms, kicking with my legs, trying always to fight my way out of the green opacity of the racing water to the light above. And losing, losing, all the time losing . . . My foot touched rock suddenly, grazingly, and I yelled in fear, but soon more than my foot was touching it; soon my body was being pressed against it. In a moment I'd be crushed against it, then swept to one side or the other, away downstream.

I had to grasp that rock, find something to hang on to. And at least now I had a trace of stability. The current couldn't do two things at once: couldn't spin and swirl me like a toy and *still* crush me against the rock! There was a small cleft. I ran my hand inside, balled it into as near a fist as I could manage, trying to anchor myself to it, then felt upwards. Miraculously there was another crack within reach . . . Two handholds. And the rope. I wrenched upwards, twisting pain into my jammed hands as I did so, got my head out of water, and managed to glance back. They'd edged a little to one side, belaying the rope against a tree, letting its strength help theirs. I levered myself upwards again; now, a yard above my head was the top of the rock, and if I could . . . but the water held my legs, streaming them away to the left, trying to draw me out into another racing stream. I couldn't drag my legs back. Could I lift one of them? Get a hold for it? Could I? To do it I had to shift one hand, and in doing so came very close to losing what precarious grip I had. But there was another small cleft, and if I could . . . I *did*! With hands securely jammed again, I heaved my body upwards and got most of my chest clear. One more heave and I was out to the waist. Another – and I was flopping on to the rock's surface like a landed fish to lie gasping and spent on the warm stone.

It was minutes before I could stand. The knot round my chest had to be loosened before I could draw a single decent breath.

'Are you all right?' Ludlam yelled, his voice close by. With no breath to answer, I nodded.

When I got to my feet it was to stand no more than seven feet from the two of them as they stood looking anxiously at me from the bank. Seven feet. And between us the green-white water raced lethally through its compressing channel. Not far: only seven feet. And all I had to do was jump. Equally, all I had to do was slip, and I'd be swept away again. I stood there waiting for strength, but it was a long time in coming. After that I stood nerving myself. I told myself that small children jump effortlessly over seven-foot puddles: all I had to do was the same. It was simple enough. But if I slipped . . .

They had the rope secure, now, tied to a tree, and kept saying, 'Come on, jump!' In the end I did. It was very easy.

There was no more hacking until the afternoon was well on. I was too tired and the other two couldn't do it. I ate and rested and smoked and drank a little Scotch and a lot of coffee, until I felt something like George Tunnicliffe again, and less like a sloth at the end of its strength. But finally conscience or something got me to my feet and the machete began to swing again.

There wasn't a hope of getting to the top of the rapid that day; the top wasn't even in sight, for one thing. I'd thought it rose straight, but as night began to drop on us, it was already dreadfully clear that at the end of the straight section, it curved away into a bend. But we worked. It was a gesture. When we stopped, I looked at Ludlam and Miss Franklin. She was weary as we all were. Her hair, though grey, had always been that shiny, somehow competent grey that bespeaks health and control. Now it straggled in perspiration-soaked tails down the sides of her face. She looked her age that day, and obviously felt it, too. If I'd taken the brunt of the work, up ahead swinging the heavy machete, neither she nor Ludlam had been idle behind me. I cut and they dragged the result away, pushing it clear of the path I was making. In absolute terms they were expending fewer foot pounds of energy, but toss the little matter of age into the equation, and I suppose they, too, were being taxed to the limit.

There was no bright conversation that night. No surprising taste sensations from among the fungi, because none of us felt in the least like hunting for them. I doubt if any of us would have had the strength even to pick them. We ate out of tins, heated water for a hot drink, and sank depressed into our sleeping-bags; we hadn't, any of us, expected to spend two nights at the same camp.

The night was by in a flash. I woke groaning with aches and stiffnesses, and not feeling much refreshed. I didn't ask either Ludlam or Miss Franklin how they felt, because there was no need. The pair of them moved like automata, in gloomy silence, breakfasted likewise, and emitted sighs to match mine at the prospect of returning to the war with the jungle, though it could be put off no longer.

The new day consisted of hour upon weary hour of the same. Stiff muscles did loosen a bit, but the heat rose, so it was swings and roundabouts: less discomfort here, more there. I felt, as the day dragged by, more like some kind of crazy unbalanced metronome than a sentient human being. Senses, indeed, ceased to matter. What did matter was the capacity to endure, and the will to get through. If either of them disappeared, we might just as well turn back. Somehow, though, they didn't; probably because having done so much, we'd disgrace ourselves by not doing a little more. And a little more. And more, and more, and more. When we did at last break through, it was unexpectedly. The view ahead had been obstructed by a rock outcrop and it had seemed just another barrier to work our way round. In fact it stood at the head of the rapid, and as we came level, the miracle lay before us: the river, green-brown and smooth-surfaced, clear for at least a mile ahead.

But there was still the portage. Heavy navvy work: goods to be humped yet again up slopes: more cursing, more wishing we'd never started, more scratches and bites, but above all a determination to move, and a common feeling that it would be unthinkable to spend a third night in the same spot. I won't dwell on that portage, nor on the aching agony of reinflating the dinghy. I'll move straight on to the happy moment when I said, 'Any more for the Skylark?' Nobody smiled as we scrambled aboard. But then that beautiful Seagull gave its little snarl of happiness and we nosed forward, and I for one at once felt a bit better.

We covered that first, visible mile, swept into the bend, and discovered that there, too, the water was free of obstruction, that we could motor steadily up against the current. For as long as we dared, we went on, the river unwinding itself clear ahead. It wasn't far, three or four miles at the most; but it was sweet. Then the same evening routine, rushed this time because we'd left it a bit late. On the other hand we were quicker and more practised at making camp, and a bit of energy had been restored; enough, at any rate, for us actually to discuss what we'd like to eat, and to take a little time preparing it.

I watched the other two as I ate, trying not to be too obvious about it. They were feeling the strain. I reminded myself not to be too patronizing towards my elders: I was feeling it, too, and probably looked as bushed as they did. Good job we couldn't see our own faces. But I was wrong about that. Miss Franklin must have had a mirror tucked away somewhere and she vanished into her tent and used it, and came out again with her hair in determined subjection, wearing clean clothes and a smile and carrying something concealed behind her back.

She was even playful. 'Guess what?'

I thought of something unlikely and said, 'Petit fours.' Not very bright, but there was no real brightness in any of us: just readiness to make the effort.

'Not precisely,' she said, 'but if you have some, this will go with them.' She handed me half a bottle of brandy.

'*Miss* Franklin!' I said in mock reproval.

'You have earned it.' Schoolmarmish as ever. Rewards for effort only – but none the less welcome. As I poured and sipped, it occurred to me that if I'd known about it earlier in the day, when I was totin' dem damn bales up the path I'd cut, I'd cheerfully have thrown it in the river to get rid of a bit of weight. Glad now, though, that I hadn't.

'There seems to come a time,' she said, 'when brandy is the *only* suitable thing. That's why I bought it.'

'Quite right,' I said, sipping further.

'But not too much!'

'Of course not.'

'It has to last. There may be another time.'

'Like this?' I said. I passed the bottle to Ludlam. He'd earned it, too. So had she, for that matter, but she showed no inclination to sample its quality.

'Will there be more rapids like that?'

'You knew there were rapids. I told you.'

'You didn't say what they were like!'

She hesitated. 'These are very bad. As bad as I've seen.'

'But you came down this river. You must have remembered something of it?'

'Not a thing.'

'Why not? I'll remember it for the rest of my days.'

'I think,' she said, 'that I wasn't quite conscious.'

'You don't know the river ahead, either?'

'Not immediately ahead, no.' Then, abruptly, 'Do you want to turn back?'

'No,' I said. Was she looking for a way out? If so, I should offer it. 'What about you, do you want to go on? If you don't, I'll – '

As so often she didn't let me finish. 'Thank you, but no.'

I thought I might as well ask Ludlam, too. He'd been distinctly un-perky the last couple of days, though he'd held his own. 'What about you? How's Jamaica sound now?'

He took a swig of brandy and gave his little grin. 'Later,' he said. 'After it's over.'

It wasn't much of a conversation, and it didn't continue, but it had done something for us. There was agreement: we were all still going ahead. Resolve remained.

Next morning resolve had multiplied in Miss Franklin. There was a fried breakfast, giving off a smell appetizing enough to tempt the dead from their graves, and it prised me out of my tent famished as a newly-wakened squirrel. As I inhaled the food, she took a piece of paper and pinned it to a tree-trunk with a knife.

I looked up at the sound. 'What's what?'

'What do you say in the army – part one orders?'

'Covering immediate activity, yes.'

She examined the paper. 'It says here, one day's leave for all ranks.'

'Eh?'

She laughed. 'It doesn't have to be all suffering. Let's move on, find a nice spot, and relax. Bathe – '

This time *I* interrupted. 'I have bathed, you remember?'

'Borneo's not always like that. There'll be a natural pool somewhere along the river. Somewhere safe and pleasant.'

'Without crocodiles,' I said.

'Only in the deltas, George.'

'Or water snakes.'

'We'll keep a look out for them.'

'You're on!' I said.

Ludlam, when he came crawling out of our tent, like a rodent after a rough night, was not averse either; in fact, he was delighted. And I can't recall a better day in my life: everything about it perfect, all the better because it looked, at first, as though disaster had struck.

We hadn't gone two miles before we struck another rapid, tumbling out of the mouth of a rocky gorge. Hearts sank audibly all around. Instead of the relaxation we'd promised ourselves, it looked as though we faced another day of slogging it out, hand to hand, with Nature's exuberance. But no: the gorge was short, the walls provided almost a staircase, with sound footings all the way up, and at the head of the gorge the river widened into what was almost a small lake that even had, to our delight, a small stretch of sand and a break in the overhead that let the sun through. We swam, all of us: Ludlam a wiry little crawl stroke, Miss Franklin the old-fashioned trudgeon, and I with my primitive, muscle-bound crawl. Fun. We even splashed each other, and laughed. We stretched out and sunbathed, ate well and cheerfully, fished successfully. For once the river here was almost leech-less, the insects merely decorative, and there were huge flowers gaping at the sunlight. It resembled one of those old films about idealized South Sea islands – though thank God without the guitars. I thought at one point in that happy day that there are plenty of things about civilization that one misses when they're not there. No pubs, no hot baths, no Sunday newspaper. But there's not a guitar or a pop group within miles, and that counts for a lot.

Evening came, lasted a few minutes, turned to night, and

even that was good, the camp was already made, the fire
going, the fish ready to cook. Pleasure continued, I can tell
you, and a certain optimism circulated, because we'd had a
good look at the maps and made some calculations. Another
twenty-five miles or so and we'd reach a part of the country
Miss Franklin remembered well and she could promise no
major rapids up there. There'd be a few short portages,
but nothing serious. Brandy for two and prayers for one
rounded off the day, and we went to sleep contented and at
peace.

But the awakening wasn't like that. There were four of
them; they were filthy, they stank, they were armed to the
teeth, and they stared at us in grim silence as we crawled
out of our tents.

CHAPTER THIRTEEN

'Wha' are ye people doin' here?' The accent came from
somewhere in Scotland, Glasgow possibly from the harsh,
emphatic tone. He was looking at me, his face flat and
expressionless. His eyes flickered momentarily in surprise
as Miss Franklin emerged.

'I said, wha' are ye –'

'We're going upriver.'

His head gave a little jerk in Miss Franklin's direction.
'Wi' her?'

I nodded, and asked a question of my own. 'Who are
you?'

'Patrol.'

'What regiment?'

'None o' your business. Ye have permission?'

'Yes.'

'Army permission?'

'Yes.'

He looked us over again, little puckers of exasperation at
the corners of his mouth. Clearly he thought they were

mad in Kuching. 'Names?'

I told him.

'Where upriver?'

I told him that too. I'd no difficulty in guessing who they were: four quiet, confident men who, for all the dirt, were soldiers to their toenails, upright and alert, same height and weight near enough, same steady eyes, weapons as natural in their hands as knives and forks. But no marks on the muddy jungle camouflage suits to indicate either unit or rank. Special Air Service. *Crème de la crème* in Her Majesty's service. Freddie Taylor hadn't told me they were here. But then he wouldn't: they come and go unannounced.

I said, 'How are things in Hereford?' Their depot is there. The grey eyes flicked at me. 'You army?'

'I was.'

'Whit aboot her?'

'Miss Franklin's a retired missionary nurse.'

'Here?'

'Yes.'

'Who's the wee man?' A jerk of the head at Ludlam.

I grinned. 'Careful. He used to wear red tabs.'

He didn't grin back. 'Where's your authorization?'

'No bits of paper,' I said. 'Check with Captain Taylor at General Walker's HQ.'

Captains and generals didn't impress him any more than Ludlam's old red tabs, and in any case he couldn't check. If they had a radio, it wasn't with them now, and probably would be valueless anyway, as Taylor had explained.

He said slowly, 'Ye'll have to gang back doon the water.'

'Why?' Miss Franklin came in when she shouldn't, her voice quiet, but all ready to be awkward.

He didn't look at her, but at me. 'If ye're a soldier, ye'll mebbe guess.'

'Action?' I asked. He didn't respond.

'We're going upriver,' Miss Franklin said emphatically.

He glanced at her then, and no doubt read determination in her eyes; he could scarcely have missed it. He said, 'I cannae order ye, but ye'd better take advice.'

'When I want advice – !'

But Ludlam cut in. 'You're tracking.'

'Dinna mind what we're doin'. It's ye people –'

Ludlam said crisply, 'Let me finish. If you're tracking, you don't want movement. They said in Kuching that there might be a war party up here. You carry on. We'll go to ground.'

The SAS man shook his head, glancing at his watch. 'Away now. Quick.'

'They're near?' Ludlam insisted.

'Just go.'

'No,' Ludlam said. A stubborn monosyllable worthy of Miss Franklin herself.

It was a quiet argument, heat hidden, but full of impatience. The Scots SAS man turned to the other three. 'Branches. Smooth out this bloody sand.'

'Urgent as that?' Ludlam said. 'Well, we're not paddling canoes, you know. That thing there is an outboard.'

'Christ!' He inhaled slowly, looking at us with cold eyes. Then he decided. 'Och, all right, we're tracking. Picked 'em up four days back and we're ahead o' them noo. If ye're soldiers –'

'Ambush,' I said.

His eyes seemed to confirm it, but he said nothing.

Already the three were at work on the sand, brushing it smooth with branches.

'Right,' Ludlam said. 'We'll strike camp. Hide the gear, stay hidden.' He pointed into the jungle behind us. 'How far back?'

'Bloody long way, eh?'

I said, 'We won't interfere.'

'Ye'll no' be able tae help it.' I could imagine how he felt. Days tracking in the jungle, a long burst of effort to get ahead, and all likely to be wasted because three awkward civilians got in the way and wouldn't move.

Maybe he read the sympathy somewhere in the back of my head as I bent to deflate the dinghy and drag it up the beach, because he came over and said, 'Ye were infantry?'

'Yes.'

'Jungle experience?'

'Limited.'

'What aboot the other two?'

'He was in Burma. Fourteenth Army. He's got plenty.'

'And her? If she was a missionary, she's –'

I said, 'She lived up here. Hid from the Japs for two years.'

He nodded, and I could see what he was thinking. It could be worse: we weren't just tourists. But he'd have been a lot happier if he'd never seen us. He helped me carry the equipment thirty yards in among the trees, stack it, camouflage it with foliage, then we returned to the little beach, where all the marks of our stay were being carefully eradicated.

'Listen tae me. Go half a mile east. That way.' There was a compass at my belt, but he pointed to be sure. 'Dinnae cross any game track, right? No stoves, no fires, no hot food, no hot drinks. Water bottles only.'

I said, 'We're hardly likely to –'

'*Listen!* No washing. Ye can smell soap at half a mile sometimes. The smell gets trapped; same as peppermint, so dinnae clean your teeth. No latrines. Dig a wee hole each time and cover it straight off. No walking about. Birds and monkeys are a dead giveaway, so be still, and I mean it. *Still.*'

'For how long?'

He shrugged. 'An hour. Two days. Who knows?'

'You?'

Just the ghost of a smile. 'We'll be around, 'at's a promise. I'll come for ye, after. Now go on.'

Obediently we moved off. Away from the river bank. The undergrowth was less fierce because the great trees hogged all the light and there wasn't much left for smaller brethren struggling beneath. We moved carefully, trailing branches behind us to cover our footprints, though in fact we left hardly a mark because the jungle floor consisted of a heavy layer of decaying spongy matter that accepted our footmarks only temporarily, swelling again as soon as the foot moved on.

At the beginning, I pulled out my knife and moved towards a tree to mark it, but Miss Franklin asked sharply, 'What are you doing?'

'Mark on the tree,' I said. 'So we can find our way back.'

She shook her head. 'Don't. Somebody else may see it.'

'We'll get lost.'

'No.' She wore a little smile. 'You might, but I won't.'

'Why not, it's all alike?' We were only thirty yards or so from the river, yet it had disappeared. Whichever direction I looked in, the view was the same.

'I can read a path,' Miss Franklin said. 'It's a trick of memory and it takes a long time to learn, but I can do it.'

I wasn't convinced. 'How?'

'I don't know. Things register. A turned leaf. The twist of a branch, small things here and there. The people who live here don't mark their tracks. I learned it from them.'

She pointed things out from time to time: a twig by a tree stump, the twist of a creeper, a fungus with an odd shape. Every few feet there was some tiny thing. But it still wasn't plausible to me: you'd need pencil and paper, and quite a lot of sheets of paper, too, to list them all.

She simply smiled at my incomprehension. 'If you lived here twenty years, George, and practised hard, you could learn it, too. Just trust me.'

I didn't, entirely. It seemed to me you'd need the memory of a computer to hold it all; on the other hand there wasn't much option, and Ludlam seemed happy. So we threaded our way onward, careful to disturb as little as possible, until we found a place where two dead trees had tilted into collapse and sunlight had produced shrubs. We reconnoitred carefully for snakes or other hazards, then crawled into a kind of gloomy bower beneath the big trunks, where the low growth concealed us.

I looked around me, and thought: two days. I must have spoken the words, too, because Miss Franklin said, 'Now – don't speak again. Don't smoke, either. Tobacco smoke lingers, too.' When I opened my mouth to protest, she put her finger to her lips.

*

Silence and immobility is a hell of a discipline. Everything rebels against it. When you're free to speak, it's possible to be quiet without strain because you know you can speak if you wish. When you know you can't, the urge becomes overwhelming. The body, too, demands movement. Muscles exist to enable us to move, and when we don't they protest: they give us twinges and little aches, and our nerves communicate messages to the brain to say stretch, turn over, wriggle.

I'd done some of it before, mainly in training, but it was a long time before, and my memory of it wasn't accurate. Recall merely said it was a bit uncomfortable; the reality is torture. There you sit, with two other people, and you look at each other. After a moment it seems necessary to say something, but you can't. The need becomes more urgent and has to be fought and the mental fighting makes the body restless, demanding movement. Try it for five minutes. I thought back to my training, trying to remember the tricks of experience that had been passed on to us, and began to practise some of them. If you can't speak aloud, you can speak inside your head. Conduct your conversations there, but *not* with your companions: talk in your mind with parents, brothers, friends, anybody who's a long way away. If you can find something to watch, watch it. Watch a fly on a window, a bee in a flower, a beetle crawling. Count legs, blades of grass, the hair on your fingers. Concentrate on *something*, and the time moves. Muscles can also be given work. Bunch your fist and the muscles tighten in your arms; stomach and back muscles can be tensed and relaxed once, ten times, a hundred, always counting slowly. Legs aren't so easy, but point your toe and push and all the muscles harden. Do that a hundred times, then do it with the other leg. It's work, and hard work at that, but it keeps mind and body in some kind of subjection.

Above all, don't look at your watch. Never? No, never, because it's always a disappointment and that kind of disappointment multiplies itself into despair.

Miss Franklin had turned away at the beginning, and I remember after a while that that, too, had been recommended behaviour. If you don't look at people, the urge to talk decreases. So I moved once, to lie on my stomach, facing away from them, and at once the jungle responded with a little burst of noise around us. Everything there was sensitive to the movement of everything else. I began to watch the jungle. Near by was a curious thing: a fungus draped in a lacy veil, that seemed to be growing as I looked at it. There was a tall, central pillar like the stalk of a tall mushroom, and the bell-shaped veil hung from it. Above was a yellowish-black cap on which a red beetle was feeding. After a while the beetle flew off, with powdery material attached to its legs. A pause, then another beetle came, fed, moved away. I became fascinated, counting the arrivals, counting the seconds as they fed, counting the intervals between beetles. That fungus was like a major airport, arrivals and departures precise and calculated, the pattern far from random. Somewhere, other beetles probably waited in some kind of holding pattern, awaiting permission to land from some obscure traffic controller.

Behind me there was no sound. I turned my head once or twice and Ludlam was sleeping, lucky devil. But he'd pay for it when night came. Miss Franklin was motionless. She could have been sleeping, too, but I was certain she wasn't. She had the patience of a lizard on a rock, learned the hard way.

My mind began to drift. I watched the beetles, still counting, still observing, but thinking about the two people who shared the silence with me, going over and over the events that had brought us here. They were odd, both of them. A woman who'd carried a letter for nearly twenty years, out of sentimentality. But it wasn't that. She was as unsentimental as they come, in most ways, and with a streak of ruthlessness more appropriate to the dictator of a banana republic than to a mission nurse. But didn't they say ruthlessness and sentimentality go together? Look at Hitler, at Himmler, at that old butcher Stalin chucking children under the chin. Why was she here, really? To see the simple tribespeople who were her surrogate children? To make sure the rubies my father had so dubiously acquired were put to the service of the Lord? For somebody who'd killed so deliberately, so cleverly, in so premeditated a way, it was difficult to credit. Yet easy, too, to believe that she simply meant what she said, because everything about her made her words believable.

And Ludlam? Those red beetles reminded me of Ludlam, as they homed in on the fungus, feeding, taking away what they wanted. He'd done it before, calculating and then acting. He'd taken the loot and the punishment and gone away. And now, here he was again, a calculating man with a well-organized mind, a man who did nothing without thinking about it first. He was here on impulse, or so he said, yet he was anything but a creature of impulse. Ludlam was accustomed to control, a planner, a man who'd wielded command. But at no point, except when he'd arrived in Kuching and forced himself on us, had he behaved in a commanding way. No, Ludlam had been content to follow, to do as he was told. He was a hard little man, especially inside his mind, so why all that twitchiness about being followed?

Come to think of it, the twitchiness had evaporated when we turned off the big river proper and into the tributary. Why? Perhaps because, as the jungle closed in, he felt safer from prying eyes.

They were unfathomable, both of them: products of strange lives and forces I hadn't experienced. But, like the beetles and the veiled fungus, they occupied my mind.

And so, at intervals, did my bladder. It was a kind of clock in itself, signalling the passing hours with pressure and relief. I could remember one bucko sergeant instructor on the subject, years ago: 'You can lie in your own urine, gentlemen. Babies do it and it does 'em no harm. You were a baby once. Remember it's yours, and it will do you no harm.'

'Niffs a bit though, Sergeant.'

'An hour ago it was tea, gentlemen, or beer or, for some of you, I dare say, it was champagne from a dancer's bloody slipper. You were glad enough of it then. Don't worry about it now!'

Smile in recollection. The reality a bit uncomfortable, though, but the bucko sergeant was as right as they usually were, and I knew the SAS men back at the river, deployed in some murderous crossfire set-up, wouldn't be worrying. That was something else to think about. Once upon a time when I was young and mad, I'd hoped somebody somewhere might decide I was the SAS type. They never did. Perhaps I was too mad for action in those days. The SAS boys aren't: they're self-contained as ball-bearings, picked for self-control and balance, and about one soldier in a hundred is suitable. I once saw four of them playing bridge in a crowded NAAFI club in Aldershot on a Saturday night. It was full of Black Watch men in kilts, and a bunch from the Inniskillings came in. A brawl started. The place just about exploded: men fighting in lumps, cursing, abuse and punches. But there was a still little place at the heart of the storm where the SAS continued to bid one no-trump and two hearts at each other, and all the drunken rowdies, as they milled about, were careful not to blunder into their table. Just the four of them, and a hundred and fifty drunken Jocks and Micks, and I doubt if there was so much as a ripple on the surface of their beer glasses, though the place turned into matchwood around them.

Lying there in silence, the first hours were the worst; after that the brain went on its wanderings, and the mental walkabouts became longer. When it drifted back, you could push it on again like a boat on a lake and let some eddy of thought take it.

I had a little water and a half-melted Mars bar when my stomach told me it was lunchtime, and the same again as night descended and while I dined insects dined off me. It was the longest day I've known, and murderously uncomfortable, but as the training sergeant had insisted would happen, it ended. I rolled myself as quietly as possible into my sleeping-bag, burrowing down deep like a nervous child beneath the bedclothes, and slept. When I woke, it was because something was snuffling at me, grunting a little, nudging at the sleeping-bag. My scalp crawled and my skin erupted in sweat. Christ, what was it? I lay rigid as it investigated me, holding the opening of the sleeping-bag tight closed, and thinking of all the creatures whose world we had invaded: everything from elephant and rhino to orang-utan and wild pig. And sun bears, with bad vision and worse tempers, and the revolting moon rat, with its white body and long nose with a pink rosette on the end and its foul stink that protects it from all the other predators.

Outside the jungle roared like Piccadilly Circus, but against its solid wall of sound, only two noises existed for me: the beat of my own heart, and the snuffling grunts of the unknown creature. If I took the initiative, whipped open the bag and popped out, would surprise drive the creature away? Not if it was an elephant, it wouldn't! There's scarcely an animal alive with reflexes as slow as man's, and if any sort of attack was made I'd be tangled in the bag. No, the only thing to do was remain still, and hope. The prodding inspection continued. I was nudged and nosed and sniffed at, and lay tense and helpless, thinking of the weight of an elephant's foot. The thing prodding at me could be a trunk, or the snout of a boar, or . . .

I was terrified, teeth clenched, trembling, soaked with sweat. Compared with the eternity of that inspection the whole long day I'd lived through was only a moment. How long before interest became hunger, or anger; how long before the realization that there was meat under the strange skin on the jungle floor? I remembered the knife at my belt and fumbled to withdraw it, then held it ready, close to my face. It was long seconds before I understood that there was quiet again. A million background sounds, but the fearful one in the foreground had ceased. Listening hard, I could hear no movement, no rustle among the decaying leaves. Was it still there? I ached to look, but dared not. The luminous hands of my watch showed in the blackness and I watched the second hand sweep unbelievably slowly once, twice, three times – ten times round the face. Surely *now*!

But I didn't look. It was as though my fingers, cramped

at the opening, were refusing to comply in my own foolishness, denying my stupid curiosity, keeping me safe despite myself. I lay in the darkness, drenched in sweat, staring at those tiny points of luminosity, willing the night away. Something must have given under the strain, because the next sharp nudge was in a nightmare and I was retching in fear, and something was ripping open the mouth of my sleeping-bag. I looked frantically upward – but only into Ludlam's unshaven face. He stared at me for a moment, then gave a little grin. 'Wild pig,' he said quietly. 'Don't worry, they've gone.'

Those were the only words spoken. I glanced at Miss Franklin and the wan look on her face showed clearly enough that she, too, had been through it. The ground around us bore traces: their droppings and the little two-pointed imprints of their trotters. I heard my own loud sigh, slumped back and stared upward into the high branches. At least the night was over.

But another day of silent stillness was beginning.

For me, much of the morning passed in sleep. I felt bone-achingly weary, foggy-headed, more exhausted than I had ever been before, and the sleep wasn't sought, it was given to me.

When I woke it was almost noon, and there were ants on my face. I dashed them away, shuddering, and was bitten two or three times. Another mouthful of water, because the horrors were beginning to get at me now. My nerves were shredded; I felt as though the whole world was composed of malevolence. Turning to look at the others, I saw Miss Franklin raise her hand suddenly, and listen. I listened too, and faintly heard movement not far away. Oh Christ, what was it *this* time? Animals, insurgents – what?

The SAS patrol came to us quickly, their faces weary, drawn with disappointment.

'Nae a sign o' 'em,' the Scot said disgustedly.

'Not coming this way, then?'

He spat. 'Mebbe they got wind o' us. Ah cannae tell. Must hae changed direction, headed off some ither way. The bastards.'

'You're sure?'

'Och, they'd have made it by now. They're awa'.'

Miss Franklin said, 'So we can go on?'

He regarded her with tired eyes. 'Ye do as ye wish. If ye want my advice, ye'll go back.'

'And if they're downriver?'

'Och, that'd be bad luck.'

'You don't know?'

'D'ye think I'd –' Just for a moment there was a tiny flare of anger, but it was swiftly controlled. 'I've nae way of knowing.'

I said, 'Can we make some food?'

He hesitated. 'Och, ye may as well. We've lost them this time. They're awa'. Have ye onny tea?'

'Yes.'

'Och, the hell wi' it. Let's brew up.'

It was over. Nothing had happened, yet there had been hour upon hour of misery and fear, all without result. We returned to the river bank and made hot drinks and hot food and fed the soldiers, too. And we washed ourselves, probably the greatest of the various pleasures. The four SAS men smacked their lips over the tea, wished us luck, and departed quietly, simply disappearing into the vastness of the forest. They had a helicopter rendezvous in nine days' time, and meantime would continue the hunt. We all knew it was probably useless now, but they weren't the men to spend nine days sitting under trees, just waiting.

But we could, for a while at least. We made more tea and sat and drank it, and then Ludlam said to Miss Franklin, 'We go on?'

'Of course.'

Interesting that he'd asked her. Also that neither of them consulted me. I thought with a touch of resentment that you don't ask the pack mule; he just carries the load.

I said, 'If anybody's interested, there are bloody bandits

about. We don't know if they're upriver or down. All we *do* know is that they aren't here.'

'And what is that intended to mean?' Miss Franklin was at her most acerbic.

'It means,' I said, 'that we wait here long enough to let them get the hell out of the way! Wherever they're going, let them get on with it.'

Ludlam looked at me and then nodded. 'Makes sense.'

She said, 'Why?'

'The Kalimantan border,' I said, 'is thataway,' pointing up the current. 'If they're going back, and remember the soldiers said they'd been in Sarawak quite a while, then they're going the same way as us. But not in a boat with an outboard. Not as fast as we'll go.'

She was impatient, all for pushing on. 'If they're not, then we're simply wasting time.'

I said, 'Think of it like this. They're armed. Their job is trouble. The outboard advertises us. Maybe shoot us up – that's the classic insurgent tactic. Why risk it?'

'Quite right,' Ludlam said. 'And a rest will do nobody any harm.'

'Rest!' She glared at us. Then she said, 'Men!' in a tone of considerable contempt.

The contemptible men grinned at each other and nodded complacently.

She'd lost and she knew it. She was also resentful, and we got a little hellfire and brimstone. 'You just want to spend a couple of days loafing about here. It's simple laziness. Goodness me, you men are all the same. When there's work to do, you look for ways of avoiding it!'

I smiled politely at her and began to set up one of the tents.

Ludlam said, 'It makes sense.'

But she hadn't finished. 'There are longhouses up there. Two of them. Don't you think those people ought to be warned that there are armed insurgents in the area?'

'Won't they know?' She'd told us a dozen times that nothing moved without those magical tribesmen being aware of it.

'They may or may not. But *we* have a duty to warn them.'

I said, 'Our duty is to survive. If we have a duty at all. I suggest we give it two days.'

'Two!'

She fretted all day, furious and impatient; she spoke to neither of us. She didn't swim and she ate apart from us. A day which ought to have been as idyllic as the first one we'd spent at this spot, turned into a sullen misery. Nobody, though, gave way: Ludlam and I because we were sure we were right, she because to give way wasn't in her.

We turned in early and morosely, as soon as darkness fell, and I for one tossed and turned, unable to sleep, partly because it was too early, partly because the whole atmosphere of the little camp was too taut to allow rest to come down upon us. Ludlam slept before I did, snoring a little and so making sleep even more difficult for me. Eventually, though, after a long time spent staring at the tent wall, my eyes must have closed.

When they opened again, Miss Franklin wasn't there.

CHAPTER FOURTEEN

For a few minutes we wondered if she was near by, feminine modesty etc, and merely called her name hopefully. But one of the backpacks was gone, and some food. Her sleeping-bag was not in her tent. She'd gone, all right, and no prizes for guessing the direction.

'Damned woman!' Ludlam muttered. 'You know, young Tunnicliffe, people have asked me all my life why I never got married. Ought to carry her round with me as a portable answer.'

Her iron will didn't appeal much to me, either, but it wasn't the time to talk about women. 'Stop philosophizing,' I said, 'and let's get packed up. We've got to get after her.'

'Let her sweat a bit.'

'For Christ's sake – she could die alone up there!'

'Maybe she wants to,' Ludlam said quietly.

I stared at him.

He went on, 'Think about it. Old maid, miserable in retirement. This is where her life was . . .'

The thought wasn't new to me. It had entered my own head the previous evening, more or less in the form Ludlam had used to express it. But it had been rejected. Little Miss Excelsior wasn't a dying elephant, wandering off alone to her graveyard; she was a survivor born, crackling with determination and intent on winning wherever she went. It didn't make a comfortable companion of her, but it did make her a highly unlikely capitulator.

There was another argument, too. I said, 'If we lose her, those rubies are lost for good.'

He glanced at me, blinking a little, and after a moment said, 'Oh yes, of course.' I had a momentary impression that he wasn't even thinking about the rubies. She *must* have got under his skin!

We packed up quickly, loaded the dinghy, I started the Seagull, then shoved off from the sand and nosed off upstream. It was true that one person, alone, carrying very little weight, didn't need to hack much of a path, and there were long stretches of river bank where no hacking would be needed. It was likely, though, that Miss Franklin was not on the bank at all, but in the jungle, moving parallel to the river, avoiding much of the heavy undergrowth that proliferated by the water. She was confident enough of her directional sense, and experienced enough in jungle travel to make faster time that way.

I reckoned she could have gone quite a distance, if she'd been going for seven or eight hours, as seemed likely, and she'd managed a mile an hour. The trouble was that we might miss her, sailing past while she stalked on alone.

I said as much to Ludlam, and he said, 'She's a stubborn old bitch, but daft she's not.'

I thought she was both stubborn enough and independent enough to abandon us and go on entirely alone, and said so. 'She doesn't need us. We need her.'

He looked at me. 'You're young. Youngish, anyway. You don't know what it's like as the strength starts to go. She won't want to walk if she can ride, I promise you.'

He hadn't seen that spare body and its easy stride crossing rough walking country on the moors in Yorkshire. Sitting there as the dinghy chattered on against the flow, I remembered how she'd covered thirty miles that day, and stayed wily and tough-minded.

As we went I began to yell her name every few yards, why I don't know, because the roar of the outboard would carry farther than any shout of mine. Ludlam kept his eyes on one river bank; I watched the other.

'We're sitting ducks, you know,' he said warningly.

'We've no choice.'

'She hasn't left us one, you mean.'

'That's right.'

'And when we find her?'

'If. *If* we find her.'

'We will.'

'Then,' I said, 'I suppose we'll go on.'

Ludlam shook his head. 'You were right the first time. Give them the chance to clear out. Don't change your mind when you're right.'

'You mean go back?'

'Yes. To where we were. Until tomorrow. Another twenty-four hours makes no difference.'

'We'll see.'

'Don't be a young fathead. This could be dangerous.' He had one of the rifles beside him as we rode, and one hand never left it. 'Decide now. Cuts out the argument later.'

Two hours and maybe four miles upstream we continued to motor along the smooth water between the huge green canyon walls of the jungle. There had been no sign of Miss Franklin, but nor had bullets chattered out at us, though our loneliness and the exposed position of the boat on the river made it seem likely. Any point on this river would make a perfect ambush, and the thought never left my mind for a moment. But we drove steadily on, beginning to wonder, now, whether we'd overtaken her. As minute followed minute the feeling that she was now behind us, that I should turn the dinghy round and go back the way we'd come, began to grow. But a mile an hour for eight hours was eight miles. Plus two to three for the time we'd been on the river ourselves – and we weren't making much more than two miles an hour against the current. No, she could still be ahead.

She must have been going hard. It was another two hours before we saw Miss Franklin. She stood by the bank watching us come towards her, a little tired, but wholly unbeaten. I felt tremendously relieved, but she showed nothing as we came near, except a little gleam of triumph in her eye, which needled me, and I said shortly, 'That was a bloody stupid thing to do!'

She flashed me a look. 'Something had to penetrate your idleness!'

I held out my hand to steady her as she stepped on board, but she ignored it, hopping easily into the dinghy.

The hours of tension had left their mark on me, and I was sure now that Ludlam had been right. We'd got away with it, but there was no certainty we'd continue to do so if we pressed on. A mile or so back, there'd been a spot for a camp site, and we'd best spend the next thirty-six hours there.

As I swung the boat out and continued turning, she said sharply, 'Where do you think you're going?'

'Back.'

'No, we're going upstream!'

I said, 'We're going – ' and got no further, because she'd picked up the rifle and was pointing it at me. Her eyes were blazing. 'Don't be silly.'

She worked the bolt, ramming a round into the chamber, and her thumb slipped the safety-catch forward.

I said, 'Don't be juvenile. You wouldn't shoot.'

'Not at you, no. But at the engine.'

'That's even dafter,' I said. 'We all need that.'

'No, we don't,' Ludlam said beside me. 'She doesn't, do you, Miss Franklin?'

'Turn upstream.' Her voice was quiet and steady.

'No.'

She said, 'I can survive here. I can find my way. Can you?'

I looked at her.

'Remember I lived a long time in this jungle. I know what can be eaten and what's poisonous. I know how to march and how to hide. And I could lose you easily.'

'All we'd have to do,' I said, 'is follow the river.'

'On empty stomachs? I could sink the boat, too, and all this with it.'

Ludlam sighed. 'Do as you're told, son. She has control.'

She sat in the bow, the rifle across her knees, through the ensuing hours, silent, vigilant and implacable.

Only once, when I burst out petulantly, 'It has to be *your* way, always *your* way!' did she reply.

What she said was, 'I'm doing the right thing for the right reasons.' After that she said nothing, wrapped in her damned rectitude until, shortly before dusk, we hit another rapid. Then, as we made camp at the foot of it, she offered another thought. 'You see. We weren't ambushed.'

'You knew, of course, that we wouldn't be,' I said sarcastically.

'I felt it.'

'Felt!'

'Call it faith,' she said.

Ludlam, busying himself with the stove, muttered, 'Useful thing in your knapsack if it works.'

'How far now?' I demanded.

'We have to reach the longhouse tomorrow.'

'How *far*?'

'Not more than twenty-five miles.'

'With this rapid to pass?'

'We have to do it.'

'Why? More feelings?'

She said, stone-faced, 'A presentiment. Something is wrong. Yes, I can feel that.'

We were ready by dawn, launching into what was certain

to be a very hard day. It was, too. An hour and a half to pass the first rapid, and the river narrower and faster above it, contained in a rock channel now, so that the Seagull had to battle harder and harder to make headway. Eight or nine miles later, there was another, and as I groaned at the sight of it, she said, 'This one's short.'

'You know it?'

'Yes. You can see all of it.'

'How far after that?'

'About twelve miles.'

There was no rifle now. She'd put it quietly away the previous night and when I'd taken the precaution of unloading it she'd told me not to bother; it had done its task. Now, somehow, it was her certainty that drove me on. I was beginning to detest Miss Franklin, but there was no denying the urgency she generated.

The final rapid was the least difficult we'd come across so far, and we passed it in little more than an hour. She was so keen to press on that she even tried to chisel me out of ten minutes' rest and a cigarette after all the hacking and carrying, but worms turn occasionally, and sometimes even a foot like hers isn't heavy enough to be put down firmly. But it was difficult to relax with the old dragon snorting impatiently all the while, and I found myself grinding out the smoke half-finished, and rising to reflate that bloody dinghy. Ludlam made himself useful by topping up the tank of the outboard. Her contribution was to urge us on.

Above the rapid the river had narrowed yet again, and flowed faster. The smooth green flow to which we had become so accustomed, was gone, and in its place was altogether rougher water. We were much higher, now, heading up the lower slopes of the interior mountains. The coastal lowlands lay behind us, but there was only the river to tell us so, because the vastness of the forest was unchanged, still climbing high from the river's banks to that dense mat of cover two hundred feet over our heads. But as we forged on through that long tunnel of shade, the air was a little less hot and small wraiths of mist twisted here and there over the water.

It was slow progress in a river now strewn with boulders; sharp eddies threatened, from time to time, to stop us altogether, and we had to find a way round, or between. The little Seagull sang out its enthusiasm, but all its power was needed. We fought our way on all through the afternoon, but as the shadow deepened, we were still well short of the longhouse.

In front of me, Miss Franklin had been fumbling in one of the waterproof bags. Now she produced a torch, and said, 'Keep going.'

'It won't last more than an hour,' I protested.

'An hour may be enough.'

An hour meant perhaps a mile and a half at the rate we were going. I said snappishly, 'If we're as near as that, walk on the water. You should be able to do it.'

At that point, though, both banks were inhospitable, with rock walls rising eight or ten feet, and there was nothing else to do but motor on into the swiftly deepening gloom. Minutes later, in the dark, we had only a bright beam of torchlight to follow and it was dense with insect life. We were unable to see more than twenty yards or so ahead. After a bit the torch showed that the rock walls on either side had disappeared and I said, 'Shine the light towards the bank again. We have to make camp.'

She turned, just a small dark silhouette now against the yellow beam. 'Can't you smell something?'

Beside the hammering Seagull I smelt only heat and oil. 'No.'

She said, 'Smoke. I can smell smoke.'

'Perhaps somebody lit a fire.'

'That's what I'm afraid of. They burn easily. Keep going!'

I sniffed and couldn't smell it. Ludlam said he couldn't either. Miss Franklin swore the smell was growing stronger and that it was wood smoke: if possible, there was an even fiercer urgency to her now.

The light from the torch dimmed gradually, until it was little more than a golden glow at the nose of the little dinghy. Even the occasional groups of fireflies in the trees shone brighter. But she hung out over the front, clasping the torch, calling, 'On, on, okay, on, left *on, on*!' until finally a small flickering light appeared, ahead of us and a distance away.

'The longhouse at Lobang Nibong,' Miss Franklin said. Her voice was low and there was no pleasure in it.

By that time I could smell smoke too!

Twenty minutes later, as we pulled to the side and clambered ashore, there was still only the single light, and we could see that it came from a small fire, dying now, and flaring only intermittently. The air was full of the smell of burnt wood though, and it clearly didn't all come from that one small source.

We stood on the mud in the darkness, and Miss Franklin began to call out in a language I didn't know. There was no answering call.

By the thin remaining glimmer, we moved forward again, then stopped, and she repeated her call.

Nothing.

We picked our way forward a little way farther, past the little fire, and now that the wind was carrying its smoke away from us, another familiar smell replaced it. There were pigs very close at hand.

They made no sound, though. And soon we discovered why. The pigs were dead. And not just dead: we found the burned corpse of one of them sticking out from beneath charred timbers. Miss Franklin swung the torch, but it gave hardly a glow now. I got out my lighter and held it above my head. In the moment before the wind snuffed the little flame, we knew the entire longhouse had been gutted.

She went on calling, her voice floating in the night, sad and unanswered, while Ludlam and I busied ourselves building up the little fire. There was another torch, and spare batteries, too, somewhere among our gear, but fumbling around in the dark I couldn't find them. But a couple of sticks dipped in petrol provided reasonable makeshift torches, and enabled us to see how complete the destruction had been.

'How many lived here?' I asked her gently.

She shook her head, tears pouring down her cheeks. 'I don't know. Two hundred or more.'

So where were they? I began to poke around in the wreckage. A longhouse is built on piles and the long living-floor is raised twenty feet or so above the ground. Beneath it pigs and poultry forage among the scraps and waste. Now it was just a big patch of fallen and blackened timbers. The whole thing had crashed in flames to the muddy soil of the river bank.

I found more dead, blackened pigs, and a few chickens with burned feathers. Every moment I expected to find a body among the debris, but a quick search produced nothing. I went back to where Miss Franklin stood and said, 'The people must have got out. Who would have lit the fire?'

She turned to me almost eagerly. 'Yes, they'd do that as a distress signal, wouldn't they? So somebody must – ' She began calling again.

It was an hour before anything happened. Then, silently, a boy appeared on the edge of the firelight, giving us a hell of a start.

Miss Franklin hadn't seen him. I called her and she hurried over. The boy backed away nervously. She said to me, 'Quick, give me some food. Chocolate if there is any.' I threw her a Mars bar and she placed it on the ground and moved away.

The boy snatched it up, but clearly he didn't know what Mars bars were. He stood looking at it, while she talked softly to him. I found another bar, tore off the paper and bit it. That gave him the idea, and he bit his too, sampling it cautiously, then wolfed the rest down fast. Miss Franklin went on talking. From the cadences of her voice she was asking questions and after a while she began to get responses.

He couldn't have been more than ten or eleven. A little brown boy in a loincloth with wide, frightened eyes, who kept glancing from her to us nervously, his feet never still, ready any second to race off and hide.

From the way he'd demolished the Mars bar, he was hungry, though. I opened a tin of beans and handed it to him as Miss Franklin went on with her soft questions.

Finally, while the boy dug a spoon into the beans, she told us what she'd learned. It wasn't much. Men had come from the forest. Men with guns. They had talked to the headman. Everybody else was sent away. The longhouse had been burned. The men went away.

Ludlam said, 'The insurgents.'

'Or another group.'

I said, 'Does he know where the rest are?'

'Scattered, in the forest.'

'But does he know?'

'He can find them. He doesn't want to go in the dark.'

'I don't blame him,' I said. 'The best thing is to tuck him up and let him sleep. Maybe they'll come back soon.'

Miss Franklin gave him a little penknife and the look in his eyes changed from fear to pleasure and he allowed us to pop him into a sleeping-bag, and promptly went out like a light, the little knife clutched in his fist. Meanwhile we built the fire higher, and waited, and every so often she would call out, soothingly, almost crooning her words at the night.

An hour passed and they began to return. First an old woman leaning on a stick limped into the firelight, stopped, then moved to stand before Miss Franklin, staring hard at her for a long moment. She spoke a word on a rising inflection, and Miss Franklin nodded and produced that always-surprising smile of hers, and a second later their arms were around each other. The old woman began to call words into the night, and gradually people emerged from the darkness to stand in a circle round the fire. We boiled water continuously, making endless tea, watching the few cups we had pass from hand to hand. Ludlam and I unpacked our food and began to give it to the children.

Then a litttle gap appeared in the silent ring around us, and two men came through it, carrying a makeshift litter on which an old man lay on his belly. Miss Franklin was beside it in a flash.

'Saram?' she said.

'Fankee?' His voice quavered and I though he was saying Thank you, then realized it was her name.

'Fankee is back.' Then, 'Bring a light.'

He groaned as she raised the cotton sheet that covered him. In one or two places it stuck stiffly to the skin, and I looked at his back, appalled. It was a mass of bloody weals.

In bits and pieces, as night wore on, the story came out. In essence, the boy had said most of it, but his brief description had given no real idea of what had gone on here two days earlier. Whether the men who'd come to the longhouse at Lobang Nibong were the same ones the SAS had been hunting, we didn't know, but there seemed no doubt they were a band of infiltrators from over the border in Kalimantan. The old headman – the *tua-ruma*, she called him – was a tough old soul, who spoke English of a sort, and once his lacerated back had been cleaned and dressed and some of Miss Franklin's brandy was warming his insides, was intent on ensuring that we didn't miss a detail.

There had been nine men altogether. They'd arrived late in the afternoon, angry because one of their number had injured his foot in an animal trap belonging to the village. I asked how they were dressed. Saram looked blank.

'Did they wear uniform, like soldiers?'

He shook his head, and Miss Franklin asked irritably why it mattered. I told her Kuching hadn't established whether Indonesian regulars were involved in infiltration and badly wanted to know.

It seemed the invaders weren't regulars. But if their clothing was haphazard, their arms weren't. Saram called over one of the men who'd seen service during the war with the Sarawak Scouts, and what he described made them automatic weapons.

They'd sought the hospitality of the longhouse for the night, and it had been granted. Other demands had followed. First, the longhouse was to accommodate two of the men permanently, pretending they were men of the village. A room was to be made available for arms and food supplies as a stores dump for raiding groups. A radio transmitter was also to be installed there. And so on.

At that, polite refusals had begun. When the Indonesians became ugly, the offer of hospitality was proudly withdrawn and the Dyaks said the men must go. They laughed and stayed, helping themselves at gunpoint to food and the Dyak *tuak*, a kind of wine. Then, drunk, they wanted the Dyak girls, but were unlucky. Guessing correctly what would happen, the girls had vanished into the forest. To show their spite, the men smashed the village's ceremonial storage jars, which were old and much prized.

Ugliness became brutality. There were kicks, punches and blows from rifle butts. More *tuak* was drunk. A pig was killed and roasted. I wondered briefly, at that, whether they were really Indonesians, because it's a mainly Moslem country and Moslems don't eat pigs. But then, they're not supposed to drink, either.

Saram said the men were pigs, also, and too drunk to care, and kept waving their rifles and firing shots. Then, in the morning with the invaders hungover and savage, the previous night's demands had been repeated. The longhouse would collaborate in the battle for Pan-Indonesia. It was to be a base for action against the Malays and their British dog friends.

Or else.

Saram, as *tua-ruma*, would not agree. His were an independent people. Sarawak was their country. They would not become the servants of Kalimantan.

The Indonesians took him outside, lashed him to the ladder which led to the upper storey, and flogged him with a long, thick ratan cane. Everybody else was herded round to watch.

They then set fire to the longhouse.

The last message, before they went away, was that they would be back. Perhaps, they said, they would return soon, perhaps after a new longhouse was built. The Dyaks of

Lobang Nibong would learn that they must do as they were ordered.

Then, firing their automatic weapons into the ground at the villagers' feet, they drove them back into the jungle, yelling, 'Stay there, until *we* say you can return!'

In the dark, they'd thought for a while that we might be the Indonesians, that the presence of a woman might be a trick. That the name of Fankee was merely a device. Fankee, after all, had not been here for twenty years.

Well, Fankee was back now, and they soon knew it. Every bump, scratch and abrasion was examined and treated. She greeted a few by name, older people she'd known years before; she asked and memorized the names of everybody else, and she treated one and all like a benevolent despot, including Ludlam, and most of all me. I was sent off with two suddenly-cheerful Dyak lads and a rifle and briskly instructed to find and fell some wild pigs for the pot. Ludlam went willy-nilly into the construction business. Having discovered that there was bamboo growing a little way upriver, she had Ludlam and the dinghy at work dragging rafts of the stuff to the longhouse. The Dyaks, declining orders from her, but accepting them as relayed by a suddenly more cheerful Saram, toiled through the long, hot day: cutting, binding, thatching. By nightfall there was shelter for everybody, rudimentary but sound, and the air was full of the smell of roasting pork.

It never seemed to occur to her that the gang might come back, and in fact they didn't, but Ludlam, that forward-thinking man, had contemplated the problem and asked questions.

'Have you blowpipes?'

Yes, a few had survived. They were old, made of *bilian*, a wood so hard it didn't burn. Any darts? No, but they could be made. Poison for the tips? That too could be made. A little group sat making things beside a pot in which something sinister was boiled. In a few hours, the village had defences, and if the marauders *had* returned they'd have had a nasty shock from a dozen men carefully concealed.

But it was Fankee who worked the miracle. She'd come less than twenty-four hours before to a place where morale was low as a beetle's thorax. In no time she had it humming again, and not only humming: those Dyaks were lively and energetic, determined, even, occasionally, laughing. Watching her I asked myself not how Britain had once gained an empire – that was all too easy to see – but how it had been lost, when people like that were doing its work.

She chased everybody along throughout the next day, too, marching round the place, organizing everything, inspecting teeth and gums, eyes and ears, rheumaticky joints and skin eruptions, at intervals of supervising work gangs and construction plans. Suitable trees were felled, stripped of bark and branches, and holes were dug to take them. Some of the timbers from the old longhouse were still sound, and they were used again. The Dyaks had the knowledge; I didn't suppose Miss Franklin had the faintest idea of the architectural niceties, but she had enough drive for everybody. By evening the main framework was beginning to take shape.

I, meanwhile, had been hunting again, and Ludlam was now in the defence industry, and the place was turning into a little fortress. Mantrap pits were dug and covered over, logs hauled up into trees to be dropped on unwary invaders. Bows were being made, and arrows, and more poison for the tips.

Even the children were pressed into action. Such of the livestock as had escaped, a few pigs and some chickens, was trailed, rounded up and returned to captivity. There weren't many left, but at least the village had a basis to build on. One boy, however, was not available: Jigah, the lad who'd been the first to respond to her calls on the night of our arrival. Jigah never left her side. Part of it was probably the hope of further Mars bars; mainly, though, it was the sense of self-importance she gave him. He was her runner, the relayer of messages, her channel of communication with Saram who actually issued the orders. She treated him with a curtness that was almost severe, told him to be quicker, to wash, to run, to do this and that and be quick about it. He grinned and adored her.

It was more than I did. Admiration, yes. Assistance to the civil population, yes. Help all one could, in fact. But I'd suffered under sergeant-majors as a youth and could do without repeating the experience.

On the third afternoon she came striding over to me and said peremptorily, 'Sure there's enough meat?'

'There's a fair amount. Nobody'll go hungry.'

She looked at the accumulated store. I'd sweated all day, stalking, shooting and carrying the assorted game. 'No. Get more.'

So I said, 'No,' for the hell of it.

'Pull your weight, man!'

'I have.'

'Now listen – ' Then she saw I was laughing at her, and something surprising happened.

She blinked and said, 'Have I been a bit overbearing?'

'A bit.'

'Mm.' She thought about it. 'I can be sometimes.'

'I've noticed.'

Then she actually gave a grin. 'Worth it, though, don't you think?'

'Yes.' I looked round the thriving scene. 'You've done well.'

'Right. Tomorrow we'll find your father's grave.'

CHAPTER FIFTEEN

We left on foot. The dinghy was required for haulage work on the river, and Ludlam was needed to pilot it. He looked at us a bit lopsided: the thought almost visibly running through his head that we were off after the rubies and he was being left out.

I said, 'Don't worry. We'll be back before nightfall,' but he only grunted.

The construction gangs were hard at work as we walked away from the growing framework of the new longhouse, taking a little narrow path into the forest, Miss Franklin in the lead and humming as she walked, while I trotted like a pet dog at her heels. She turned left, I turned left; she stopped, I stopped. I thought of the old army selection schools where qualities of leadership were assessed, and decided they'd have marked my papers 'Z-minus, return to unit'.

She began to relax a bit, though, after a while, explaining the lie of the ground, the words floating back to me over her shoulder as she marched on.

'From here the river flows round in a big loop, roughly U-shaped. If you think of that letter U, this longhouse is at the top of the left arm. There's another at the top of the right, and a third at the base. I used to work from a little place in between, from which I could visit all three.'

'Equidistant?'

'No. I was about three miles from two of them, and six or seven from the other. That was in the late 'thirties, and then again at the end of the war.'

'Wasn't it lonely?'

'Lonely?' She made it sound as though the thought was new to her. 'No. It was, well, peaceful. And busy, too. I looked after more than a thousand people. I could walk to each of the longhouses, do my work, stay if I needed to, return to my little camp. Yes, peaceful.'

'And dangerous – a woman alone?'

She said, 'No. Never. These are wonderful people.'

Not too long before, these wonderful people had been headhunters and books I'd read about Borneo suggested that during the war they'd taken it up again, at the expense of the Japanese.

'No trouble with the flora and fauna?'

'Very little. They're not so fierce in Borneo, you know, for some reason. There aren't many big carnivores, apart from the clouded leopard, and you're very lucky indeed to see one of those.'

'Did you?'

'No. I never did.'

We moved steadily, but without hurry. There was plenty of time in the day, and she'd stop occasionally to point out the marvels. Once we saw a pangolin, a scaly ant-eater like a small dinosaur, covered in scaly plates. At our approach it curled instantly into a ball, curving its armed tail over its head, and lay still, grey and shiny like dull steel, and I wondered what predator could tackle it. A foot or two away was a termite mound, thrumming with activity.

'That's his food,' Miss Franklin said. 'When we've gone, he'll make short work of it.'

At first we followed a hunting trail, but soon we moved off it, slipping between the great trees, walking round them, never walking in a straight line, our feet silent on the thick rug of decaying matter. She moved easily ahead of me, certain of her direction. Alone I'd have been lost at once; but Miss Franklin never hesitated.

Once, glancing back, I saw a centipede about eight inches long, marching purposefully behind me. What's more, it seemed to be keeping up. I mentioned it and she turned to look. 'Nasty brute,' she said, and stamped on it hard as its whole front end reared up at her. She explained briefly. 'They attack.'

I said, 'Yes,' and thought privately that they weren't the only ones.

She had an eye like a hawk and kept drawing my attention to brilliantly camouflaged beauties whose camouflage wasn't quite good enough: a horned toad that looked like a leaf, and was deeply offended when its disguise was penetrated, a mantis nymph that looked like an orchid and could, she told me, look like almost any other flower at will. She was an odd old lady, but she loved this place.

Two hours after we set off, or a little more, another sound became faintly audible in the pattern of jungle noise: falling water.

She halted then, and turned to me and her face was

glowing. 'My waterfall,' she said. 'Listen. When I heard it, I always knew I was home.' And then, 'Come *on*!'

It fell about twenty feet: a little tumbling cascade down a rock outcrop to a narrow stream below. There was a clearing, too, for some trick of nature had pushed an uneven floor of rock upward to form a small circle forty yards or so across where the trees could not take root. She crossed it, to a small level table on the far side where a few rotting timbers lay among such small plants as could cling to the rock, and stood looking down at them.

'This was my home. Isn't it a beautiful place?'

It was: just a small break in the jungle's immensity, a place where the sun could break through the vast canopy above, where clear water tumbled through rock. The green here was bright, not the darker colour of the endless shade.

I said, 'Where?'

'Over here. I'll show you.'

She'd buried my father close by the waterfall, in a cleft in the rocks. I stood looking down at a small clump of wild orchids, and she said, 'There was a gap in the rock there, and it seemed perfect. I had no coffin, of course, but I lined it with branches and laid more over him, then filled it up with earth. It was as much as I could do, you see.'

I've said before that I barely knew him. That over the years he'd crossed my thoughts only occasionally; but to be there, to see the spot, was unexpectedly moving. I began to say, 'You did –' but there was a catch in my voice and I had to start again. 'You did very well.' She was small. She had been weak from illness and he was a big man. I said, 'Thank you,' and thought that when my time came, I'd rather be in a place like that than in some unkempt cemetery full of tilted tombstones – death showing its grey teeth. This was a place of life.

'What sort of man – no, how did *you* see him?'

She gave a little sigh. 'Human, I think.' Then, 'Dishonest, I suppose. And brave.' And that rare grin flashed. 'Like you, really. Let's pray for both of you.'

And we did, she more naturally than I, but in that place,

to my surprise, it came easily, even to me.

Afterwards, as we walked back to the longhouse, the pilgrimage complete, we talked about plans. The longhouse at Lobang Nibong was, she said, the wrong place for our base. Having got them started on re-building, it would be better to move on to the other leg of the letter U, to the longhouse at Tunggal. The journey from there to the clearing was easier, and in any case, the clearing was technically in Tunggal territory.

We decided we'd spend one more day helping with the building, then move, to let the village complete its own work, and recover its confidence in the process.

A good deal had been recovered already, though. Organization was returning. Clothes were being washed and food prepared, and the boy Jigah came skipping towards Fankee to tell her he'd prepared tea and rice for her return.

I said, 'You've made a conquest.'

'So has he.' She ruffled his hair and told him he should be doing something useful.

Strange. I quite liked her again.

Ludlam, in contrast to his surliness that morning, also seemed pleased to see us. He must still believe that we'd been on a ruby hunt because he asked, 'Find anything?'

'A grave,' I said. 'We weren't looking for anything else.'

Thirty-six hours later, we packed our things into the dinghy and set off round the loop of the river towards Tunggal. We had a stowaway on board, too. Jigah had begged to be allowed to accompany Fankee, and Fankee had said no. He'd then approached Ludlam – age equals seniority equals authority among the Dyaks. Ludlam also said no. I came last on the list, and he'd clearly considered me carefully. When he approached me, he offered the penknife as payment of fare, and it worked. Not that I accepted the penknife. I knew I was being silly and sentimental. It was a good decision, though, however unsound the reason.

I had him tucked under the storage bags before Miss Franklin came aboard, and when after a couple of miles he came eeling out with an enormous grin, the issue was won. She bent her brows upon him in a great frown of disapproval, but he could read behind it and the grin intensified.

We went ashore at the longhouse on the bend of the U, for Miss Franklin to renew old friendships. The people there fed us and pressed Fankee to stay, but she declined, promising a longer visit on the return journey. Then we pushed on. The journey on to Tunggal took longer than we expected, partly because the river seemed to flow faster and faster, partly because, for once, the Seagull let us down. It was only a blockage in the fuel feed pipe, but an hour or so was lost, and the result was that it was well into the afternoon before we rounded a long sweep of the river and saw the big, flimsy-looking structure of Tunggal longhouse against its jungle backdrop.

A crowd quickly gathered at the little wooden jetty there and we came to it feeling a bit like visiting royalty, because Fankee had been recognized while we were still yards away, and the villagers at Tunggal quickly became excited. It was an excitement that lasted. The headman was not merely an old friend: he'd been with her part of the time when she was in hiding during the war, before leaving to join Harrisson's force in active harassment. At the feast that night, he wore a little row of medal ribbons slung from his neck, and I was inclined to be amused until I recognized the little emblem of a mention in despatches.

I got slightly tight on *tuak*, and so did Ludlam, and we retired early to the beds prepared for us in the longhouse. It was my first sight of the inside of one of these odd structures, and I looked round interestedly, if a little blearily. A big verandah looked out over the river, and beneath us cheerful fires burned and hymns were being sung, but as one stepped back inside, there was hardly any light at all. A few carefully shielded lamps burned at intervals along the massive hallway which ran through the whole hundred-and-fifty-foot length of the building. There were small screened divisions – they could hardly be described as rooms – along the rear, to give individual families some separation from their neighbours. I was surprised by the height of the roof above me, by the smokiness of the air, and by the dogs and the chickens that prowled hopefully along the hardwood boards of the floor.

I don't remember much more of that night. *Tuak* beats sleeping pills, and punishes the unwary, too. What I do remember very clearly is awakening in the morning. A sow was snorting beneath, and in momentary confusion I was back in my sleeping-bag in the jungle, with my hair standing on end. But sense took over and I lay listening as the jungle's sounds died away outside with nature's night shift going off duty. An owl called a few times near by, then fell silent. Then cocks began crowing in the rafters overhead, and somewhere near to me a dog began scratching. A little while later, wild birds began to greet the day in the trees all around, and soon there were footsteps along the boards as the longhouse-dwellers rose to begin a new day.

We were fed, then shown round, and it really was a most extraordinary place. Afterwards Miss Franklin said, 'Do you like it?'

'Yes,' I replied. 'But everything's a bit public.'

She said, 'Private, too. That's the beauty of it. There's no loneliness here. People meet the whole time, perfectly easily. But if somebody wants to sit and brood for a bit, nobody will bother him.'

'Better than Birmingham, then?'

She grimaced. 'Here, they know how to live. We don't any more. We're separated too much.'

We left early to return to Fankee's private clearing, reached it in about an hour and a half, and sat on the rocks to drink hot coffee out of a Thermos bottle and consider the problem of the search.

It was clearly a very considerable one. We sat sipping at our coffee and trying to make sense out of a landscape we couldn't even see.

Ludlam approached the problem systematically. 'Look,' he said, 'here's a badly injured man. He was conscious, was he?'

Miss Franklin said of course he was, or how could he have moved?

'What I mean is, was he rational?'

'Certainly.'

'All right. He's injured and lost. Probably doesn't want to leave the plane, because of what's in it. Who would? But he knows his only chance is to find help, and the chance is a very thin one indeed. His thigh was broken, you said?'

'Yes.' Her mouth was thinning, and she glanced at me, her disapproval of his cold approach manifest.

'So he couldn't walk. Had to crawl. Maybe hop a bit if he could. Well, nobody in that state goes uphill if he can go down, right?'

He was briskness personified, ticking off the points on his fingers. 'So – the best chance is an up-gradient.' Ludlam pointed to the waterfall. 'There's a stream, and streams flow downhill. We can conclude the ground rises over there. It does, doesn't it?'

She was staring across at the light patch of wild orchids marking my father's grave, and he had to ask again.

She nodded almost absently. 'Yes, it rises over there.'

'Anywhere else?'

I said, 'No. We've approached from two directions, and both ways we climbed a bit to get here.'

Ludlam's little hand slapped at his thigh. 'Over here, then. East. Now there's the matter of distance. Question is, how far did he crawl?' He glanced at Miss Franklin like a commander at a briefing looking for data.

She said, 'Oh God!' Her lips quivered. 'He crawled, as you put it, until he *dropped*!'

Ludlam gave her a glance. Casualties are part of the job. Emotion isn't. The attitude was apparent in his eyes. He said formally, 'I'm sorry if this is too direct for you. But it's best if we save time.'

'A mile's a hell of a way, here,' I said.

Ludlam nodded. 'Maybe it was less than that. It's even possible – ' he tilted his head back and gazed up at the patch of sky above us, where heavy grey cloud seemed to hang low over the treetops – 'it's even possible that he might have seen this patch as he came down. Can't be many holes like this in the canopy. Do you know if he *did* see it, Miss Franklin?'

She shook her head. 'He didn't say. I didn't ask.'

Ludlam's expression showed he thought that a serious omission but I remembered her description of his last days: his intermittent lucidity, his rising fever, her weakness and feeling of helplessness. I said, 'Let's just assume it. It gives us a quadrant. One mile radius from here, where the ground rises. We may as well start there as anywhere else.'

We'd reduced it as much as we could, but it was a big area to search: nearly a mile and a half at the outer edge of the quadrant, and solid jungle, with every square yard to be walked over: a DC 3 is a big aircraft, but the jungle covers quickly and completely.

We set off along the southern extremity of our quadrant, I at one end of our little line with Jigah at my heels, Miss Franklin in the middle, Ludlam at the other end. He and I each carried a machete to mark the trees we passed. The plan was to walk a mile directly away from the little clearing, then turn left along the curve of the quadrant for a mile and a half, then head back. If there was time, after that, we'd go out again, paralleling our route, working gradually inward towards the centre point.

We were about ten yards apart. Any more and we might miss something; less and the search would be lengthened. That was the optimistic intention. The reality was different: above the waterfall the character of the jungle changed and soon we were forcing our way through high ferns that turned out to have hooks underneath their feathery fronds – hooks that scratched and scraped at the skin and left irritation behind. Most of the time there were ways past and through and round the ferns, but often we had to stop and slash them out of the way. It was clear, too, that undergrowth of this height could easily conceal the wreck. So could the fallen trees we encountered from time to time. I tried counting paces as we went; we had to know when the mile had been covered; but our steps were so irregular, our direction so uneven, that I knew that method was useless.

I called to Miss Franklin, 'Can you judge the distance?'
'Yes.'
'Accurately?'
'Yes.'

She spoke firmly enough, but her heart wasn't in it. The energetic Fankee of the longhouse had disappeared, and the starchy, disapproving Charity Franklin was back among us. She might like the idea of finding the rubies and making a gift of them to the mission she had served so long, but the search offended her. I know how she was feeling because I felt a little of it myself: the unhealthy sensation of being a scavenger, of intending to live off the dead. Somehow it went deep into me, distilling into a kind of depression. No matter how often I told myself that the stones were my father's legacy, not much different from inheriting a house or a business, I couldn't shake it off.

The ineffectual nature of the search was depressing, too. It was plain enough that in this mass of vegetation, in the half light of the jungle, we could pass within feet of wreckage and not see it. The ground here was rippling and uneven, criss-crossed by dozens of hillocks and hollows, and some that were much deeper – small ravines, in fact.

We ploughed on, cutting the trees to leave a marked trail, and much-marked ourselves in our brushes with those damned ferns. Once, when we halted for a moment's rest, Ludlam said, 'This is like fighting your way through straw with fish hooks buried in it!' It was a very precise description.

We managed to complete that first tour of the quadrant by late afternoon, but it was at the price of extreme weariness, and the walk back to the longhouse was completed on wobbly legs. Young Jigah had stood it best, but then he'd had no hacking to do. Next day, we decided, we'd move the tents up to the clearing.

The days that followed were exact replicas of the first,

differentiated only by growing tiredness and depression. We spent eight days fighting our way round and round that quadrant, finding nothing, and knowing always that we might already have gone past the wreckage without seeing it. It may seem impossible that we could have missed something as big as a wrecked plane, but to see that area was to know it could happen. Probably the wings would have been torn off on impact with the trees. The fuselage, big as it was, might have been telescoped and crushed as it fell. The ferns and creepers swarmed over everything and the feeling that they were only too ready to swarm over us was never far away.

We'd agreed from the beginning that the Dyaks were not to be involved. They were simple people, but not fools, and if they knew there was a fortune at hand, they'd want their share. For different reasons, none of us wanted that. For Ludlam and for me it was a matter of simple greed; for Miss Franklin, loftier considerations applied.

'It would upset the whole area,' she had said, 'if one village were suddenly to become a great deal wealthier than its neighbours. Furthermore, sudden riches would put impossible strains on a longhouse community. The money would be far better applied by the mission. It would do good over a wide area.'

'Spoken like a good bureaucrat,' Ludlam muttered. Fortunately she didn't hear him.

After nine utterly exhausting days, we decided a break was sensible. We'd go back to the longhouse and relax for twenty-four hours. There we could swim in the river, collect some more stores, and get away from each other for a bit; we were starting to get on each other's nerves.

But that wasn't quite how it worked out. We'd no sooner got back there than I began to run a fever, shivering and shaking, burning hot one minute and freezing the next. Fankee, the great healer, filled me with pills of various kinds, and in a couple of days the shakes and the temperature went away. But I was weak as could be. My arms and legs seemed to weigh a ton each; if I tried to sit up, I failed; if I was raised, I felt dizzy.

When the worst was over, and I was merely immobile, lying flat on my back on my pallet in the longhouse staring for hours at the high smoky thatch, Ludlam and Miss Franklin left me and continued the search, but I doubt if they went at it very hard. They said they were going to extend the southern edge of the quadrant, and they put a firm face on it, but they were both tired, contemplating the exertion reluctantly. I knew in my bones that they'd find nothing, that nobody was going to come clambering up into the Tunggal longhouse yelling 'Eureka!'

But I also knew that a few more days would take us to the point of abandoning the search, to the point where we all became so dispirited that sooner or later someone would say, 'Let's go home,' and that once the words were spoken, it was only a matter of time. I made myself get out of bed, forced down food I didn't want, drove my heavy limbs to simple exercise, and in a day or two was managing to mooch round the longhouse, learning that Miss Franklin's point about a working society was well-made. Once, in my little London flat, I'd had a bad dose of 'flu and been alone and miserable for days. Somebody from the bank came to visit me once, staying half an hour, and that was that. Here, though I was a stranger, my welfare was watched over. Children came to play beside me, and with me; as I moved about there were smiles and cups of hot food thrust at me. Everybody I met would stop, assess the degree of improvement, and nod approval.

Not much English was spoken, though, except by Buran, the headman, a delightful old boy with beautiful manners, who visited me three times each day and insisted that the moment I was well enough, I visit him. That meant a walk to the other end of the longhouse, where he had a kind of rudimentary two-room suite from which all administration and justice was carried out. When I finally managed to stagger along there, we sat round his log fire, which burned in an earthenware trough on the floor, and talked mainly about the army. He didn't know why Fankee had returned, and was far too polite to ask, but I was Fankee's friend, so he was interested in me. We talked about the wars we'd fought, idle old-soldier reminiscence, all of it. He knew about the Indonesian brutality at Lobang Nibong, was angry and horrified and had sent a group of young men to help. It reminded him, he said, of a similar visit to Tunggal by the Japanese in 1942. They had been brutal, too, and had paid for it later.

'How?' I asked.

He shook his head to dismiss the question. 'Those times are gone.'

I persisted, somewhat idiotically: guessing what had been done, and wanting for some macabre reason to hear about it. 'You defeated them later?'

'Yes.'

I hesitated, then said, 'Heads?'

He looked at me. 'It was the old way.'

I told him I'd heard of the deeds of the Dyak warriors against the Japanese and how remarkable it was that a modern army had been so much disrupted by warriors with no real equipment.

He said the taking of heads caused fear in the Japanese. The custom had been dead for years, but the brutality had resurrected it for a while. It was a weapon.

Then he changed the subject. Later I brought it up again. Buran disapproved, that was clear. He had not been at Tunggal when the patrol was destroyed. If he had been . . .

I wasn't exactly obsessed, but was conscious of a kind of sick fascination. Now I knew there were heads, here at Tunggal, I wanted to see them, and began to wander through the long, rambling structure, looking for them. I'm not normally morbid; perhaps some kind of aftermath to the fever had made my mind as unsteady as my body, I don't know. Anyway, I didn't find them; not, at any rate, until late one night Buran said sadly, 'You want to see the heads?'

'Yes.'

He asked why.

'I don't know.'

He looked at me in silence for a long time. 'It is not a good thing.'

'I know.'

I suppose it was because I was a guest that he gave in. He took my arm, and led me to a space at the rear, a dark room partitioned off from the rest. Inside, he turned and pointed. I looked up towards the smoke-blackened rafters, and saw nothing for a moment or two. But then I made something out: seven dim, dark, round shapes, hung in a kind of circle, high above me. They didn't look like human heads, or indeed anything at all. They could have been gourds, or coconuts. Seven blackened things.

Buran said, 'Now you have seen,' and led me away.

In the night I wakened with my mind full of them, disgusted with myself. There was a terrible urge to go back to that room and stare at them again, and I had to fight it down. I lay there feeling like some mad thing in a horror film, one of Boris Karloff's nastier creations. In the morning the feeling was still with me. I resisted it for a while, but something was drawing me back, and my feet just took me there, to stand looking again up at the little ring of seven heads, almost hidden from sight under their sooty covering.

I wondered about the ritual of head-taking, and why they were hung in a circle. Why put them in so dark a place? They were trophies, and man puts his trophies where they can be seen.

It was very strange. Something gripped me in that place. I stood there, head tilted far back, looking at them, until I began to get dizzy. The heads seemed to move, to turn, the circle to spin, and I had to lower my gaze and shake my head to restore a sense of balance.

The dizziness passed almost at once, and I looked up again, but now with a sudden realization of what I had seen. I was no longer looking at the heads as heads, but at the circle they made.

I went straight to Buran's room.

He saw me in the doorway, and said, 'Do not think about them.'

'I'm not, any more. But I have a question. Where did you get the wheel?'

CHAPTER SIXTEEN

It, too, was blackened: a dim, sooty, circular shape, half hidden by drooping strands of thatch, and the heads suspended from it on strings distorted its outline so much that in the dimness it had remained unrecognizable. That brief moment of dizziness had given it movement, or I'd never have known what it was. Yet my subconscious must have identified it far earlier, or why had I been drawn back so strongly?

The whole thing was uncanny, and a little shudder ran down my back as Buran stood beside me and once again we looked up into the high gloom of the longhouse roof.

'It *is* a wheel?'

'Yes.'

'Where did it come from?' The world may be full of wheels, but the jungles of Borneo aren't. 'How did it get here?'

'From the forest. Many years ago.'

'I'd like to see it. May I?'

Buran said, 'Try not to think about the heads.'

'I'm not thinking about them. It's the wheel I'm interested in.'

He gave me a doubtful look.

I said, 'I only want to see the wheel more closely.'

'It is not to be moved.'

'Then can I get up there? On a ladder?' Ladder was a word he hadn't encountered. Steps he understood.

He didn't like it. He was a very civilized man, but he was a Dyak, with respect for the taken heads bred into him. A head brought with it the courage of its owner, to be added to the warrior's own courage. There are plenty of civilized people who touch wood from superstitions as ancient and inbred.

'Steps,' I pleaded, 'so that I can see the wheel. I will touch nothing.'

In the end he agreed. A ladder was brought – a rickety affair of bound steps and frighteningly flexible poles – and I climbed up slowly. I didn't much trust my own physical state, and trusted that ladder a good deal less. The heads swung gently about twenty feet above the floor, but until the light fell on them it was only in imagination that they had form. With the light they were abruptly real. Through the coating of soot, features remained clearly discernible. One still wore spectacles over fallen eyelids; two others had moustaches. They were macabre enough to turn a butcher's stomach, yet for all that, there was a curious tranquillity in the expressions on the dried and blackened faces.

I'd promised Buran not to study them, and I didn't. Carefully dusting away soot, I examined the wheel. It seemed to be fifteen to eighteen inches across, and with a heavy rubber tyre that had not perished enough to lose its shape. The wheel itself was metal, though what metal I didn't know. It might be steel, though if it came from an aircraft, aluminium was more likely. I tried to remember the Dakotas I'd seen and flown in. This seemed altogether too small to be a landing wheel from a large aircraft. But the picture in my mind's eye, of a Dakota at Brize Norton years before, standing waiting for us to board, reminded me of something. We're accustomed, nowadays, to big jets with a cluster of landing wheels at the point of balance and a tail high off the ground, but the old Dak dates from earlier days. The Dak had a tail wheel. I reckoned a tail wheel might be just about this size.

Climbing down, I could feel my heart beating with excitement. I thanked Buran gravely and said I had been very careful not to touch the heads. Then I said, 'Where, in the forest, was it found?'

'This is important?'

'To me, yes.'

'Why?'

I thought, suddenly: to hell with keeping them in ignorance! We weren't going to find the plane by ourselves;

already two weeks had been spent searching and no trace had been found. We needed all the help we could get. Buran listened grave-faced as I told him about my father's disappearance, about Miss Franklin nursing him until he died, about the letter she'd carried for me all those years.

When I'd finished, he said, 'It was in the forest. I do not know where.'

'Who, then? Who found it?'

He thought for a moment. 'The man is dead.'

I felt my shoulders slump, but persisted. 'The aircraft itself must be somewhere. Do you know of any wreckage?'

He shook his head.

But an hour later, as I leaned disconsolately against the verandah rail, he came to me with one of the men. 'This is Kelang. His father found the wheel. Kelang was with him.'

'Do you remember where?' I could hear the excitement in my own voice.

Kelang shook his head, and I felt my stomach contract in disappointment. But Buran talked to him and suddenly Kelang smiled and nodded. It wasn't that he didn't know, merely that he didn't understand the question.

The two of them talked rapidly, question and answer, then Buran turned to me, smiling. 'He knows the place. He will guide you, when you are strong again.'

I felt stronger already, and said so. Buran shook his head. Tomorrow perhaps. He would not allow Kelang to take me until then. Another day would make a difference to me.

Then would he send somebody to ask Fankee and Ludlam to return? He would.

They were both drawn and weary when they came back that evening; even Jigah seemed downcast. They'd been out searching when the messenger arrived and he, like a sensible bloke, had simply sat at the camp and waited for them, so there had been a day of pointless expended effort. But hope works wonders, and when I explained about Kelang and the tail wheel, the adrenalin began almost visibly to flow through the pair of them, as it was flowing through me.

We left early next morning, taking with us equipment to set up camp, and full of a bright optimism that lost lustre steadily as we tramped in Kelang's wake over all-too-familiar ground: straight along the trail across the neck of the U, then turning towards Miss Franklin's little clearing. When we reached it, Kelang led us up the rocks beside the waterfall, forcing his way, as we had done so many times, through the head-high ferns. We passed trees that bore the marks of our own machetes, fern fronds we had cut. It was all ground we had covered laboriously.

Kelang finally stopped at the foot of a tree, and pointed at the ground. His meaning was all too clear, but Miss Franklin asked him to be sure. Then she grimaced. 'Yes. The wheel was here.'

It should have been such a great moment, but I think we could all have wept. We were near enough in the centre of the arc of our original quadrant, and we'd searched here that very first day, when we were fresher and more alert. We'd all known it was possible to miss the wreckage, but not here, surely. Not on the first day!

Standing there in the forest's gloom, we were deeply despondent at that moment. All around us the ancient, giant trees reared like pillars into the high, dark canopy; we were like a small funeral party in a vast cathedral, suddenly and brutally aware of our own helplessness in all this immensity.

In a desultory way, we began to search again, but with no real expectation. If anything was there it was thoroughly covered. A kind of film sequence was running in my head, in which my father, knowing he was going to crash, was dropping lower towards the trees. I'm no pilot, but it was obvious he'd try to keep the nose up, so that the tail made the first contact, in the forlorn hope of skimming across the matted treetops. Well, the tail wheel had been ripped off, and fallen here, but it told us nothing; not even the direction in which he'd been travelling. It merely gave us a centre point for a search area.

Later we went back to the spot where the tail wheel was found, to eat a dispirited meal, and afterwards I stood leaning against a tree, smoking a cigarette, frustrated and angry. Without quite knowing it, I was banging the heel of my fist angrily against the bark.

Kelang murmured something.

'What did he say?' I asked Miss Franklin.

'That you must not be too sad. Fathers die before their sons.' There was a nice edge of irony in her voice.

I inclined my head, and said, 'Thank you.'

Then he spoke again, and Miss Franklin's head snapped round to look at him.

I said, 'What now?'

'He says he shares feelings with you. It was near here his own father died.'

'Ask him how,' I said, but she'd done that before I spoke. She was listening carefully.

At last she said, 'He fell.'

'Fell!'

'Kelang's grandfather was with him. Kelang's father was apparently trying to climb a tree, and he fell and was killed.'

'Are the Dyaks climbers?' I asked.

'No.'

'Then why?' I was looking upward now, my mind racing.

'He doesn't know.'

'And his grandfather. What did he say?'

'Kelang says it was long ago. He has no idea. His grandfather didn't talk about it.'

I studied the huge trunk against which I was leaning. It was bare of branches for at least a hundred feet, but then they spread from it, and from its neighbours, tangled and intertwining, so densely that no direct light came through. How much higher did it go? Another hundred feet – another hundred and fifty? Away up there was an immense mattress of leaves and branches, that was supported by these tremendous hardwood trunks much as the piles in the river bank supported the structure of the longhouse itself.

I said slowly, 'Is it possible that the plane didn't crash *through* the trees?'

Ludlam looked at me in astonishment. 'You mean it could still be up there?'

'I don't know.'

But was it *so* impossible? There could be anything up to thirty yards of solid cover in that endless raft of foliage floating high over our heads. Many of the branches were two feet thick, even more, some of them, and it was all hardwood, strong as girders. If the Dakota had floated down into it more or less level, wasn't it just conceivable that the trees could have taken its weight? That they *continued* to support it?

I tore my gaze from that green-black canopy. 'Ask him where his father fell.' I closed my eyes and crossed my fingers, and hoped.

Kelang was replying to Miss Franklin's question.

'*Does he know?*'

As she nodded, Kelang was already rising to his feet. We all followed him as he picked and forced his way for about a hundred and fifty yards. He stopped then, and pointed to a tree. Kelang smiled habitually, but he wasn't smiling now.

'It was from this tree that his father fell,' Miss Franklin said.

We glared up into that damned greenery until our necks ached. If the plane was up there, then some part of it, *surely*, would be visible. The suggestion of a shape, a single line straighter than any line nature makes, a glimmer of light reflected from metal or glass. But the foliage was as opaque as deep water, and indeed I felt almost as though I were looking upside down into a dark green lake.

We moved from spot to spot, hoping that changed angles might reveal something. We tried hurling a few sticks up into the trees, but they didn't even reach the lower branches. The analogy with a deep lake grew more accurate: if the plane was up there, the jungle had it hidden beyond a surface.

Ludlam, the pencil and paper man, finally said, 'Let's look at the facts,' and we chopped a clear space for ourselves at the foot of the tree and sat down.

'Right,' he said. 'One, this place meets the first criterion.

It is within a mile of Miss Franklin's camp, and the land slopes towards it. Two: the tail wheel was found over there, a hundred and fifty yards away.'

'If it *is* a tail wheel,' I said.

'All right. A query beside that. But even if the evidence is entirely circumstantial, it's difficult to see why any kind of wheel should be found in a place like this. We know the wheel is small and that it has a thick rubber tyre. If we were in a city somewhere, it could have come from anything, but we're not in a city. We're in the vicinity of an aircraft crash. But the query stands.

'Next, Kelang's father. The Dyaks aren't climbers. This isn't palm country. People don't shin up and down trees the way they do in Jamaica, because the trees are simply too damn big. But he *was* climbing. And anybody who sets out to climb a big brute of a tree like that must have a damn good reason. Okay so far?'

'It looks,' I said, 'as though he told nobody, anyway, except his own father. I asked Buran if he knew of a crashed aeroplane and he didn't.'

Miss Franklin looked at me quickly. 'I thought we'd agreed not to mention the crash!'

I shrugged. 'Having found the wheel, it seemed pointless not to ask.'

Her lips tightened, but she said nothing.

I went on, 'It looks to me as though Kelang's father was doing the climb on the quiet. Would a Dyak do that?'

Miss Franklin thought about it. 'A discovery would give him standing. You saw how the wheel was hung up. Yes, it's quite possible.'

'Right.' Ludlam was bringing the meeting to order. 'If Kelang's right, it was this tree here that he tried to climb. Not over there, where he found the wheel, but here. That seems to argue that he could see something. He found the wheel, then he saw the plane; that's what it looks like, to me. Anybody disagree?'

I said, 'No, it's perfectly feasible. It doesn't follow that it was the plane, though; it could have been anything: broken branches, even.'

'Would you try to climb up there to investigate a broken branch? They're snapping off all the time as we very well know. No – he must have seen the plane. That was twenty years ago. In twenty years the jungle can cover anything. It's covered the plane. *I* think it must be up there.'

'So do I,' I said, 'but it's thin evidence. A man fell out of a tree twenty years ago. How do we know it's this tree? Because Kelang says so? Well, okay – but how good is his memory?'

'Very,' Miss Franklin said. 'Rely on it.'

'There's only one way to find out,' Ludlam said. 'We have a go.'

'What you mean is, *I* have a go!'

He didn't bat an eyelid. 'You, young Tunnicliffe, are the obvious candidate.'

It was all very well to make a decision. Executing the damn thing was going to be a great deal trickier. I'd been looking at that tree merely as one interested in what it might conceal; now I had to face it as an opponent, and a formidable one at that.

The trunk was a good sixty inches in diameter, bare as a pole and straight as a pillar. If I'd been one of those athletic Canadian loggers one sees in the documentaries, climbing like monkeys with a long belt round the tree and spiked boots to give grip, it might have been simple. But I'm not, and it was going to be very difficult. A fire-engine with a hundred-foot extending ladder would have been handy, but the nearest one was probably in Singapore. I thought longingly of a helicopter: it might be possible to charter one in Kuching, and have a look at the tree from above. If we did that, though, the story would be out with a vengeance. I went over the possible alternatives, and was left with one option only. A rope.

Well, there was the new, sound nylon one I'd bought in Kuching. All *I* had to do was shin a hundred feet up a rope! . . . and I swallowed at the realization because I've never been much of a one for rope-work, even in the gym. I can do it, but I'd rather not. Like Kelang's late-lamented father, I'm not a climbing man.

All that, though, was still a distance away. There was a problem to be solved first. I said, 'Okay, we have the rope. How in hell do we get it up there?'

Ludlam looked at me, then at the tree, then at me again. 'You've got a point.'

'Too bloody right I've got a point!' Master Ludlam was the sort of planner who sent an indent to the stores depot for a dozen grappling hooks, size six or whatever, and a line-firing gun, à la commando operation. Listen, now, gentlemen, here's how the objective is to be approached and taken . . .

Miss Franklin, more accustomed to primitive parts, said, 'Bow and arrow?'

'We haven't got either, and if we had, I'm no archer. Are you?'

No, she wasn't. She'd have a go, of course, being daunted wasn't part of her stock-in-trade, but she wasn't going to be much use.

I stood and stared at that bloody monster of a tree, and at its surrounding brothers, and got nowhere. Here and there a creeper twisted round a trunk, and Ludlam pointed to one, fatuously. 'Do you,' I said, 'think I'm Tarzan?'

In the end I borrowed his paper and pencil and began making a list of our equipment, hoping that something in it would give me inspiration. Stoves, sleeping-bags, several Thermos flasks, rope, knives, fish hooks, fishing lines, gew-gaws for gifts. I sat and went over that list again and again, getting precisely nowhere.

I got up, tied the rope to a biggish stone and tried to hurl it up by sheer brute force, and a bird high in the foliage gave something surprisingly like a contemptuous laugh. I didn't blame it; the stone got about a third of the way before the weight of the rope dragged it back. Kelang cut a length of branch from a struggling sapling and gave us a demonstration of spear throwing, and that didn't work either. All these efforts were observed by a bunch of pro-boscis monkeys who sat in lofty safety, so unimpressed by our efforts that they scarcely bothered to move when we threw things. They looked not unlike Mister Punch and seemed to share his sardonic approach.

Reading for the tenth time that list I'd made, I solved one problem. The weight of the rope, even though it wasn't heavy, held back anything we might try to throw. But there were those two rolls of fine nylon filament for fishing lines that Miss Franklin had so thoughtfully bought and not yet given away. The filament wasn't much thicker than thread. If that could somehow be propelled up first, with one end left tied to the rope . . .

Stone and spear were tried again. They still didn't work. It would have taken the throwing arm of an Olympic javelin champion to manage it, and even he would require a run-up, and neither the Olympic arm nor the run-up was available.

Ludlam fashioned a bow of sorts, using several twisted strands of filament as a string, but as every boy learns, home-made bows aren't very good, and home-made arrows are worse.

Arrows, though. *Arrows.* Suddenly my mind was back in my misspent youth, and something my father had once made for me that he'd said was a secret weapon from Yorkshire; and after the first one was lost or broken, I'd made one or two myself. He'd called it a throwing arrow, and it had been a marvellous toy for a boy, though oddly enough few boys I ever met seemed to have heard of it.

I hunted round for a sound piece of wood, and began to shape it with my knife. A good throwing arrow is about fifteen inches long, thick at the tip, and tapering gradually down towards the flight. Ideally you need a bench and a vice and a plane, so naturally, I made a mess of the first piece of wood.

'What on earth is *that*?' Ludlam said as I whittled busily at the second attempt.

'Throwing arrow.'

'Hmm.' He looked at it, and at me, doubtfully. 'How's it work?'

'You throw it.'

'Yes, but – '

I said, 'What part of the world are you from?'
'Kent.'
'And where were you at school?'
'King's, Canterbury.'
'Far too posh,' I said. 'This is ragamuffin stuff.'

I worked more carefully this time. No slips of the knife, and slicing the slivers away carefully until it sat nicely balanced on my outstretched finger, with the heavy third on one side and the tapering two-thirds on the other. Always for me the tricky bit had been splitting the thin end for the flight, but the knife was sharp and the touch delicate for once and I managed it. The flight was made from my cigarette packet. I then cut a little notch in the wood about five inches below the flight.

'What's that for?' Ludlam's nose was about six inches away, in imminent danger of being sliced off if the knife slipped.

'You mean,' I said, 'that in all your experience of war and weapons, you've seen nothing like it?'

'No.'

'Well, that,' I said, deepening the notch a little, 'is the magic bit.'

All I now wanted was a piece of string about two feet long, and of course we hadn't one. The filament was too thin, the rope too thick. We had sophisticated materials: what was needed was the string from a Christmas parcel.

'String,' I said, looking for ideas.

Heads were shaken.

Well, something else might do. 'Elastic?' I said daringly to Miss Franklin.

'No,' she replied neutrally. Whether that meant refusal or unavailability was not disclosed. But she had an idea, all the same. 'Would a bootlace be long enough?'

It was. With the little ferrule cut off, I tied a knot in the end, laid the lace across the notch in the arrow, then passed the rest round the shaft, over the knot and down to the blunted tip, holding the tautened lace pinched against the side of the tip, with thumb and forefinger, and the remainder gathered in my palm.

The arrow was ready to throw.

The principle is simple enough: the loop at the notch applies thrust behind the point of balance, and the extra weight of the heavy, forward end is sufficient to prevent the arrow tumbling over and over in flight.

Now the target: there was a heavy branch growing out from the left side of the tree, bent down a little by the weight of its subsidiaries, and almost clear of the others. If I could flight the arrow over that, with the filament attached, so that the arrow dropped the other side . . . We spent a bit of time unreeling filament, trying to arrange it so it wouldn't snag on anything.

But it did. The arrow flew up a few feet, then stopped and fell back. We spent more time fiddling with the thin filament, then I tried again. It was on the fifth attempt that the arrow flew high into the tree – and stayed there.

Cautious tugs on the line failed to dislodge it. A stronger one snapped the filament. Fishermen know the feeling well. I settled down to make arrow number two, and set the others making three, four and five. Jigah, to his fury, wasn't trusted with a big knife and his gift penknife wasn't up to the job. It was an extremely frustrating afternoon. All four arrows vanished, one by one, into the canopy because I wasn't throwing very straight, and though a couple of times we managed to tug them down again they finally went up and stayed up.

So there was more manufacture, more vexation, until at long last I achieved the miracle and an arrow sailed over the right branch and came down the other side. Pulling on the filament, I drew the nylon rope up and over the branch and back down to the ground.

Ludlam gave me a bright little nod. 'You're in business,' he said.

It was too late for that day, though, and I wasn't sorry. Tomorrow would be quite soon enough.

As we walked laboriously back, I was thinking of possible ways to make the climb a bit safer: a rigged-up bosun's chair, perhaps, or loops for my feet, or something on those lines. Borneo chose that moment to underline the hazards.

Just ahead of us, something long and thin launched itself out of a tree, seeming to swim through the air in a kind of curve.

I said, 'Was that a snake, by any chance?'

Miss Franklin said it was, and gave me a little lecture about them. 'They flatten themselves, and draw in the ventral scales, you see. It makes a hollow along the body and lets them glide. I think there are three kinds.'

'Are any of them venomous?'

It was one thing Miss Franklin didn't know.

CHAPTER SEVENTEEN

Contemplating that climb, and I spent most of a largely-wakeful night thinking about it, the hazards seemed to multiply. That flying snake had put the wind up me in a very comprehensive way. What else lurked in those tree-tops? Were the monkeys aggressive? All you'd need, a hundred feet off the ground and clinging on with both hands, was a couple of angry monkeys biting chunks out of your face! But there was no ducking out. Neither Ludlam nor Miss Franklin was up to it, and we could scarcely ask Kelang to risk following his father. If anybody was scheduled to go farther the following day, it was me. No doubt Miss Franklin would find another suitable cleft in the rocks, another lot of orchids to mark the spot and a few heartfelt prayers!

I wasn't a hundred per cent fit yet, but had certainly been recovering fast, and the percentage was probably some-where in the nineties. I'd fashioned a rough bosun's chair out of rope and one of our bright nylon backpacks with holes cut in it for my legs. As I put it on, next morning, Ludlam gave a little snort and said I looked like a kid in an orange nappy. I told him security was the watchword, not beauty.

I was prepared, by then, but not ready; one never is

quite ready for a thing like that: not when life is at stake. I managed to postpone the evil moment by demanding a cup of coffee from the flask, and a cigarette.

Miss Franklin, as she invariably did when I smoked, said, 'You really should give it up.'

I replied, more or less seriously, 'This cigarette may well be my last,' and she saw the point and let me smoke it in peace.

After that, though, there was no more delaying. One final check on all the knots of the bosun's chair, then suddenly my feet were off the ground, with all of them hauling on the rope and the chair beginning to move upwards in a series of little jerks. It was slow progress, because after every heave the rope had to be belayed round a big fallen branch we'd dragged to the spot for the purpose. The branch weighed a good deal more than I did, and provided a safety margin of a sort, but Lloyds wouldn't have classified this trip an A1 risk.

It's relatively easy beforehand, when it's all in the mind. You know there's a hundred feet of space and very little margin and when that's said, everything is said. Things change, though, as you swing up there and the people below grow smaller and the branch above grows nearer and you look up and there's a big black bird with a curly yellow bill like a pickaxe cocking its head to one side and wondering if this is the new flavour of the month.

Levity, but I wasn't feeling any. My guts were in my gob, as that Irish stepfather of mine used to say. When I reached that branch, now about twenty feet above my head, I was going to have to clamber on to it. Then stand up. Then start climbing.

Christ!

No sign of the aeroplane yet, and the branch coming nearer . . . I began to try to work out some kind of route farther into the tree. There'd be one hellishly awkward big step first, but after that it might not be too difficult if I could forget about the height. I could see one long straight limb going up almost vertically, with a good number of smaller branches going off it. With luck . . . The big bird startled me by taking off and flying lazily by only a few feet away, a good deal less scared of me than I was of it.

A few jerks more and my hand touched the branch.

I sat for a moment, working out the move, then hung on tight with both arms and hooked one leg over it, bosun's seat and all. The next thing was to haul up enough rope behind me to make ties as I went upwards. That done, I stood up with monumental care, leaning against the trunk. The branch I wanted was almost round the other side, nearly a yard away, and higher, and reaching it entailed a kind of splits and I bloody well didn't want to try it. I told myself sternly that if I didn't, nobody else would and stuck a leg out experimentally into space. Hammers and pitons would have been useful, but this was primitive climbing in a primitive place, with no mechanical trickery to reduce the risks. *One*: stretch out leg; *two*: find foothold; *three*: try to test it without overbalancing; *four*: transfer weight. I did it, breathed again, and tied more knots.

So far so good. I began to climb that canted branch, making loops every foot or two, with my breath rasping in my ears and sweat that was half-heat and half-fear cascading out of me.

A sudden, hammering thought caught me immobile, clinging to that branch. What an idiot I was! What idiots we all were! There was no plane stuck up here in the trees. That kind of thing couldn't happen; we'd simply made ourselves believe it! And in all our talking and questioning, over and round and through and over again, we'd all managed to ignore something important.

Simple Question: How on earth could a badly injured man have climbed down?

Simple Answer: He couldn't.

Simple. Multiple injuries, she'd said; broken thigh and ribs. However well he could fly, he couldn't fly without an aeroplane. Big black birds might sail down, but injured men certainly couldn't, however clever, brave and resourceful.

It was time, I thought thankfully, to go down. From

where I clung at that moment, the prospect of returning empty-handed to London looked distinctly inviting. I was actually taking a first downward step when I glimpsed something, stopped and stared! The very tip of the Dakota's flat tailplane peeped at me from about twenty feet above my head.

I remained very still, staring at it, half-convinced it must be an illusion of some kind; that some unlikely conjunction of plane and angle, leaf and branch, had been sufficient, in that dim light, to appear what it was not. Yet it was a clean line. No more than a foot or two to be discerned, but clear and defined. Climbing with slow, deliberate care, I inched towards it, still unconvinced; it would not have surprised me if, at any second, the shape had vanished, become part of the tree again.

But it didn't. As I came nearer, it was possible to see small, flaky curves of the camouflage paint that had partly peeled away. When finally it became possible to reach up and touch the thing, there *was* metal under my finger. *Simple question:* How *had* a badly injured man climbed down? Because that was what he'd done. No simple answer now.

The Dakota seemed to lie as though on a cushion. Its weight had pressed down upon the branches, spreading them wide to make this springy green platform high in the treetops. I tested the tailplane's firmness to be sure it would take my weight. Then clambered through the damp foliage to stand crouching on it, and from there was able to see almost the whole length of the aircraft, though the view was badly obstructed. Over the years hundreds of branches, forced aside but fighting for light, had climbed upward again beside the fuselage until now it was almost as though the old Dakota had deliberately been wrapped in a cocoon of foliage. Turning awkwardly, I saw that the tail fin had been torn and bent over just above my head. The wings I couldn't see at all: they were too far away and there was too much in between.

For quite a while I crouched there, spellbound by the weirdness of it, by the uncanny fact that it was here at all, damaged but relatively whole, fifty yards above ground in the middle of endless tracts of primary jungle. A dozen streams of thought swept through my mind: the extraordinary fact that we'd found it, the closeness, now, to real riches, like something from a pirate tale. But above all I thought of the man who'd brought the Dakota here: of my father, elated at the wealth he'd grabbed, flying off to what must have seemed to him like a heavenly wealth. The war's discomforts all behind him; the means for life-long comfort; escape into a new life only hours of flying away. And then, perhaps very suddenly, the abrupt knowledge that the aeroplane was failing. Had it been engines, fuel – what? It must have been sudden, or he'd have tried to turn, surely, to a landing at Kuching. But no chance of that. The realization that nothing lay below him but the trees: the frantic attempt to set the Dakota down among them. Impossible, no alternative, yet he'd almost brought it off.

Now, twenty years later, birds chirruped and called around the green grave of the silent aircraft, and he lay beneath the wild orchids a mile away. And it was I, *his* son, who . . .

Twenty years in which I'd given him scarcely a thought. Now my mind was full of him. His letter lay in my pocket, his picture across my sight.

Faintly, from below, I heard shouts, but didn't answer. The long, hollow corpse of the Dakota waited and it seemed important that these minutes, this time, should belong only to me, and to him; an almost religious feeling. A few feet away, the door in the side of the fuselage gaped open, partly screened by the fronds climbing past and over it. I began to make my way towards it, moving horizontally rather than vertically, but climbing all the same. It was like a traverse on a rock face, but more dangerous, because the footholds here were often on slimmer branches that gave under my weight. In the mass they supported the great weight of the plane, but individually they were pliant and treacherous. Reaching the doorway, I pushed and pulled at the climbing branches to make a way through, then reached for the sill, clambered through, and stood nervously just inside the opening, listening to the thousand creaks and whispers in the branches caused by the small increase in weight. The aircraft seemed to move a little. Was it possible its balance was so tenuous . . . ? Better not to think about it.

I'd thought she lay level, but she didn't. There was a downward slope, not steep but appreciable, from tail to nose. When I moved it was to follow the line of least resistance, down the incline towards the cockpit, over the damp, mildewed floor. At once the rubber of my boots slipped and I fell on my bottom, and as I did so, grasped in reflex at something on the floor. It snapped in my hand: the rotted remnant of a webbing strap. As I rose I could see the rest of it, the harness from which it had come, secured to one wall of the fuselage and leading towards the door. Careful now about my feet on the slippery floor, I bent to examine it. This had been a parachute harness. My father must have fastened it, streamed the parachute out, and used it to climb down, hoping it would let him reach the ground. Possibly he'd knotted the cords to make a long rope, and tried to climb down. Then a new thought came. Maybe he'd come through the actual crash more or less unscathed, and injured himself getting down from the tree. A long climb down and thin rope that wasn't quite long enough – or it could have broken, and the fall inflicted all the injuries. There'd been no sign of a rope, or parachute silk, but twenty years would have rotted natural materials to nothing in the damp of the jungle.

I puzzled over it for a while, but this was a mystery, would remain a mystery, and it was, in any case, of concern only to me. I walked with care down the cabin to the cockpit, past a long thin packing case, to where the flimsy door stood wide open, and looked inside.

Then recoiled.

A skeleton sat strapped into the co-pilot's seat, the skull thrown back to grin at the roof!

*

Rotten remnants of clothing still hung about the bones, and I looked at it more with shock than surprise. Long ago, in Jamaica, Ludlam had told me about the day my father had taken off in the Dakota with his false documents and his red treasure, and Colonel Toshiba of the Imperial Japanese Army wearing a glengarry bonnet and the uniform of the Shanghai Volunteer Force. A disintegrating webbing belt held a knife in a rusty scabbard. A couple of brass buttons, green with verdigris, clung to the remaining rags of uniform, and as I rubbed them, a crest showed through. During the war, they'd always talked about grinning Japanese, and here was Toshiba left to grin for ever.

I've used the word uncanny before, and I doubt there's a better to describe my feelings then. But I was here for a purpose, with work to do, and sitting rapt was no part of it. The aeroplane had been found, so one search was over. Now another began. Somewhere in this dead structure, this tomb in the trees, was the collection of rubies for which the first George Hawke Tunnicliffe had died. Now the second George Hawke Tunnicliffe must set about finding it. From the beginning of this trip, finding the aircraft had been the difficulty. If we managed it, the rest would be simple. A single floor beam had been removed, a mould made, and a new beam recast in printing metal, with the stones embedded in it. I'd thought it would all be easy; a few quick scratches at the beams to distinguish aluminium from printing metal. Then, with the beam identified, cut it free. Soft metal, so no problem.

But now, standing with my back to the cockpit, looking along the fuselage, it became clear how difficult the search would be. The long, teak packing case almost by my feet would contain the Japanese torpedo that had been the ostensible reason for my father's flight. Somehow, miraculously, it had not been torn completely free on impact. The big crate lay partly awry but still chained to rings bolted into the floor, though it rested upon a row of hardwood planks intended, no doubt, to spread the load.

Before leaving England, I'd done some research on the Dakota's structure: elementary stuff in the British Museum reading-room, because I had no access to design plans. Remembering it now, I could understand the size of the job ahead of me.

The beams lay beneath the floor: part of the structure of the aircraft but not, apparently, essential to its integrity. That was part of the reason why beams had been chosen for the various pieces of smuggling. Another was the fact that in order to get at one, a section of the floor had to be taken up. They must have reasoned that inspecting Customs men had better things to do than tear up the floor of the C-in-C's own aircraft.

What faced me was a huge load of work. The torpedo would weigh – what? A ton, or more. The crate was seven good paces long, so more than twenty feet of the floor, and most of the more substantial beams, lay beneath the torpedo.

So: more calculations, if that's a proper name for the process. These were the factors: first, the torpedo weighed *at least* a ton. Secondly, the Dakota itself had an all-up weight of a bit more than eleven tons. Thirdly, the Dakota was poised up in the treetops. It might be firmly wedged, or it might be balanced, perhaps even delicately balanced. What would happen if I succeeded in moving the torpedo?

Nice question. Eleven tons could start moving in the branches; moving, furthermore, with me inside! And if they moved enough, and began to slip, or to fall, I'd be trapped inside with a ton of tumbling torpedo.

That, anyway, was the general direction of my thoughts. There were others. Could I get help? Neither Ludlam nor Miss Franklin could even make the ascent. Nor could Jigah. Nor could we reasonably recruit Kelang or any of the other men from Tunggal. For me to risk my neck was one thing. I'd be doing it in the hope of reward. In any case they weren't climbers. Up here they'd probably be useless anyway.

What tools did I have? Very little except the machete, and no prospect of getting more, apart perhaps from an axe. Then it occurred to me that some at least of these problems would have faced my father. He, too, would have

had to raise the floorboards and cut out the beam. He'd
have intended to do it *after* the removal of the torpedo, of
course, but he'd have had to do it himself. I began to hunt
round the interior of the fuselage, and this piece of reason-
ing, at least, proved correct. A little oiled-cloth roll containing a rusty hacksaw, a screwdriver and a few spanners,
some blades wrapped in waxed paper, and a big pair of bolt
cutters, was tucked away beneath the pilot's seat.

Better. But no crowbar, and it was a crowbar I'd need
to have any hope of shifting the torpedo.

Before starting work, though, I ought to let them know,
down there on the ground, that I'd found the plane. They'd
be wondering, and with justice, what had become of the
wandering boy. I went to the doorway, and paused there,
listening again to the creaks of the branches – just how
critically *was* the Dakota balanced? – then shouted at the
top of my voice, 'I've found it! Searching now!'

There seemed to be some sort of answering shout, though
I couldn't be sure with the background noise so continuous.

Duty done, I began my search the coward's way, putting
my faith in luck. No point in tackling the torpedo unless
I had to. So I started at the tail. The floor panels had been
bolted down for twenty years, so the bolts were stiff. The
screwdriver fitted and though it turned a few of the bolt
heads, most of them refused to move; when I applied more
pressure, the notch often stripped. Taking out what bolts
I could, I then began work with the machete, hacking at
the panels, chopping round the bolt locations, watching my
own sweat drip down to form a little puddle on the floor.

More than an hour went by before I could lift that first
panel. When I did, five floor beams were revealed below.
I breathed a small prayer, and scraped hopefully at them
with my knife, then swore. An hour's hard labour, then
less than half a minute to discover that all five were
aluminium. Not enough faith behind the prayer – maybe
that was the trouble!

The next panel was bigger and wider and presented the
identical problem with the bolts, and this time there were
more of them. It was 1 p.m., the sticky heat at its height,

and the work brutally hard. Slogging away with the tools, I'd lifted two panels in almost three hours, and uncovered only aluminium beams.

The snack I'd brought with me consisted of coffee, a tin of cold beans and a cigarette, and soon I was back at work. By the end of the long afternoon, I had raised three more panels, and inspected a total of twenty-one pure aluminium floor beams. If they *were* pure aluminium: they looked light and almost flimsy yet resisted like tungsten steel. None, though, was printing metal.

I called it off, then, and took a little rest before beginning the climb down. Had there been more water and more food, I'd have spent the night up there with Colonel Toshiba. I'd spent the day on my knees, and figuratively was still on them, and his ghost would not have disturbed my slumbers. But the descent had to be made, and duly was: frightening, as expected, because all the spring and most of the sensation seemed to have left my weary limbs, and the drop to the ground now looked twice as long. Imagination, yes; but that's how it looked.

They could all see from my face that no exciting discoveries had been made. But the different reactions were interesting. Ludlam said, 'At least we've found it, and tomorrow's another day.' Considering they'd spent this one picnicking pleasantly, while I flogged myself to death, it seemed pretty cool. Miss Franklin thought that really I could have let them know a bit more! and I smiled my smile at her and apologized nicely. Kelang said nothing, but looked at me sadly, which was an improvement on the others. The boy Jigah, though, held my hand as we trudged back to camp. Sympathy, and very welcome.

We held a council of war. Position explained, diagrams drawn, much discussion: general agreement, after all, that I'd done the right things. Only perseverance now needed. But I was Percy and the verance would be all mine. For them another picnic; for me it was back to the salt mines. In the morning every bone and muscle ached, but if, as the Bible says, taking thought can add cubits to the stature, then I was stronger if not bigger, because I'd thought a good deal, especially about the torpedo. This time I was going up armed with rudimentary equipment and scientific principle, as well as hope. I'd cut a couple of thick hardwood poles, each about eight feet long, plus a bundle of shorter, thinner ones, straight as I could find them, all a couple of feet in length. Also I'd hacked a few rough wedges.

Getting the damned things up there wasn't without its difficulties because they seemed to snag and catch on every leaf, twig and fork, and manhandling them across and into the plane was a sweaty, dangerous operation. I may gloss over it now, but I promise I'll never forget it. Even considering what was to come, it was as hair-raising a thing as I've ever done in my life.

But at last I got them inside the fuselage and could set to work. Lever and roller, that was the principle. George Tunnicliffe's puny strength couldn't hope to shift the torpedo, but George Tunnicliffe with levers was puny no more. George Tunnicliffe proposed to lever up one end of the packing case and slide one of his thin poles underneath, and repeat the operation until it rested on rollers. Primitive rollers, but rollers none the less. *Then* watch St George defeat the monster!

I got my breath back after the climb, then bent to the task. Would she come up? She would! I tapped the roller in place with my toe at one end, then began on the other. Aha, my beauty! Rollers now in place at each end. Half a dozen more went in, spaced at intervals, and a good thing that crate was made of Burmese teak that hadn't rotted! In an hour or so, the torpedo was ready to be moved.

Not, of course, without hazard. That goes without saying, and I faced the prospect of changing the balance of the aircraft with what I think is known as trepidation: mouth dry, hands sweatier than ever, and the little tremor in my lips that always manifests itself in me when the going is palpably tricky. Once I moved it there would be no escape if the Dakota began to shift on its perch. Diving out of the door wasn't exactly to be recommended, though perhaps

less certainly fatal than remaining inside. But even that
escape route wasn't available; I was as far from the door as
it was possible to be, my back almost against the bulkhead
that blanked off the cockpit. So when I applied the lever
to one end of the crate, I felt a little as though I were
beneath the guillotine and pulling the release handle. If it
went, I went with it!

I took a breath and committed myself, moving it an
inch. Branches creaked and cracked a bit, but there was no
desperate lurch. So far, so good. I tried it again with the
same result. And again, each time kicking in the wedges.
When I'd moved the crate a foot, and one of the rollers
was free, I went to the far end and tucked it in place there.
As an afterthought, I moved gradually towards the tail
to test whether my own weight made any difference.
Apparently it didn't; the fuselage moved not at all, though
the vast net of branches outside was protesting.

Gradually, the torpedo was inched up that slight incline,
with my wedges slammed in at every movement to stop
it rolling back at me. Nearly three feet to go before that
first floor panel was exposed, but I began to feel that with
reasonable luck, I'd get away with it.

At the very last heave, the Dakota seemed to give a little
groan. There was a tiny pause, as other groans answered
from the trees, and suddenly she shifted a fraction. Not
much, but it was enough to stop my heart for an instant.
Had she changed position and settled? Or was she about to
topple? I stood there, scarcely breathing, as the chorus of
sounds from the branches sang on and on. There was no
further movement; or none discernible.

I mopped my brow and went to work, lifting the load
spreaders to get at the floor panel. As before, some of the
bolts could be turned, some could not, and it was back to
the old routine of crash, bang and wallop, hacking with the
machete and cutting with the bolt shears, but now I had
the lever to help lift the panel once one end was clear:
still backbreaking labour at those temperatures, but at least
I was now working in a more hopeful area. By noon I had
it free and could haul it clear, lean it against the side of

the fuselage, and bend to look at the floor beams.

Six of them were visible here, and I was on my knees, bending to scrape at the first with my knife, when a sharp, nerve-shredding screech seemed to paralyse me. Two proboscis monkeys had come in through the door and were glaring down the fuselage at the intruder in *their* refuge. They honked at me angrily and one began to move towards me, mouth open, teeth bared, arms raised threateningly, displaying all the aggression at its command, its long nose raised to the horizontal each time it barked. They're supposed to be shy, but these two clearly weren't. I grabbed my lever pole and waved it threateningly and that halted them. The bigger snapped large yellowish teeth at the pole, and didn't retreat. So I had to advance. I didn't want to hurt them, but they clearly had designs on me; above all, I didn't want to go past the end of the crate, where my weight might affect the balance of the aircraft.

I got them out eventually. That was the second and, as it turned out, the last of my brushes with local wildlife, and both had been more frightening than dangerous, but the incident hadn't done my nerves a lot of good. That first ghastly screech still seemed to ring in my ears as I scraped once more at the floor beams. The first had the dull grey of weathered aluminium, and so had the second, the third and the fourth. I remember glancing at the torpedo and thinking: what happens, you bastard, if I move you again?

It wasn't necessary, though. The fifth beam was made of soft metal and the machete chipped a lump off relatively easily, to reveal a clean silver shine beneath. I squatted back on my heels, mopping at my brow, staring at the length of metal which, if Ludlam had been right, contained gem stones enough to make me rich. All I had to do was cut it away.

The hacksaw blade bit into it easily, though the sawing position was awkward, and I kept banging my wrist on a projecting piece of metal. It also made a lot of noise, squeaking and squealing as I dragged the blade back and forth.

That noise, I think, must have prevented my hearing the other one. When I stopped for a moment, though, the sound was clearly audible, *and* unmistakable: it was the clattering roar of a helicopter.

I listened, thought about it, and decided to ignore it. Then I changed my mind. This would be the army dropping in, Captain Taylor's compliments, no doubt, to see we were all right. Well, we were fine, thank you, and Miss Franklin and Ludlam could go back to Tunggal and deliver the necessary assurances, including something convincing about my own failure to be present.

But they wouldn't leave me alone here. I had to tell them to go. I approached the doorway more than a bit cautiously, without sending the Dakota crashing, and shouted down. They shouted back, too, but no words were audible. I swore unpleasantly because I'd have to clamber down to get within decent shouting range, and that meant I'd also have to climb back. Distinctly *not* amusing, that thought: but necessary. We didn't want the army wondering, or, worse, investigating.

So down I went, until I could see them all, standing looking up at me.

I yelled, 'You go. Leave me here.'

Miss Franklin gestured me down, and Ludlam called, 'You too!'

'No. I'll stay. Come back for me when they've gone!'

There was a bit of an argument, but I was in a position to dominate it, so I won, and off they went, the four of them, in a little column through the ferns. I climbed back to the Dakota, hoisted myself back in with my usual prayer, started down the fuselage, and noticed something tucked into the space beneath the cabin floor. I hadn't seen it before, simply because I'd been facing the wrong way, but now I hauled it out. It was a small, steel attaché case with G.H.T. punched into the metal by the handle. It had rusted a good deal, but wasn't locked, and though the hinges squeaked, it opened easily enough.

There wasn't much inside, but what there was proved

interesting: Australian discharge papers in the name of
Wilfred Hirst (I grinned at that name, because it enshrined
a couple more celebrated Yorkshire cricketers), my father's
flying log (difficult to see why he'd intended to keep *that*,
if he had, when he was in the process of changing his
identity) and the Dakota's own maintenance log. There
were also some shards of glass that had once been a bottle
of Johnnie Walker. The bottle must have broken in the
crash. Pity. It would have been smooth old whisky by now,
and I'd have enjoyed drinking a memorial toast in it.

I squatted there thumbing idly through the old, damp,
discoloured papers; idly, that is, until something leapt out
from one of them and left me with my mouth hanging open
and a lot of very unpleasant thoughts racing through my
head!

CHAPTER EIGHTEEN

It wasn't much, really: just a few figures on an old piece
of paper. But those figures made a number, and it was a
number I wasn't likely to forget, because the last time I'd
seen it had been in Singapore, in blood-red paint, on the
wall over Miss Franklin's bed!

So somebody in Singapore had known the Dakota's serial
number . . .

No need to guess who, either, and no prizes for working
out the obvious. The trail led straight to Ludlam. After all,
he'd known the aircraft in Burma, when my father was
flying it legitimately. Miss Franklin could be ruled out. She
hadn't been acting as she gaped at the words and figures
on her bedroom wall. Ludlam, though, had certainly been
lying when he'd said he hadn't been in Singapore. I'd
thought so at the time, when he'd shown me his air tickets
as proof. They hadn't really been proof at all, though: it
would have been easy to fly from Jesselton in North Borneo
to Singapore, then fly back. But *why*?

I sat on the torpedo crate, tried to work it out, and got nowhere. He'd been puzzling from the beginning, of course, though of late there'd been nothing new. The last time he'd behaved strangely was at the beginning of the river trip, when he'd seemed so worried we were being followed. What the *hell* was Ludlam up to? He'd set the whole thing up from the beginning, virtually sending for me, telling me about my father and the missing loot, pointing me in the direction of Borneo. Why? Not just the rubies. He might want them, but it had to go deeper than that: the Singapore episode went way outside the issue of the rubies.

My God, but when he came back I'd choke it out of him!

Ratlike as ever, he gnawed away all afternoon inside my head. I did no more to the beam and sat there with my eyes on it and my mind on him. The Ludlam of recent days had, I now realized, been a very different character from the man I'd first met in Jamaica. *Then* he'd been alert, probing, aggressive, intolerant. Here in Borneo all that had vanished, and Ludlam had been content to follow, chipping in occasionally it's true, perky sometimes; but in general he'd been a passenger.

I drank some coffee and smoked a few cigarettes, trying to analyse. In reality he'd had little option but to be a passenger: Miss Franklin was the guide, I was the muscle, he was just . . . well . . . along, waiting for us to . . .

Waiting, I thought. Waiting for what? For us to find the rubies? Then what was Singapore all about? Or was he waiting for something else? Why, on the river, had he been so concerned about being followed? So concerned *then* – but not later! Once we'd branched off the main river he hadn't seemed worried.

Hang on a bit . . . at the beginning, he hadn't known where we were going, had he? Because we deliberately hadn't told him. And that was when he'd been so twitchy about being followed.

It hit me, then, fair and square right between the eyes. He'd wanted to be followed, even arranged it! Ludlam hadn't known where we were going, but it wouldn't have been difficult, in Kuching, to discover the places in Sarawak where Miss Franklin had worked. There were only three, after all, and he knew we were going to one of them. Once we entered that first tributary our destination was known . . .

The question *why* wasn't answered, but the rest fitted uncomfortably closely. I was certain now he'd wanted us to be followed.

But by whom?

And something else – if Ludlam had been keeping quiet and waiting for something to happen, well, something *had* happened. A helicopter had arrived. I'd blithely assumed the army was on patrol, and maybe it was.

But –

And it was a very big but.

As time went on, my worry grew. I kept glancing at my watch, calculating the time needed to reach Tunggal and return. Time went by on a rising tide of anxiety. They could have been back by now, I thought, and a little later: they *should* have been back! Then it was only an hour or so to darkness and two facts hammered in my brain: they weren't back, and the helicopter was still there.

I was marooned now, a hundred and fifty feet off the ground; soon it would be night, and Heaven knew what was going on! Like a snake, an unwelcome thought slithered into my mind: I ought to try to get down. I booted the thought out. To get down alone would be impossible. My stomach churned at the idea. Back it came. If I . . . *No*, damn it, I'd kill myself! I wouldn't even think about it.

I did, though, and increasingly . . .

Strong nylon rope, an extra turn round the branch, providing additional friction to act as a brake, lowering myself, able to control the rate of descent. I'd done it before on battle courses. Yes, and I'd had rope burns, and the nylon, though strong, was thin and would cut. In my mind's eye I could see myself all too clearly, swinging, falling as my father must have fallen.

But it drew me. I had to know what was going on down

at Tunggal. And, like the man drawn to the cliff edge, I was tugged by my own mind towards that awful descent.

Nor was there time to delay. I wouldn't reach Tunggal in the light, anyway, but at least I would reach the camp. From there, there was a track, and I had a torch.

I shinned down to the big branch where my home-made bosun's cradle was secured. My heart rose into my throat as I looked down at the jungle floor far below.

Already, on the previous hauls, the rope had cut deep into the bark of the big branch in three places, two of them adjacent. I slotted the rope first into one, then round the branch, then into the other, then struggled into my mutilated backpack-cradle. The old oilskin bag that had contained the tools I now wrapped round my hands for protection, not that it offered much. Deliberately, I didn't look down; that first look had been more than enough and another would probably break what nerve I had.

Don't hesitate, I told myself. *Go!*

I lowered myself off the branch, the rope held in my hands, and coiled round my right arm, and began to pay out a little. Instantly my whole arm was under crushing pressure. Gritting my teeth against the pain, I fed it slowly through my hands. After ten feet, the pain was hellish, and the realization came that it would be impossible to go slowly; if I did, the pain would soon be unbearable, and willy-nilly I'd fall. Smooth and fast, like a parachutist's fall. Steeling myself, I began to let the rope slide faster, doing what little I could to let the wrapped oilskin take the strain as the rope burned hotly through my hands and over the arm.

Suddenly there was blood on my hands and the oilskin was fraying as the rope bit through it, and there was pain like fire in hands and arm.

I tried to slow the descent, but at once the pain was infinitely greater, and I had to loosen my grip. I seemed to be rocketing down, far too fast, and the rope, as it passed in front of my face, was stained with blood.

How far now? Forty feet . . . thirty . . . I was close to

passing out with pain, longing to let go; the thought of falling was now less appalling than the agony in my hands. Twenty. I'd kill myself if . . . but I could hold on no longer. I clamped my feet together, let go, fell, rolled, yelled as my body crashed down, and every bit of breath whooshed out of me.

Dazed and aching, but alive, I got to my knees, then rockily to my feet. I felt bruised all over, hands and arm hurt like hell, but I was down, and staggering off towards the camp. Miss Franklin's medical pack was there, but I didn't use it. Years ago there had been an army doctor in Korea with a theory that milk was the stuff for burns, and there was tinned milk among our gear. I knocked a hole in a tin of Carnation and poured it over hands and arm, rubbing it in gingerly. Then, carrying the tin for further applications, I set off for Tunggal.

He must have been put there to watch, lurking in the dark. I never saw him, but he'd probably heard me crashing about long before he saw my torch which, by then, was pretty low. But he had a torch of his own, which he shone first into my eyes and then, briefly, on the machine-pistol that pointed at my midriff. I didn't see his face, but the machine-pistol gave a little jerk to indicate that I was to walk ahead and when I emerged from the trees it was easy enough to see the situation. An armed man stood at the foot of each of the three big ladders leading to the upper floor of the longhouse, where the balcony was empty. On the cleared flat between the longhouse and the river, a fire burned brightly, and several men hunkered down beside it. On the river, the firelight showed a pontooned helicopter riding at anchor. But it wasn't a British helicopter, and the armed men were not uniformed soldiers.

The insurgents had come to Tunggal!

A jab in the back from my captor's machine-pistol propelled me towards the fire, and two of the squatting men rose, came towards me, and rapidly tied my hands behind my back. They were silent, brisk and highly efficient, and when it was done I was shoved past the fire, my legs were kicked from under me and I fell heavily on the trampled earth.

They watched as I rolled over and achieved a sitting position. Then they moved towards the fire, unconcerned. Turning my head I saw Miss Franklin a few feet away; her hands, too, were tied. I began to edge across to her, walking on my bottom, expecting to be stopped, but nobody even looked in my direction.

I said, 'Have they hurt you?'

'No.'

'Where's Ludlam?'

The words spilled out, swift but quiet. 'That's what I don't understand. When we got here the Indonesians were waiting. I was tied up like this, but he – '

'Go on,' I said grimly, scenting what was coming.

'He seems to know the commander!'

'He does, does he?' Nothing about Ludlam would surprise me any more. 'Where is he now?'

Her head gave a little jerk. 'Just over there.'

There were the two of them: Ludlam and another, a heavily-built, fat man sitting cross-legged on the ground ten yards or so away. They were eating, apparently without talking.

'What happened?'

'It was like this when we got here. They've herded everybody up into the longhouse. The whole village is up there, except Buran.'

'Have they hurt him?' I was thinking of what had been done to the headman at Lobang Nibong.

She shook her head. 'I don't think so. They tied him up, too, but I can't see where he is.'

We were talking in not much more than whispers. I told her about the aircraft's number and, almost as an afterthought, that I'd found the floor beam.

Miss Franklin said, 'We're going to be robbed.'

'I know.'

It was then that Ludlam rose and came towards us, the other man following. He wore a rumpled bush shirt and was inclined to waddle, but there was nothing comic about him. The firelight gleamed on a round, impassive face in which the eyes were almost invisible behind slabs of subcutaneous fat.

Ludlam gave his little rat's grin. 'Clever lad, young Tunnicliffe,' he said. 'Never thought you'd get down. What's that, rope burns?'

I said nothing.

'Find' em, did you?' He bent and looked into my face. 'Not that it matters. They'll be found easily enough. Colonel Singsong here knows where they are.'

'Who is he?'

'The Colonel? If your hands were in condition, you could shake hands with a friend of your father's, couldn't he, Colonel?'

'What do you mean?'

Ludlam chuckled. 'Longish story. He wasn't a colonel then, of course. Sergeant aircraft artificer in those days. Sergeant Ching Song and known as Singsong. Mentioned him to you, I remember.'

I remembered, too. Very well. Ching Song was the Malay-Chinese who'd built first the gold, then the rubies, into the aircraft. How in hell had *he* materialized?

'Makes you think, does it?'

'Yes,' I said. 'I started thinking too late altogether.'

'Your trouble is you can hardly think at all, young Tunnicliffe. Told you that before.'

'Oh, stop it!' Miss Franklin burst out. 'Stop playing cat and mouse! What are you doing? What are you *going* to do?'

'Shh. I'll tell you. You see, the good Colonel and I –'

'Colonel in what?' I demanded.

'Indonesian army. What else? Be patient. Don't interrupt. He and I are a bit in the same boat. I've been running through my funds in Jamaica. He ran through his a good bit faster. Fond of a game of fantan, the Colonel was, and dedication to that pastime comes expensive. After the war he drifted down to Djakarta and helped boot the Dutch out, and when Sukarno's lot became the regular army, he just went up and up. Clever with his hands, the Colonel.

Told you he was Rolls-Royce-trained and that kind of thing comes at a premium. Then it turned out he was even better with his brain.'

He looked it, too. There was a still watchfulness to Singsong.

'So what now? Kill us?'

'No need, old lad. Up sticks and off, that's the general principle.'

'With –'

'Of course, *with*! Afterwards you hop into your little boat and go back to Kuching. In your case though, it'll be *without*.'

'But why?' Miss Franklin said uncomprehendingly. 'You'd have had your share.'

'Not enough; not enough, you see. I'm an old crook, as you very well know.'

I said, 'I suspected –'

'Been surprised if you hadn't. Christ, anybody with half a brain would have known I smelt of stale haddock. But you're lazy-minded, as I've told you before. If it's more convenient for you to put it out of your mind, out it goes.'

True enough. 'So you –'

He interrupted again. 'Into Colonel Singsong's helicopter and off we go. The good Colonel's retirement is comfortably underwritten, and I don't have to worry either. Not exactly unassailable in purely moral terms, I suppose. But legally, well – possession's nine points, as they say, and it's more finders-keepers than straight theft.' He looked at me, a grin showing his little teeth. 'I think I can see some sluggish stirrings in that mudpool under your scalp. You're trying to work out how I did it?'

'Something like that.'

He chortled. 'Your forehead's in knots with effort. Give you a clue. Start thinking how I knew about old Fankee here. While you're doing it, the Colonel and I will reminisce.'

Ludlam turned and began to stroll away, saying to the silent waddling Singsong, 'Spot of Scotch appeal to you?'

I watched them go, thinking: he couldn't have known

about Miss Franklin, could he? *Could* he?

Beside me she said suddenly, 'He said that for a reason.'

'What reason could there be?'

'I don't know, but . . .' Her voice tailed away. Then, 'We know it's not true.'

'Do we? How do *I* know whether anything's true about any of you? Damn it . . . !'

'If he knows it's not true, and we know it isn't, who does that leave?'

'Singsong, I suppose.'

'Yes. He has to convince Singsong.'

'Why?'

'I'm not sure. But you saw how Singsong behaved. They're old friends, Ludlam said, but did they look it? Ludlam is full of bonhomie, but Singsong isn't.'

I thought about that. Old friends. Brigadier J. C. H. Ludlam, DSO and et ceteras on the one hand; and on the other, Sergeant-Artificer Ching Song. No, not friends.

Miss Franklin said, 'I think Singsong is suspicious of him.'

'Why?'

'He'd be foolish if he weren't.'

'Because?'

'Because from the look of things, Ludlam has turned up – and quite out of the blue, too, it seemed to me – to give him a share in the gems.'

It could be true: *if* Ludlam had come out of the blue.

She said, 'You didn't see, did you? You weren't here. When we arrived we walked straight in. All this was unexpected. Though Ludlam had seemed a bit excited on the way here. Ludlam shouted to ask if Ching Song was here. He was standing quite close at the time, and Ludlam didn't recognize him.'

'That means nothing. They could have been in touch. They wouldn't exactly exchange photographs.'

Miss Franklin shook her head. 'I'm sure I'm right. Ching Song was surprised, I know he was.'

'So Singsong's suspicious of Ludlam. All right. But I'd think it was the other way round. Ludlam's the one at risk. When Singsong gets the stones, there's nothing to stop him leaving Ludlam here with us, is there?'

'No.' The word came out slowly, speculatively.

'Well, then.'

She said, 'Ludlam knows that, too.'

'Bound to.'

'In that case . . . what can he be telling us?' and as I opened my mouth to speak, 'He's telling us things aren't what they seem, isn't he?'

'You could have fooled me!'

'Is he fooling Singsong, though? If so . . .'

We couldn't get hold of it. I wasn't sure there was anything to get hold of, but Miss Franklin was convinced Ludlam was up to something.

Later Ludlam came back into the circle of firelight, heading towards us, with Ching Song right behind him. 'Worked it out yet?'

I said, 'Do you have to keep us tied up?'

'I'm not letting you hop off, young Tunnicliffe, and you'll try it if I give you half the chance.'

'Put us in the longhouse then. It's guarded.'

'And let an experienced officer –' he gave a little chortle at the phrase – 'and let an experienced officer organize the natives? Think again. No, you're here for the night, and tomorrow you do the monkey act again. Back up the tree for you, my lad.'

Angrily I said, 'Do your own dirty work!'

'No, no, no, no. I'm too old, and the good Colonel's too old also, and a bit bulky besides. So you're volunteering. Know your way round up there, after all. Mind you, you'll have company, extra pair of hands and all that, one of them with a pistol in it. Miss Franklin stays here so we know you're behaving yourself. Quicker the job's done, quicker we're off, so it's to everybody's advantage.' He paused. 'We fed you yet? Dear, oh dear, I'll fix that. You need your strength. Oh, and by the way, don't try any silly nonsense, will you? Bullets will fly.'

Our hands were untied while we ate some rice concoction and re-tied immediately afterwards. Two of the raiders moved into position just behind us, where they could watch and, if they understood English, listen.

'You really won't do anything silly, will you?' Miss Franklin said.

'I would if I could see any way –'

'Just sleep. Tomorrow's another day.'

'What a cheering thought!'

But then she whispered something almost under her breath, and it was a very interesting piece of information indeed.

We were off before first light. Colonel Singsong wanted to use the helicopter, and took it badly when it was explained that from the air we wouldn't even be able to find the right tree. I told him he'd have to walk, and enjoyed saying it.

Five of us, plus equipment, made up the party: Singsong, me and three guards, one of whom was to go up the tree with me. Ludlam, who was to be left behind, presumably at Singsong's insistence, explained why I was to be accompanied: 'You're the bolshie type, young Tunnicliffe, and at this late stage I'm not having you hide the rubies away somewhere out of sheer spite. So behave yourself and nothing happens to you or Miss Franklin. You get the rubies – if you haven't found them already, and *I* think you have – and then you bring them down. All right?'

There was nothing to do but obey instructions, carry my share of the load, and derive what satisfaction I could from Colonel Singsong's sweaty waddle and laboured breathing.

That – and think about Miss Franklin's whispered words the night before.

CHAPTER NINETEEN

There were hopeful moments on that hike when I thought Colonel Singsong wasn't going to make it. That body of his had grown too accustomed to restaurants to be much use on jungle trails, and he wheezed and grunted and we had to stop a dozen times to let his blood pressure simmer down before it blew his head off. Yet while the body was pathetic, the will that drove it was not. Behind the sweat that streamed down his face, the little dark eyes were hard and aware, and they rarely left me.

When we reached the foot of the tree, he sat down heavily on the ground and stayed there for several minutes pulling himself together. While he rested, one of his men set up a light machine-gun a few yards away and squatted behind it, covering me. I could imagine Ludlam's briefing: 'He's not bright, but he can be a bloody fool, so watch him carefully. He's taken on armed men before.'

No way of taking on this lot. They were pros and alert for trouble. I lit a cigarette and waited for Singsong to recover.

He struggled to his feet eventually, with help from the other two. With a big square of sweat-soaked silk, he continued to mop at his face as he surveyed the tree and the long loop of rope to which my makeshift cradle was attached. Then he produced a large folded paper and opened it out. 'This is a structural blueprint of the Dakota aircraft.' Rolls of fat circled his knuckles as the finger prodded at the sheet. 'The beam is here, in this position, at Station one-five-six point five.'

I stared at him. 'Station *what*?'

He said impatiently, 'The number represents the distance from the median station at the tip of the aircraft's nose. The beam is located one hundred and fifty-six point five inches to the rear. No need to measure. It is level with the propeller boss.'

So that, I thought bitterly, was the answer. That damned number, which had baffled me so totally from the time I first read my father's letter, gave the exact location of the rubies! If only I'd had the sense to find out more about the aircraft . . . if I'd known even yesterday. I'd have saved hours of sweaty work *and* got the rubies out before Ching Song arrived. If . . .

He was snapping his fat fingers. 'Listen carefully. I spent more than twenty-four hours securing the beam in place.

It will not be easy to cut free.' He pointed to a big canvas bag one of his men had carried from Tunggal. 'This will do the job quickly, and I am interested in speed.'

'What is it?'

He ignored the question. 'First my man will go up into the tree ahead of you. You will follow. He will take this thing with him, and he will be armed. He will watch while you cut the beam free. You understand?'

'Yes.'

'Good. Embedded in the printing metal is a steel tube. The floor beam is seven feet long and the tube one foot. It is located on the base of the beam at a point nine inches from the fuselage former on the port side of the aircraft.'

I nodded.

'It will be necessary for you to cut the whole beam free. When you have done so, you will cut out the tube. The rest of the beam is of no value. The guard will take the tube from you, and return to the ground. You will remain inside the aircraft.'

'And once your man's down, you cut the rope and I'm stuck up there?'

He regarded me steadily. 'Be quite clear on this. Whether you live or die is of no interest to me. I have no particular wish to have you die, and if you obey my instructions, you will live. But if you do not . . . you understand?'

'More than you think,' I said. 'I bet your men don't know about the rubies. You're using me for this job so they don't get let into the secret.' I turned to the man beside me and said, 'There's a fortune in rubies up that tree.' His eyelids didn't even flicker. To Singsong I said, 'If they knew, they'd see you had a convenient heart attack, wouldn't they? And divide up the proceeds!'

Expressionless, he said, 'When I have that tube, I and my men will return to Tunggal, and we will all fly out.'

'Ludlam included?'

He ignored that. 'So you will live if you obey. But I warn you that if you make some stupid attempt to interfere, you will not descend alive.'

I pointed to the machine-gun. 'He won't have much of

a target. Won't be able to see me, for a start.'

Singsong glanced at his watch. 'Two hours from now, if the tube is not in my hands, the tree will be dynamited. When it falls, the aircraft will fall with it. We will then retrieve the tube from the wreckage.'

'Your man might be up there.'

'Yes.'

'You'd kill him, too?'

'I have already told you, I prefer speed and no bloodshed. But don't doubt that I will do what is necessary.'

I didn't doubt it for a second. Ching Song wouldn't be squeamish about trading two lives for a fortune.

He waddled over and squatted beside the LMG while two of the guards began to haul the other one up. The man in the cradle looked nervous, as well he might; and he looked a hell of a lot smaller by the time he reached that first big branch and began to shed the harness. He was also encumbered by that big bag – what on earth was in it? – and by his gun. Climbing would be tricky for him, though the line I'd secured up there would make his ascent easier than my first one had been.

The cradle was swinging down again, as I watched him negotiate that step from one branch to another. Singsong said quietly: 'Don't waste time.'

A minute or two later, gingerly gripping the line in painful swollen hands, I was ready to be hoisted. He gave a nod to the men on the rope, my feet left the ground and slowly I swung up through space into that giant tree. As the trunk went past me, I was thinking that there seemed to be a lot of ways to die in Sarawak; I'd encountered one or two, and dodged, but I couldn't see myself dodging this time. I glanced down. Ching Song was crouching at the foot of the tree taking small brownish cylinders out of a cardboard box. Gelignite.

All his talk about my surviving was purest moonshine and I knew it. When the guard and the tube came down, the tree would go up, and me with it. Singsong wouldn't take chances, why should he? The country he was in was fighting a tough little war against Indonesia, and he wouldn't feel safe until the helicopter had lifted him back over the mountains, into Kalimantan. There he could breathe, as easily as his corpulence would allow, and count his money; here he stood a chance, however slim, of encountering patrols. That was why speed mattered.

I tried to think of some way out, but there was no question that he had me thoroughly bottled. Even if I could do something about the guard, Singsong still had the whip hand. A few minutes from now, well before I reached the Dakota, he'd have the explosives wired up, and be sitting well away, ready to push the button at the first sign of anything untoward. He'd fret about the delay, but that would be later, *after* the big bang.

I reached the branch, slipped out of the cradle, and performed my splits round the tree, then began to work my way up that straight, thrusting branch, and across the leafy traverse. I glanced at my watch as I climbed through the door into the fuselage. Thirteen minutes. Getting faster.

The guard stood well back towards the tail, the butt of his machine-pistol tucked under his arm, and as the old Dakota took my weight as well as his, his eyes gave a little flicker of fear, because the floor gave a definite lurch and outside the branches creaked and moaned. Christ, I thought — it's going to crash down without aid of gelignite!

He pointed towards that mysterious bag, which lay in the middle of the floor near the door, and then towards the nose. I picked it up and moved as directed, and quickly too, to get some weight forward again. I set it down beside the crate and again felt the plane shift a little beneath my feet. By God, but she was delicately poised now! My hands were sore and swollen, usable, but only just. It took a good deal of careful tugging to open the drawstring of the bag, and a good while to get over the first reaction to what was inside: a chainsaw! I glanced at the guard. He was still at the far end of the cabin. What if I started it, and threw it at him? Sense, fortunately, prevailed. I wouldn't be able to throw it that far for a start; secondly, he'd empty the magazine at me the moment he saw me begin the movement.

I examined it. Petrol-powered, lanyard for starting. Made for cutting wood, though, not metal. Still, Singsong knew what he was about, and had obviously brought the thing along to make a quicker job of removing the beam. The skin of the Dakota was thin aluminium, so this chain of blades would probably chew through it easily enough. Probably all too easily. I needed time to think, time to try to find a way of using this situation, and this bloody machine would cut the time back savagely.

The guard yelled at me, gesturing with the pistol. No language I understood, but the meaning was clear: get on with it!

A little brass screw in the fuel tank cap opened the air hole. I turned it, opened the choke lever, and took hold of the lanyard handle. The first pull sent agony through my hands, and I gave a grunt at the pain. When it had ebbed a bit, and the guard had yelled at me a few more times, I tried again and the saw roared to life with that murderous blade snarling smoothly round the sprockets.

It was painful even to pick it up, but that had to be faced: the thing was far safer in my hands than jumping round loose by my feet. All the same, I felt as though my hands were full of red-hot coals as I lowered that racing blade to let it rip at the mounting of the floor beam, and prove Ching Song right. The saw jumped about excruciatingly in my hands, but it chewed through the metal as though it were paper. The bottom of the beam fitted snugly into the concave inner surface of the airframe, and the saw rapidly sliced a track alongside. In a couple of minutes I'd made a cut from side to side and could see through to the greenery below.

That sight gave me pause for thought, and I looked closely at the saw-cut. The Dakota was a notably rugged aircraft, but it was of monocoque construction. So long as the integrity of the structure was maintained, fine. But cutting through the skin, as I'd just done, was like tapping an eggshell with a knife-blade. With that cut, the airframe's integrity was gone.

Desperately I tried to think of some means to make use

of the fact, but nothing came to me. If I began to slice vertically upwards, sooner or later the Dakota's nose would snap off. But I'd be dead before that.

I moved across and began to make the second cut, on the other side of the beam, and beneath me the metal gave a few small squeals of outrage. The nose might tear off anyway, and then . . . I shivered. Already there was one seven-foot cut in the skin, and now I was making another. As the saw-blade chewed away, the coals in my hands became white hot, not red, and the pain drove me to hurry. Only by finishing could I get rid of the saw!

With the second cut made, there was a three-inch slice clear through the floor and the metal squealed again as I moved, more loudly this time. I had only to cut round the ends of the beam.

Two or three minutes was all it took. I'd wedged the bolt-cutter handle through one of the circular holes drilled for lightness in the beam, so that it couldn't fall away. Now, with relief, I flicked off the fuel and waited for the motor to starve. As it stopped I flung it down and began to try to comfort my hands under my armpits. The pain remained, like pulsing fire, for quite a while, and from the tail the guard yelled at me to go on.

When, finally, the pain had stopped attacking all of me and was concentrated in my hands again, I bent and hauled the beam out on to the cabin floor. Nine inches from the port side and, one foot along, and on the base. I touched the cool metal, knowing my fingertips were less than an inch from the rubies that had cost my father his life, and now looked like costing me mine.

But nothing was visible. The steel tube was entirely hidden inside its casting of printing metal. I'd have to cut again to get that section out. I swore, and reached again for the saw, gritted my teeth, and started it. Two cuts in and one along. With my feet holding the beam firm on the cabin floor, I tried to forget the pain for as long as it took to get the cuts made. Gleaming swarfs curled away as the racing chain tore into the soft metal, then once more I could get rid of the saw. The tube, still encased, lay separated now from its hiding-place, and I picked it up, shook it, and listened. A small rattling: the sound of riches.

The guard shouted, coming towards me, halting three or four yards away, indicating that I should toss it to his feet, and I obeyed dully, half numb with pain, and wondering how many thousands of pounds I was tossing away. Something I'd never know. In any case, rubies would be no use where I was going.

As he picked it up and walked towards the door, all sorts of noises began. Everything was straining now: towards the tail the branches rasped and groaned; behind me the fractured airframe squealed more loudly.

He turned in the doorway, the silvery bar of metal tucked into his belt, then swung himself out, and I flopped down on the crate, nursing my hands, knowing I had no chance now. He'd be down in a quarter of an hour or so. And then . . . well, and then there would be an explosion and I'd die.

After a moment I went to the door. A daft idea had struck me: would it be possible to climb from this tree into one of its neighbours? But looking round, I knew it wouldn't work. I wasn't a monkey and this tree was so vast, its branches so widely spread, and so intertwined with its neighbours' that when it fell the ripping and tearing would affect all the others, perhaps even knocking some down. Below me the guard was just completing his traverse. Soon he'd be reaching that vertical branch that for him was a ladder to safety.

I was in my coffin. About to die, with a skeleton for company, and a chainsaw, and the crate with that old Japanese . . .

. . . with a torpedo!

I went to it quickly. The crate sat on its rollers, held in place on the slight downslope by the wedges I'd driven in. Just beyond it was the long narrow cut in the fuselage. Beside *that* was the chainsaw!

Hope flared then, for a few seconds, but it wasn't sane hope. Though I knew nothing about torpedoes, I'd been around enough armouries to know that large explosive devices don't travel armed. If this one had been going to go off, it would have done so twenty years before, when the Dakota came down. Fuses and firing pistols are fitted just prior to use, and not a second before; there are elaborate rules and procedures governing the matter, and court-martial awaits those who break them by a millimetre.

Hang on a minute, though . . .

Hadn't Ludlam said this torpedo was being sent to Australia for examination? Yes, he had. It was a new type. So would it be sent with a bit missing? Hardly.

So somewhere in this plane there had to be the detonating mechanism! But where? Inside the crate? Surely not. But where else could it be? I'd been over the damn Dakota from nose to tail. It *must* be in the crate.

I grabbed for the chainsaw, and yelped with pain but made myself hold it. If I was going to die soon, damn the pain! It started first bang, and I attacked the end of the crate nearer the tail, watching the teeth tear into the hardwood, willing it to go faster. With most of the end chopped away I saw a long shape encased in what looked like oiled wrappings, but they'd collapsed with the years and the shape of the propeller showed. I flicked my lighter, and in the little jump of flame saw a small box, tucked down below the torpedo's tail.

Lifting it out gingerly, I put it on the floor and began prising at it with the machete. It opened readily enough, and I looked at the contents with a weird kind of pleasure. The thing was about a foot long. At one end was a steel cap; and below it was a threaded section, and below that was a straight, smooth, greenish pipe. Greenish with age: this was copper. Inside would be what? – fulminate or something like it. This was the firing pistol. I put it down very carefully indeed and took the chainsaw to the forward end.

Which first? Enlarge the slit in the fuselage, or cut the end of the crate? Prudence said: fuselage. As I ripped at it I think I was half out of my head, partly with pain, partly with the knowledge that what I intended with suicidal. All

I knew was that I was going to fix Ching Song as he'd fixed me! Those rubies had claimed two victims already, and I was going to be the third. Well, then Colonel bloody Singsong and his men were numbers four, five, six and seven!

I sliced upwards from the floor extending the cut through the thin skin beside one of the fuselage formers until it reached shoulder height, then started on the other side. The saw juddered painfully every time the tearing teeth jarred into the steel wires securing the cabin trim in place, and they pinged as they broke like so many violin strings. Now the other side. As the saw-cut rose up the wall the whole section above my head suddenly started to buckle. Christ, had I overdone it?

I swung the chainsaw round and set it to the end of the long crate. The cabin was all noise now: tearing metal, engine, the shriek of the chain teeth ripping at teak. I cut down, round, up, to make a U at the front end of the crate, and behind it the rounded dark shape came into view: the nose of the torpedo, shrouded in its oiled tarpaulins. With the U-cut completed, I took a step back and looked at it. Damn! The wrapping was wired tight round the thing. I began to cut away the top of the crate. The old teak was thick and hard and the two four-foot lengthways cuts and one across were an eternity of pain.

But now I could get at the wires. Bolt-cutters clipped through them, but the tarpaulin was thick and heavy and I couldn't see where the edge was. I needed something to cut that tarpaulin. The saw? A chainsaw on a torpedo, when the explosive inside might be unstable? If only I had a knife, but Ching Song hadn't left me a knife.

A knife! Something to cut . . . there was nothing. Yes there was, though! I knew where there was a knife – and it was out of reach, on the rotten remnant of Colonel Toshiba's belt in the co-pilot's seat.

I swung round to look. Ahead of me the cabin roof had buckled; the floor beyond the hole where the beam had been now sagged a good two feet lower than where I stood. If I stepped down on to it, the whole nose section, half torn free as it was, might tear off completely and fall, taking me with it, with the torpedo still in place.

But without a knife, the tarpaulin couldn't be cut and the torpedo couldn't be armed!

I could even see the knife. Eight feet away, and it might as well be on the moon! But Christ, there was no other way! How slowly would the metal tear? One quick grab, and . . .

I stepped down, stepped forward, grabbed . . . and the whole nose section began to turn and tilt. I flung myself and the knife back at the step, got my arms and chest over the edge and clung, with the jagged sharpness of rough cut edges slashing at my clothes and through them to my flesh. Frantically I tried to haul myself up, my feet now with nothing to push at, and above me the skin of the aircraft buckling and tearing as the heavy nose section drew it down. I got a leg over the edge, rolled and scrambled up beside the torpedo and began to hack at the canvas.

Where would the bloody guard be? I glanced at my watch. Eleven minutes since he'd left the plane. He'd be on the branch by the rope, or very near it. And below they'd be waiting.

I scrabbled and sliced at the coverings. There'd be a hole somewhere for that firing pistol. Where, though? In the nose, probably. But when I'd cut through, it wasn't there. One long clean cut. I dug the knife through, blade upwards, and sliced, peeling the material back.

There!

Two feet or so back from that rounded nose a small brass cap covered a socket. Shaped for a hand grip, but my hand wouldn't turn it. How? Grip with the handle of the bolt-cutters – try that.

It slipped. I tore a piece of canvas, wrapped it round the flange, tried again. My hands painful beyond bearing, but a final pain, intolerable but to be tolerated. Just for a moment. Movement. And it moved again, and then I was turning it, hurling the freed cap aside, sliding the firing pistol carefully in, tightening . . .

Ready.

Now the chainsaw again, slashing through that buckled

aluminium, and the nose section lowering. It had to go completely, though, or the torpedo wouldn't fall.

It ripped, held, ripped again. Oh God, if it was supported, I was finished! It canted round, pulling the roof down to my head, to my waist, turning, tearing . . . suddenly gone, dropping off clean, leaving no more than a two-foot gap between roof and floor. I flung the chainsaw through it and kicked at the wedges holding the crate. Anything could happen now. A new tilt to the mutilated Dakota could send the torpedo plunging towards the tail.

One out. One to go. I kicked at the last wedge again, knocking it askew, then half away. The crate lurched. Another kick and the wedge flew away to the side.

At once the crate slid forward. I grabbed the lever and tried to help. It moved, stuck, moved again. I heaved up with the lever; she rolled, and I sweated and levered again. The crate slid down – and jammed in the narrow mouth between roof and floor.

But the torpedo didn't. A ton of smooth metal was on the move, slipping through that gap with nothing to hold it. Twenty feet of death, unstoppable, now . . .

I seem to remember hearing shots, but I can't be sure. I heard branches cracking as the monster fell, and then I was falling as the wrecked fuselage, freed of the weight of both the nose section and the torpedo, began slowly to pivot. I was tumbling, somersaulting down it towards the tail as the warhead exploded.

CHAPTER TWENTY

I can only guess at what happened. Miss Franklin glimpsed the end of it, but she'd been knocked over and wounded by the explosion and couldn't be sure.

How come she was there at all? Ironically, we had Ludlam to thank, though not just Ludlam: she'd had a part in it, and so, for that matter, had I.

So many things had come together in a short space of time in that lost patch of jungle that it's almost impossible to know where to begin.

With the Dakota, perhaps? As I say, it's purest guesswork. The old aeroplane must have been held up largely by its wings. That's all I can think, anyway, and as the tail pivoted downwards, it would have formed a cross weighing eight or nine tons, beginning to slip down through the branches as the torpedo reached the ground, but with the strong wings acting as a brake. Then the explosion, tearing away the huge tree's hold on the earth, and the tree falling, but slowly because other trees gripped it, and the Dakota falling with it, with everything in a crazy kind of slow-motion that ended with the old plane still largely intact, thirty feet or so off the ground, on a mountain of foliage.

I just don't know. I wasn't even conscious when it happened. Blast may have had something to do with it : a moment of lift at the right instant. Miss Franklin said the old Dak hit the fallen treetop as though it was landing on a cushion. She also says it doesn't pay to try to analyse God's works, and certainly He's the only one who knows.

Like the Dak, I finished up in the branches. Some trick of force must have shot me out of the narrow hole at the nose of the plane. I came to quite certain I was dead until assorted aches and pains convinced me I wasn't. More were accumulated in the scramble down to the ground. I was dizzy and dazed, with a blinding headache where my skull had cracked against something.

And then I heard her calling my name.

That's my story, such as it is. She told me hers later, and I listened with my mouth hanging open, and afterwards, when I decided this story should be told on paper, asked her to write down her part of it. She didn't want to, but I insisted as best I could, and here it is, exactly as she set it down in that bold clear hand of hers.

'It would be wrong to say I was entirely happy with either of my companions on the journey in Sarawak. The former

brigadier, Mr Ludlam, struck me at once as thoroughly unreliable and unlikely in any circumstances to prove trustworthy. As for George Tunnicliffe, he is a pleasant man and
undoubtedly has courage, but I found him to be too easily
upset. Accordingly, and also perhaps because I am by nature
self-contained, I kept my own counsel so far as that was
possible.

(The truth is that I should never have agreed to return,
but Tunnicliffe was insistent and persuasive, and when he
suggested that in assisting him to find the precious stones
so improperly acquired by his father, I should become
entitled to a share which could be put into God's Work,
I reluctantly assented.)

Since he has apparently already recounted most of the
events that befell us, I have no need to go over them again.
His account will, no doubt, be over-emotional, but he is
quite straightforward in most things, and will probably
be reasonably accurate as to fact. There were, however,
certain matters and events of which he had no knowledge
either because he was not present, or for some other reason.

The first of these occurred on my return to Tunggal after
we had heard, but of course had not seen, a helicopter. On
the journey back, which took two hours approximately, it
appeared to me that Mr Ludlam was in a state of some
eagerness but that he was endeavouring to suppress it. I was
naturally concerned about what was to come and, in view
of his general character, also suspicious.

I therefore instructed a Dyak boy named Jigah, who had
attached himself rather impudently to our party, to remain
a distance behind us in case anything untoward should
occur. It would have been wholly wrong to allow a boy so
young to become involved in any unpleasantness or danger.

On arrival at Tunggal we found that the helicopter had
brought a group of Indonesian irregular troops, that they
had taken control of the longhouse and that all the people
of the village had been ordered to the upper floor and were
now under guard.

I was somewhat shocked, though scarcely surprised, by
Mr Ludlam's conduct. As soon as we had been taken

prisoner, he began to shout that he wished to speak to a man named Ching Song. The man was present, and Ludlam addressed him in familiar terms, though it appeared to me that at first he did not recognize Ching. I was unable to hear much of what they said to each other, but what I did hear suggested that Ludlam proposed to give many of the stones to Ching (whom he addressed always as 'Singsong' or 'Colonel Singsong') in return for being flown out of Sarawak and into Kalimantan in the helicopter. This was confirmed in a subsequent conversation Ludlam had with Tunnicliffe and with me, late that evening.

However, something rather fortunate had occurred shortly after darkness fell. The Dyak boy Jigah, having obeyed my instructions not to accompany us right to Tunggal, had waited until dark, and then reconnoitred the position. I was sitting alone (I suppose because of my age they saw no reason to waste a man's time guarding me) some little distance from the other people present, and Jigah contrived to circle round until he was able to speak to me from the shadows at the edge of the jungle.

He asked what he should do. I told him at once that he should return home to Lobang Nibong and inform his headman, the *tua-ruma* as he is known, that a group of irregulars from Kalimantan was now at Tunggal. It seemed to me that these might be the men who had burned down Lobang Nibong, and that the village should be alerted.

Later, when to my surprise Tunnicliffe arrived at Tunggal and was captured and we were able to talk, I mentioned Jigah to him because the boy had attached himself to Tunnicliffe, who had quite wrongly encouraged him.

Next morning Tunnicliffe was taken from Tunggal by a small party of irregulars accompanied by Ching. It was their intention to compel him to recover the precious stones.

I was kept sitting on the ground, with my wrists tied, from early morning. Mr Ludlam did not speak to me at all, or come near, though I was in some discomfort. Much of the time he simply stood ostentatiously in the middle of the bare ground before the longhouse.

I have thought about what happened next. Excitable people might think it intensely dramatic, though the reverse is true, because it was accomplished quite quietly. Yet something must have caught my attention, for I turned my head to see one of the Indonesian irregulars with his hands at his throat. He collapsed as I watched him, and at once I saw another man on the ground near by, and looking round it was clear that all of them were being attacked simultaneously. There is, of course, only one weapon that is both silent and immediately deadly, and that is the blowpipe. The Dyaks use it for hunting and show inordinate skill and accuracy in bringing down game. I also recollect how efficient a weapon it proved to be on occasion against Japanese troops in the late war.

I understood almost at once that the attackers must have come from Lobang Nibong upon learning from the boy Jigah of the presence here of Indonesians. Presently, the men of Lobang Nibong emerged from the forest. They were almost shamefully triumphant at the success of their attack and I confess that for a moment I was afraid they would revert.

[*By 'revert' I assume Miss Franklin means that the Dyak warriors might have taken heads. G.H.T.*]

However, I managed to stand and called out to them, and seeing that I was tied they came quickly to cut the rope at my wrists, and their attention was happily diverted.

Mr Ludlam had not, of course, been attacked and he came to where I stood and said, with a most unpleasant smile, 'Now for Singsong!'

I asked the men to hold him and they did so. I informed Mr Ludlam that the Dyaks were perfectly capable both of restraining him and proceeding in pursuit of Ching Song.

He shouted that I must listen to his story and at first I refused, knowing how accomplished a dissembler he could be. He began to beg. I believe he thought I might instruct the Dyaks to kill him.

So I let him speak and he told me a story of deviousness

so extreme that in the end I had to believe him, if only because such a tale could not be made up on the spur of the moment.

Ludlam said that after he left prison and went to live in Jamaica he was recruited by one of the secret agencies of the British government and that he worked as what he called 'a freelance' in Jamaica for a number of years. However, when the island achieved independence, his services were no longer required. He said he was extremely unhappy at this and felt it was a reflection on his abilities, pride in those abilities, in my opinion, being his besetting sin.

At all events, he attempted to remain in touch with his intelligence superior, and he said that some time before he went to Borneo he learned from this man that the Head of Operations for the Indonesian incursions into Sarawak was a man who had served in the Royal Air Force in Burma. The man was Ching Song.

Ludlam told me that he began to try to devise some means of meeting Ching Song in circumstances that might enable the intelligence services or the army to take him prisoner, but that there appeared to be no way. Ching Song remained either in Djakarta, or in a secret jungle headquarters in Kalimantan.

Ludlam was not apparently without funds; his motive was vanity. He wished to prove himself again by achieving a coup. He realized, naturally, that the British services would very much like to capture Ching Song, but also they had made clear their doubt of Mr Ludlam's ability to assist. He had to remain in Jamaica, unhappy and unemployed.

When he read in *The Times* airmail edition of George Tunnicliffe's exploit in preventing a raid on the bank, it became clear to him that here was something to attract Ching Song's attention. He issued an invitation to Tunnicliffe to visit him in Jamaica, and explained to him the circumstances of Tunnicliffe's father's disappearance. When Tunnicliffe returned to Britain, Ludlam hoped, without serious grounds for hope, that Tunnicliffe might be tempted to go to Sarawak to try to discover where his father's air-craft crashed.

It was the purest coincidence that I, too, had recognized Tunnicliffe's name and written to him. Ludlam at the time knew nothing of that, or of me.

But when he received from Tunnicliffe a letter announcing the intention of going to Sarawak, Ludlam believed his opportunity had come.

He told me he believed his problem was to let Ching Song know of Tunnicliffe's presence without at the same time giving Ching Song grounds for suspecting that a trap was being laid for him. Ludlam said he knew from the newspapers of intense Indonesian intelligence activity in Singapore. He flew to Jesselton in Sabah, then on to Singapore, and there informed the *Straits Times* of my and Tunnicliffe's presence there. The newspaper interviewed and photographed us, and Ludlam believed the report would be sent back to Djakarta by Indonesian intelligence. Such a report, if it reached Ching Song, would of course alert him and cause him to speculate why the son of Squadron Leader Tunnicliffe was now going to Sarawak, where Ching Song knew the plane had crashed with the rubies on board.

When the report appeared, however, Ludlam felt it was too small, that it might escape attention in the Indonesian consulate, and that he must do something more. He could not send the report himself, lacking an address. He therefore determined upon a more dramatic happening. He invaded my room in the hotel in Singapore and there created a scene designed to attract the attention of the press once more. The aircraft's number, painted in large figures on the wall, was put there because Ching Song would certainly know it. He even telephoned the *Straits Times* so that their representatives would go to the hotel quickly.

The number, of course, though it mystified both Tunnicliffe and me, meant nothing to us.

Ludlam then returned to Jesselton and proceeded from there to Kuching, arriving a day or two before us. In

Kuching he devoted his time to discovering at which mission stations I had served, in order to have some approximate idea of our ultimate destination. It seems he had no difficulty. At the museum he mentioned me to one of the staff and the information was given to him. There was, after all, nothing secret.

I insisted that our destination be kept from Ludlam because I distrusted him profoundly. He therefore did not know, until after our departure, where we were going, but he believed that by this time Ching Song would have arranged with the Indonesian sympathizers he controlled in Kuching to have us watched closely.

In the early part of the journey upriver, Ludlam was noticeably nervous and said he was afraid we were being followed. In fact what he wanted was to be sure that we *were* being followed. He told me he never was sure, though he thought that a helicopter that twice passed over us on the river was likely to contain Ching Song's observers.

[*Miss Franklin, conscientious as always, here included a long passage describing what happened first at Lobang Nibong and at Tunggal, and our search for and discovery of the aircraft. Since I have already told that part of the story, I have omitted it here, and taken up her narrative again at Tunggal, after the attack. G.H.T.*]

When Ludlam had finished, I was reasonably certain he had spoken truthfully and I did not doubt for a moment that the commander of the Indonesian irregulars would be an important prize for the British army. I asked Ludlam what he now proposed to do, and again the unpleasant side of his nature showed itself. He again produced that odious grin, and said he intended to obtain the rubies as well as Ching Song.

I told him I disapproved of his priorities, but that appeared not to concern him. He intended to wait for Ching Song's return to Tunggal, take him prisoner, relieve him of the rubies and fly in the helicopter to Kuching. When I mentioned George Tunnicliffe, Ludlam merely said that Tunnicliffe had descended the tree unaided once, and would doubtless be able to do so again.

This was not to be tolerated. If the rubies were to come into our hands, the division of them was already decided. Also I thought it likely that Ching Song could not be trusted to deal fairly with Tunnicliffe.

I therefore insisted that we go to the place where the aircraft rested in the high canopy, and try to ensure that nothing happened to Tunnicliffe. There was no reason, I told him, why Ching Song could not be taken prisoner there instead of at Tunggal.

He protested but had to agree, and we set out immediately, taking with us three of the blowpipe bearers from Lobang Nibong, as well as two of the weapons we had taken from the fallen irregulars. I confess that for me the Dyaks' presence served a secondary purpose, in that they would concentrate Ludlam's mind on his duty.

We made all speed, and reached a point not far from the site in about an hour and a half. We stopped for a moment, then, when we realized that a roaring noise not far ahead came from some kind of motor. As we moved on, I took the lead until we came to a position from which the tree was visible.

Events then occurred with quite extraordinary speed, but I believe I have a clear recollection of the sequence they took. Much of the fern near the base of the tree had by now been cut down, or trampled, so that it was possible to see almost everything that occurred.

Ching Song stood a little back from the tree, looking up. One of his men was on the high branch. I heard Ching Song shout, but was unable to understand him, since the motor was still making a noise that rendered the words incomprehensible. The motor then stopped quite suddenly, and Ching Song shouted once more, ordering his subordinate to drop something: the rubies, obviously.

I saw something silvery thrown down, Ching Song snatched it up instantly, and began to twist at it, and then Ludlam quite suddenly pushed past me and rushed forward. I had never imagined for a moment that he would do such a thing, and was momentarily off balance when I heard firing and saw that he had shot down the two of Ching

Song's men who were at the base of the tree. He stood pointing the weapon at Ching Song and holding out his hand.

It was as Ching Song handed the thing to Ludlam that I heard the crashing in the branches above. I was running forward at the time, to ensure that Ludlam did not murder Ching Song too, but most fortunately I was still a short distance, perhaps twenty yards, away.

I remember quite distinctly seeing a long black object emerge from the foliage of the tree and fall to the ground. There was a very loud explosion. Something struck me painfully in the shoulder, and I was blown off my feet. The Good Lord chose to protect His servant, and I was not killed though that is something of a miracle. As it was, I was able to rise to my feet in time to see that enormous tree begin to fall.

It came down very slowly indeed at the start, tearing itself free of its neighbours only gradually. The fall then halted as it came to rest against another and equally magnificent neighbour. By this time it was tilted perhaps thirty degrees out of the perpendicular. It seemed to rest for a moment, then again began to fall, but the process, though inexorable, was quite remarkably unhurried, as though the forest was letting its child die gently.

The trunk was near the ground when I saw that the aircraft had been shaken loose and was falling, too. It must still have been partially in the tree's grip, however, because though it was falling tail first at one point, it appeared almost to fly upwards for a moment, before landing on its belly in the mass of branches that made up the top of the tree.

I am rather ashamed that the spectacle so caught my attention that for some space of time I ceased to think about anything else. Of Ludlam and Ching Song there was no sign at all, and clearly the explosion had blown them to pieces. The man on the bough must have fallen at the time I was blown over, because he now lay where the tree had been. I went forward to see if he might still be alive, but he must have been killed instantly in the fall.

Until then, I had not realized that I was actually wounded; the blow on my shoulder had been somewhat painful, but now, as I touched it, my hand was bloodied. I was standing, rather stupidly, looking at my hand when one of the Lobang Nibong men spoke, and pointed, and I saw George Tunnicliffe emerging from the tangle of branches where the aircraft now lay.

Those are the events as I remember them.'

She had signed it 'C. Franklin'. Of course.

And that is the end of the story, except for one minor item: minor, that is, in terms of hopes and expectations. I don't know if you'd call it a freak blast effect, or an act of God. But whatever had hit Miss Franklin was now embedded in the scant flesh of her left shoulder and had to be removed, rather painfully, with a knife. Stoically she probed for it herself, and produced a bloody, irregular bit of shrapnel, which she held between finger and thumb. As you've perhaps guessed, it was a ruby. But not a huge and valuable one, merely a small fragment.

For days afterwards I searched the area looking for the rest, but needles in haystacks are nothing compared with rubies in primary jungle.

That tiny jagged fragment was all we had. Later, back in London, we had it valued. Twenty-five pounds, the man said, and he insisted he was being generous.

Duncan Kyle

'The outstanding thriller-writer discovery of the seventies.'
Evening News

WHITEOUT! 75p
A CAGE OF ICE 80p
FLIGHT INTO FEAR 80p
TERROR'S CRADLE 80p

Fontana Paperbacks

Geoffrey Jenkins

Geoffrey Jenkins writes of adventure on land and at sea in some of the most exciting thrillers ever written. 'Geoffrey Jenkins has the touch that creates villains and heroes—and even icy heroines—with a few vivid words.' *Liverpool Post* 'A style which combines the best of Nevil Shute and Ian Fleming.' *Books and Bookmen*

A BRIDGE OF MAGPIES 85p
A CLEFT OF STARS 70p
THE RIVER OF DIAMONDS 85p
THE WATERING PLACE OF
   GOOD PEACE 75p
A TWIST OF SAND 75p
HUNTER-KILLER 85p

Fontana Paperbacks

Alistair MacLean

His first book, *HMS Ulysses*, published in 1955, was outstandingly successful. It led the way to a string of best-selling novels which have established Alistair MacLean as the most popular adventure writer of our time.

SEAWITCH 85p
THE GOLDEN GATE 85p
BEAR ISLAND 95p
BREAKHEART PASS 80p
CARAVAN TO VACCARÈS 80p
CIRCUS 75p
THE DARK CRUSADER 85p
FEAR IS THE KEY 80p
FORCE 10 FROM NAVARONE 85p
THE GOLDEN RENDEZVOUS 85p
THE GUNS OF NAVARONE 85p
HMS *ULYSSES* 85p
ICE STATION ZEBRA 85p
THE LAST FRONTIER 85p
NIGHT WITHOUT END 85p
PUPPET ON A CHAIN 85p
THE SATAN BUG 85p
SOUTH BY JAVA HEAD 85p
THE WAY TO DUSTY DEATH 80p
WHEN EIGHT BELLS TOLL 85p
WHERE EAGLES DARE 85p

Fontana Paperbacks

Desmond Bagley

'Mr Bagley is nowadays incomparable.' *Sunday Times*

Fontana Paperbacks

Fontana Paperbacks

Fontana is a leading paperback publisher of fiction and non-fiction, with authors ranging from Alistair MacLean, Agatha Christie and Desmond Bagley to Solzhenitsyn and Pasternak, from Gerald Durrell and Joy Adamson to the famous Modern Masters series.

In addition to a wide-ranging collection of internationally popular writers of fiction, Fontana also has an outstanding reputation for history, natural history, military history, psychology, psychiatry, politics, economics, religion and the social sciences.

All Fontana books are available at your bookshop or newsagent; or can be ordered direct. Just fill in the form and list the titles you want.

FONTANA BOOKS, Cash Sales Department, G.P.O. Box 29, Douglas, Isle of Man, British Isles. Please send purchase price, plus 8p per book. Customers outside the U.K. send purchase price, plus 10p per book. Cheque, postal or money order. No currency.

NAME (Block letters)

ADDRESS

While every effort is made to keep prices low, it is sometimes necessary to increase prices on short notice. Fontana Books reserve the right to show new retail prices on covers which may differ from those previously advertised in the text or elsewhere.